The Faenum Quest

Book 1: Mortus

by

Dennis K. Hausker

Published by
Melange Books, LLC
White Bear Lake, MN 55110
www.melange-books.com

Mortus, Copyright © 2012 by Dennis K. Hausker

ISBN: 978-1-61235-318-0

Cover Art by Caroline Andrus

I'm dedicating this first book of the trilogy to my nephew, Craig. We share a love for the epic fantasy genre and this great adventure my character lives is my tribute to the awesome giants who blazed the trail for the rest of us.

Mortus
Dennis K. Hausker

David Cray suffers a trauma which ends the life he's known on Earth. An unknown uncle shows up to convince him to travel to his father's planet where he begins a life journey that starts as a quest to the dark fortress of Mortus. He gathers a group of friends who share his trials, tribulations, and his hopes. Dave begins to transform as his buried heritage from his father develops and that includes magic and power. Dave comes to Faenum unprepared in virtually every way. He's constantly surprised by what he encounters, he performs miraculous acts he can't explain, he doubts his decisions and feels overwhelmed by events and people in his new world. Dave becomes the de facto leader of the quest, but leads them into a trap and galling captivity. They escape from Mortus eventually but they're much changed people, never to be the same again.

About the Author
Dennis K. Hausker

Dennis Hausker is retired from a career as a medical insurance specialist for an insurance company. Post retirement he works part time as a financial consultant and he is the finance chair person at his church. He has been married since 1968. He and his wife met at Michigan State University from which they graduated in 1969. She is a retired teacher who volunteers helping adult's with learning impairments. Dennis is a veteran of the Vietnam War. He served at Long Binh as a finance clerk paying field combat units. He loves to write with his preferred genre being Epic Fantasy, although he has the goal to also write books in other genre's. He is very grateful for the business partnership he has established with Melange Books in terms of their professional support services and encouraging friendly atmosphere. His hope is his stories will be captivating, unique, and compelling for the reader.

Website: www.denniskhausker.com

Endings and Beginnings

David Cray sat at the kitchen table staring vacantly out the back window at the tree line by the back of the lot. Steam rising from the coffee mug blurred his vision, giving him an ethereal view of the woods. He'd looked at those same trees and daydreamed often as a child that just out of his sight lurking in the forest were strange creatures waiting to draw him into wild adventures and terrifying danger. Now, as he looked, he didn't see adventure on the horizon, only loneliness and despair mirroring the searing pain in his soul.

A car pulled into the driveway. He got up from the table and walked to the front door and waited. After a few moments he opened the door just as Pastor Bryant stepped onto the porch.

"Good morning, Dave," he said soberly.

"Morning," said Dave quietly. "Come in, sir."

"My wife is waiting in the car, Dave."

"Oh," Dave replied with a look of confusion, like his mind couldn't connect any of the dots, "I've got coffee…"

"We should be going. We don't have much time before they open the doors. Remember, you have private time scheduled before everybody else comes in."

"I know. I poured some coffee, but I wasn't really drinking it anyway. I'll go pour it out and we can go. I'm sorry if I'm in a fog. This is all a little overwhelming for me."

"I understand, son."

He walked to the sink, rinsed out the cup and put it into the dishwasher. His mother would not have allowed any stray cups or dishes to sit in the sink and this was her house after all.

The pastor eyed him sympathetically as they turned and walked out the front door. Dave locked the door slowly. He was in no hurry to make this trip.

Dave got into the back seat of the pastor's black Buick.

"Hello Mrs. Bryant," he said.

"Hello David," turning her head and gazing sadly.

The pastor and his wife spoke to each other softly on the drive. Dave sat in the back seat staring out the window. He saw the large building which was their destination when they made a turn at the street corner and then turned again into the parking lot. A man in a black suit came out of the home to greet them.

"Hello Bob," said the pastor.

"Reverend…everything is ready for you. People have started to arrive early. We've got them waiting downstairs so Dave can have his private time."

Dave accepted a handshake from the man and nodded to him.

"We're going to take you straight in," Bob explained. "Take all of the time you want."

"Do you want me to come in with you?" asked the pastor.

"I think I'd like to be alone at first, at least for a few minutes."

"That's fine, son."

Dave followed Bob to a parlor room. Bob opened the door and led him in.

"If you need anything, let me know, I'll be right outside the door."

"Thank you," said Dave quietly.

Bob stepped out of the room and closed the door.

Dave paused a moment before he turned and walked over to the casket. His mother looked serene, at peace at last. It was tempting to imagine her as merely asleep, but that pleasant thought faded quickly. She was gone from his life forever and there was nothing he could do to bring her back. The enormity of that fact struck him like a sledgehammer and he struggled with his powerful feelings looking down at her. His underlying distress flamed to life within him.

"Mother," he whispered painfully, "what am I going to do? I'm alone now."

He gently touched her face with his hand stroking her cheek. Her pale flesh was cold.

"It isn't fair," he whispered painfully.

He wanted to see her open her eyes, his emotions were in turmoil as he stood looking at the only family he had.

The odor of the flowers was overpowering. That infuriated him because he was already angry and he had no outlet for the rage.

The funeral director had given Dave his mother's wedding ring. He had it in his pocket, but it gave him no comfort. There was nothing to console him in the grief of his loss.

He took out his handkerchief and wiped his eyes.

"I'll stay here with you, Mom," he whispered protectively. The thought of ceding her to the burial crew incensed him, but it was futile misdirected anger. There was no person at fault here. Losing his mother in her early forties seemed impossible to him with her so young, yet it had happened nonetheless.

Dave stood for several more minutes staring at her. She was gone. Only her lifeless shell remained behind. Finally, he went to the door.

"Could the pastor and his wife come in now, Bob?"

"Certainly Dave..."

Dave went back to the casket and stood waiting. He heard the pastor and his wife come into the room after a few minutes and they walked up beside him.

"What would you like us to do for you, Dave?"

"Maybe a little prayer…?"

They all joined hands and closed their eyes before the pastor began to speak.

"Merciful father, please hear us now in our time of loss. We're mere mortals and we don't understand times like these when our lives are torn apart and we suffer such loss and grief. It's easy for us to lash out at circumstances we cannot control and blame those who don't deserve it, lose our faith and stumble in our walk on the path. We feel alone, Lord, but we're never alone for you are with us always, especially now at our greatest trial. For, though we're brought down to our knees in our pain, you will carry us through the dark valley and into the light. Please comfort your son David for he's mourning the loss of his mother who's been called up to join with the angels in heaven. Grant him the knowledge that someday he'll be reunited with her again through your grace and your power to live for all of eternity. We ask this in your most precious name. Amen."

"Amen," they said.

"Thank you, pastor, I appreciate that. My mother loved the church."

"She was an incredible person, Dave. We'll all miss her."

That statement affected Dave deeply bringing his pain to the forefront with the finality of her death. He swallowed the huge lump in his throat.

It took him a little time to recover his composure as Mrs. Bryant eyed him tearfully.

"I'm so sorry, Dave," she said compassionately.

He couldn't utter a word and dabbed his eyes again.

"Well," he said after a few moments, "I guess I'm ready for them."

"Are you sure?" asked the pastor.

"I'd like to get it over with. I hope that doesn't sound bad."

"I understand completely. Actually, I hear that quite a bit. These are not easy things to handle."

Dave waited with Mrs. Bryant while the pastor went to get the well wishers. Dave took a deep breath to steady his turbulent feelings as they filed in through the doorway.

They were mostly friends and co-workers of his mother. There were also some of his school acquaintances. Dave shook countless hands and said *"thank you"* to endless condolences. The people gathered into groups and sat down in the chairs talking with each other. Dave heard laughter often as they talked about their lives and their plans, but by then he was numbed emotionally. His Mom was gone so what did it matter?

He stayed through the entire day with the exception of a brief trip outside to grab a very quick meal. An evening surge of people came after work before the room finally emptied out. Dave sat alone in the front row just before it was time to leave. The pastor and his wife were downstairs talking to the funeral director when a lone man came into the room and went straight to the casket. Large, with thick curly hair and a thick beard, the man was a stranger to Dave.

The mysterious, new arrival whispered to his mother and seemed to be in real distress. Dave got up and walked over to the man.

"Did you know my mother?"

"I did," said the man with difficulty. His genuine grief reignited Dave's own painful feelings.

"What happened to her, Davey?"

"She got cancer...fought it for years and there was a point where I thought she was going to beat it, but one day it just spread all through her body and she went downhill quickly. It was murder for me to stand by helpless and not save her."

The man started to sob and put his hand on Mary Cray.

"I'm so sorry, Mary," he groaned in misery. "I was inadequate for the task and I failed you."

"I don't understand. What are you talking about? Who are you?"

The man was lost in grief and took time for him to compose himself.

"David, I'm your uncle. My name is Bralan, your father, Doran, is my brother."

"My father, I never knew my father. Mom wouldn't talk about him. I thought that he abandoned us or something."

"NO!" snapped Bralan, "he didn't abandon you, David. There's a great deal that you don't know."

"I'm all ears," said Dave, his ire starting to gather.

"We can't talk here. I'll attend the funeral service tomorrow. After the burial, I'll come to the house and we'll have a long talk. You have decisions to make, nephew."

"I really never thought about what to do afterwards."

"You have no choice about that. You'll be forced to decide."

"You say there's a great deal I don't know. Will you tell me the whole story about my mother and father?"

"I will, but I must leave now before they see us together."

"Who?" asked Dave, glancing around the empty room.

Bralan walked quickly out of the room. Dave tried to follow him, but when he got to the hallway Bralan was gone.

The pastor came up the steps.

"Are you ready to go home, Dave?"

"Yes sir, thank you."

They went out to the car for the drive home. Dave looked around for any sign of his uncle.

"Do you want me to pick you up tomorrow, Dave?"

"I've imposed on you enough, Pastor. I'll drive my Mom's car tomorrow myself. I'm very grateful for everything you've done for me, but also for what you meant in my mother's life. She drew a lot of strength from your sermons."

"Thank you, David. You like to think you make a difference."

"You did for her, reverend."

Dave got out of the car and waved as they drove away. He went into the house and sat down on the couch, curious about the new relative in his life.

"I've got an uncle?"

Restlessness and sadness gripped him. He got up and walked slowly around the house looking at his mother's belongings, items she would never use again. They were reflections of the simple life she lived. None of them was particularly valuable or ostentatious, as it wasn't her way to be showy. It was very depressing; such a waste of a good life cut short and made no sense.

"There are so many evil people walking around, but the good people are struck down early," he muttered regretfully.

He went into her bedroom. A comb and other personal items were neatly arranged on her dresser where she'd left them. Clothes hung in the closet, untouched for months after moving to the hospital for a last ditch and an ultimately futile surgery, and finally hospice. He remembered clearly the day that she left the house for the last time. She knew it was her end, but displayed courage and resolve in spite of her looming dark fate.

"Davey, don't worry about me, I'm ready for whatever happens. I've come to peace with my life and my mistakes. I'm sorry I can't be here to see you and my grandchildren, son. I'll be with you in spirit always, never forget that."

Dave sat down on her bed and lay back staring at the cracks in the ceiling paint and stains where water had leaked from a pipe. He dozed off lying on top of the covers fully dressed, exhausted from a sleepless week of stress and worry and didn't awaken until morning to a loud knocking on the door.

Jumping up, he hurried to the front door.

When he opened the door Uncle Bralan said, "Good morning, David." Bralan was dressed in an ill fitting suit that looked very odd. He didn't seem to be the type who wore suits.

"Morning, Uncle Bralan."

"You had a difficult night, David, I'm sorry to wake you, but time is not our ally."

"I'll make a pot of coffee," said Dave, rubbing the sleep from his eyes. "The funeral service today is early so we'll be back fairly quickly. I told them I didn't want a protracted service. You can ride with me, because I've got Mom's car."

Dave went to the kitchen and rustled about for the pot, the coffee, and cleansed mugs straight out of the dishwasher. Uncle Bralan strolled about the house looking at everything closely.

"Do you want to watch the news?" Dave asked.

His uncle looked at him curiously, like his question made no sense.

"The news, you know, on television?"

"Oh," his uncle replied. "I've never gotten accustomed to that aspect of your society, this technology."

"My society…?"

"I'll explain. First though, tell me about your life, your mother, and your future plans."

"There isn't much to tell." He poured the coffee and handed a cup to his uncle. "I hope you like your coffee strong."

"I do. That's the only way to drink coffee."

"Mom has always lived here in the Midwest. The only time I didn't live here was when I went south to college. She got the cancer soon after I left, but she never told me. She wanted me to finish school and get my degree and knew I would drop out of school and come back if I found out about her disease. After I graduated and came home, it was too late. She had a brief rally when I came around, but it didn't matter. The cancer seemed to explode overnight and she went downhill in a hurry."

He paused and glanced at Bralan who had a haunted expression on his face.

"She never had any grand goals for herself," he continued. "She doted on me and I know I should feel bad about that, but I don't. Her love got me through the rough times not having a father. I got teased when I was young, before I started to grow and I got some size and they left me alone. I had a lot of anger back then. She helped me to cope with it instead of letting it consume me. Without her, I think I would have been fighting all of the time. As it was I had more than my share of fights."

"Are you still angry, David?"

"About some things, yes I am."

"What about you and your life?"

"I had trouble picking a major in college. I played sports for fun and I was really good, but when it came to academics, I had trouble getting

11

enthused about any particular subject. I was smart enough, but wasn't motivated and finally graduated with a social science degree. With the economy in rough shape, there are zero jobs out there and I have no idea what to do about a career. Mom was content to live a simple life. She didn't make a great deal of money and her job was average, but she didn't care. As long as I was taken care of, that was all that mattered. I wanted to return the favor and take care of her so she could take it easy, but I never got that chance."

"Do you have a girl, someone that you desire for a mate?"

"No, I date, but there's no one special to me. Being unemployed, I wouldn't even think about marriage."

He paused and sipped his coffee.

"Tell me how you know my mother."

"This is going to sound unbelievable, David. I don't ask you to take anything I say just on my word alone. Later, I'll show you proof. I simply ask that you hear me out until I finish. Please don't interrupt me with questions. If you have any when I'm done, you can ask me then."

"Okay," said Dave.

"I know that I look different from other people. There's a reason for that. I am different, as was your father. We were not born on Earth. We were born on a planet far from here called Diasporia. That planet suffered a great calamity that forced all of the inhabitants to flee annihilation in the ancient past. It was centuries before life could return to the planet. The new residents were immigrants, drawn from many other worlds. The current residents know the planet as Faenum, which comes from their word for refuge. My people were scattered on other worlds and only a relatively small number of them chose to return to our ancestral home. You must understand that I'm talking about fundamental differences between Earth and Faenum. They're not in the same universe. Here the laws of nature are different. Where you have technology as your standard, on Faenum, there is no technology, but instead there is magic."

"What?" Dave asked, skeptically.

"No questions yet, David. The proof of magic is that I'm here standing before you. I didn't come here in a space vessel. We don't fly to other planets. You wonder how your father and your mother could have met and fallen in love. Your father was brilliant and he was gifted beyond any of us. He perfected his craft and then developed new skills and abilities. It was he that delved into the ancient records of our forefathers and learned the great secrets of their migration, and he learned about the vast powers they wielded. With that power, he learned about other universes and conceived of traveling outside of our own universe. He took a great risk on his first effort to accomplish such travel, because if he was wrong he would have died in the attempt. That endeavor brought him here to Earth, but he was sapped of strength and in bad shape. It came to pass that he arrived near your mother's house. She happened upon him lying unconscious in a forest, took him to her home and nursed him back to health. Their bond grew rapidly. Doran learned from his mistakes in that first attempt, so he fixed the process to make it safe to travel again. He was able to bring Mary back to Faenum where they were married and then they came back to Earth and had a wedding here too. Unfortunately, they had too little time together. Events on Faenum required your father to take action against an enemy too terrible to contemplate, but there was no one else to do it. Since there was no guarantee he could prevail, he sent his pregnant wife back to Earth where she would be safe, but they both knew their lives together were over. He gave her his love, but he told her that she should not tell you about him. Rather, she should raise you here where you were safe from the perils on Faenum."

"So, what happened to him?"

"No one can be sure. He went on a quest, a suicide mission to breech the dark fortress called Mortus. No one ever chooses to go there and no one that has gone there has ever returned."

"If he knew there was no chance to succeed, why did he go?"

"He had no choice, David. We don't know what occurred when he went there, but we do know he had an effect. The peril that threatened us was blunted, though not eliminated. There's some form of stalemate that resulted from his efforts which endures to this day. What my brother did, we'll never know. He was the most powerful of us all. If he couldn't conquer his foe, then none of us can. We exist now in something of a limbo, like the stalemate will expire at some point and the enemy will fall upon us again, but next time with us helpless to stop them."

Bralan looked at Dave who sat transfixed.

"I wouldn't tell these things to just any person of the human race," he continued. "There would be no point. What occurs on Faenum doesn't

13

impact Earth. If we were wiped out for all time, none on Earth will ever know, or care."

"From what you're saying, there's nothing that we could do from Earth anyway. You must have a point you're getting at."

"Although you've always lived on Earth and you see yourself as one of them that's only half true. You have mixed heritage and therefore a stake in Faenum. If you choose to live out your days on this world, that's your choice to make, but if you wish to come with me and return to the world of your father, we're hard pressed to deal with our enemy. Your presence would be a great boon. Here you're bound by the laws governing this world. Back home, you would revert to the innate attributes you gain from your father."

"Magic…?"

"Yes, I would need to teach you to find it within yourself, and then teach you how to wield it."

"So everybody has magic back there?"

"No, most do not, but I'm sure that you're blessed."

They looked at each other.

"You can think about this difficult choice, but I must tell you Dave that time is very short. I must return to my world soon. If you choose to stay here, that decision is irrevocable. Once I leave, I won't be coming back. Don't make a hasty decision nephew, but be clear on what you wish to do with your life."

"I gather things are tough on Faenum."

"You have no idea. We'll protect you at our keep until you're acclimated, trained and ready for the hazards of life on Faenum."

"Maybe this was an omen. I've got nothing going here. The only person that I was tied to is gone. Maybe I'll give this a try, uncle."

"I'll leave you after we get back from the service. There are preparations that I must make. I'll return tomorrow. If it's your decision to leave Earth, settle your affairs. I don't know if you'll ever return."

Later, when he got home and his uncle had left, Dave thought about the bizarre story he'd heard and tried to think about his life on Earth. There was, in fact, nothing holding him here. He called his mother's best friend.

"Listen Madge, I'm going to be moving away. I don't really have need of any of my mother's things. I'll write a paper to authorize you to sell the house and her stuff. Take anything of hers that you want and take

14

a big chunk of the proceeds for yourself for doing this for me and then you can donate to whatever charities that my Mom liked. I know this sounds impulsive, but I do have a plan. Thank you, I love you and I appreciate your doing this for me. Don't worry about me, I'll be fine."

* * * *

He received a number of calls after that, all from concerned friends offering to counsel him about his "hasty" decision.

"You didn't waste any time, Madge," he muttered to himself as he listened to the message from the pastor he'd let go to the answering machine. By the time that Bralan returned the following morning, there were ten messages on the machine.

"Are you ready, David?"

"Probably not, Uncle Bralan, what's going to happen?"

"I'll create a bubble of power to encase and protect us for the translocation to Faenum."

"Does it hurt?"

Bralan smiled. "It's a strange feeling, not one that I'd call pleasant."

"That's encouraging."

"I'm going to put my hands to your head. Your human side dominates your mind at the moment. You need to have access to your other mind, your Faenum half. You need to be able to understand the language of Faenum. Opening this mental door will do that for you. I think, too, it will enable your innate abilities."

"If I have any," Dave muttered skeptically.

Dave closed his eyes as his uncle touched his head and felt a warm glow seeping into his head. For a moment he felt weakness and nausea and stumbled. His uncle held him up in an iron grip. The glow soaked deep into every part of his brain. When his uncle took his hands away Dave felt much different. Scents were sharper, colors more vivid; he felt a tingle throughout his whole body and felt full of energy.

"How do you feel, David?"

"I guess I'm okay, I can see really clearly."

"I've just spoken to you in my native language and you replied in it also. I've given you the ability to talk on Faenum when we arrive."

"Thanks. I wish that you'd been around when I was taking math classes in college. This is the fastest I've ever learned anything."

"I couldn't help you with that. I can only impart what I know."

"Bummer..."

"It's time, David."

Dave looked around the house one last time.

"I'm ready, let's do this thing."

His uncle started to whisper and they began to glow. The glow expanded surrounding Dave and felt warm, comforting. As the glow grew in intensity, the background darkened and faded out of sight. Dave felt the nausea return and then experienced vertigo, like he was falling out of an airplane.

In the midst of the blazing aura, he could barely see his uncle.

He wasn't sure how long they traveled in time, while gritting his teeth to endure the unpleasant sensations.

Suddenly there was a severe jolt. He felt like he was falling out of control and lost sight of his uncle.

After a few moments, the bubble popped with a loud concussion and Dave fell down on a forest floor bumping into a person lying under a heavy blanket. It was very cold and there were light snowflakes in the night air. The impact knocked the air out of his lungs and crashing into the person caused a scream and a flourish of movement.

Dave tried to orient himself, but had a splitting headache was wobbly and off balance. The camper leaped to their feet and suddenly Dave had a sword pointed at his chest.

"Whoa!" Dave yelled, putting up his hands.

"What are you, Intruder?"

Dave blinked his eyes and peered in the darkness at the sword wielder.

"I'm Dave."

"Are you a god?"

He realized it was a female voice, although he couldn't see her face under her heavy hood.

"No, I'm not a god."

"You appeared in a burst of sound and light. Why have you come to my camp? Have you come to slay me?"

"No."

He tried to shift out of his awkward position. She brought the sword point against his chest.

"I was just trying to sit up so we can talk."

"I don't trust you."

"Well, we can't sit like this all night. Will you let me sit up?"

16

"If you make any move against me, I will slay you where you sit."

"Fair enough..."

He slowly levered his body around and sat up. She kept the sword pointed at the ready.

"What now?" The cold air cut through his light clothes and he began to shiver. He was still wearing clothes from Earth: blue jeans and a shirt.

She said nothing, but simply watched him.

"Why do you not protect yourself? Do you have strange powers that you plan to use to assail me?"

"I'm sorry to disappoint you. I'm just me. I just came here from my world. I was traveling with my uncle, but something happened and I got spilled out here. I've never been here before, I have no weapons, and as you can see I'm not dressed for this climate. You can let me freeze to death, or you can be a nice person and help me. I've got nobody here."

She thought about his words and lowered her sword.

"I still don't believe you, but I will not ignore your request for my help. I'm a nice person, as you say."

"Thank you."

"If you believe you'll lull me into complacency so you can perpetrate evil against me, know that I'm diligent at all times. I'll end your life quickly if you try anything at all."

"You've already made that point. I got it the first time."

"You speak strangely."

"What's your name?"

"I don't give my name to strangers."

"What should I call you?"

"Don't call me anything, go away from my camp."

"Go where? It's night here, wherever here is. You've got weapons and I've got nothing. I've got no choice but to stay here. I can't wander around lost in the dark."

"What is that to me?"

"I don't know you, but I have the feeling that you're not cruel. I'm going to trust you."

She looked at him thoughtfully and glanced around as they heard the roar of a beast on the move in the forest.

"Perhaps I'm a fool, but I think that you're also a good person, so I'll grant you my trust. It's a sacred gift. If you try to take advantage of me, I will not hesitate to slay you."

17

"Maybe we should get some sleep and forget about the slaying," he said tentatively. "We can figure it out in the morning."

She eyed him closely as she sat down and pulled her covers over her. Dave watched her a moment. His shivering was getting intense and he slid over beside her.

"What are you doing?" she shouted, pulling out a dagger.

"It isn't hard to figure out. Either I sleep under that blanket with you or I freeze to death. It's your choice."

A hostile look came over her face.

"Don't think to surprise me. I'll have blades in both of my hands."

Dave eased down beside her and carefully brought the heavy blanket over both of them.

"Thank you," he whispered.

New World

When Dave opened his eyes into the dim light of dawn, the ground and their blanket was covered with snow; he was lying on his side snuggled against the back of the woman with his arm flopped over her. She was on her side sleeping restfully.

"*This could be a problem*," he thought to himself and tried to gently take his arm away, but still awakened her.

She suddenly smacked an elbow to his ribs, knocking the air out of his lungs.

"Ah!" he shouted painfully.

"What are you trying to do?" she snapped.

"Nothing...We were sleeping together for warmth. I think you broke my ribs!"

She eyed him skeptically. "For a god, you complain a great deal."

"I'm not a god, I told you. I'm scrambling here. Put yourself in my shoes. One minute I'm in my own world and the next thing I'm dumped into your camp unprepared for anything. You keep pretending I'm a threat. Do you see any weapons of any kind? Did you not notice me shivering from having on the wrong clothes? Have you ever seen clothes like these?"

"No. They're stranger looking than you are."

"Thanks," he said facetiously. "Why don't you drop the threats? I'm not doing anything but trying to survive."

Eyeing him thoughtfully, she went to her pack and set out some food. She ate some dried meat and chunks of cheese and drank some water.

Dave watched her feed and waited to see what she would do.

She wouldn't look at him. Finally, she turned her head and glared.

"Is it your plan to eat up my food too? I have too little for me."

"You would be getting more food anyway, right? Now we'll just get food for both of us."

"You cannot stay with me," she huffed.

"Where am I supposed to go? I don't know where I am, and I certainly have no place to go. This is your world, not mine."

She looked at him sourly before she reluctantly handed him a little meat and cheese, and then a few swallows of water from her gourd.

"You're an infant," she complained, "less than an infant."

"Sticks and stones," he muttered.

"I hear you. Your words make no sense, but I know that you insult me."

"Wrong, I'm not the one on the muscle here."

"What? What does that even mean?"

"It means that we should get up and get about our business," he said. "If we need food, let's go get it."

She looked like she was going to argue further.

"What do we do next?" he asked, ignoring her hostile mood.

"Is there anything that you can do?" she asked, scornfully.

"I'm a fast learner."

"Very well, I'll teach you to hunt for food. Don't think that means you may follow me around forever. You may stay with me until you can fend for yourself, but no longer than that."

"Sure, I'll take it. Maybe you can also teach me about your land and your people in the meantime."

She shrugged her shoulders and walked away. Dave hurried to follow her when it became obvious she was not going to wait.

"So, this planet is called Faenum?" he asked rhetorically.

She glanced at him like he was an idiot. "Of course, if you're not from here, how did you know that?"

"My uncle told me. He's from here. My father was from Faenum, my mother was from Earth."

"Earth...?" she asked, testing the word. "That's a poor name."

"Why do you say that?"

"It sounds dull, like saying Mud - I come from the planet Mud," she answered.

Dave started to chuckle. "I guess you've got a point." He saw a slight smile on her face.

They came upon an animal trail and paused.

"Don't attempt to chase down your prey," she explained. "They can easily elude you. Wait for them to come to you."

He followed her as she climbed a large tree nearby. Once she seated herself securely on a sturdy branch, she notched an arrow in her bow. They didn't wait long before an elk trotted up the path, paused just out of range and looked around, as if it could sense them.

It stood immobile for a long time before it finally took a few tentative steps in their direction. She pulled back the bowstring and fired, striking the animal and bringing it down. They hurried down to the ground and raced to the thrashing creature.

Quickly pulling out her knife, she silenced the animal. It was the first time Dave had seen anything killed and he stared uncomfortably at the scene as she worked. She suddenly stopped and looked at him.

"We must hurry, the smell of the blood will draw predators…" and then handed him a large knife.

"Do what I do," she said as she started to dress the kill. "We'll take what we can carry. We have little time before the scavengers close in. We must be well away before they get here."

They sliced up meat and stuffed it into some carrying pouches.

A nearby roar split the air.

"We must go now," she said. Dave grabbed the pouches and chased after her sprinting form as she ran at full speed up the path. She veered off the path and they climbed a rise. Just as they left the path, Dave glanced back at the carcass and saw a blur of movement as a massive furred beast snatched up the remains in a huge maw and dragged it into the trees.

"What was that?"

"Silence," she said. "We must move quickly."

They hurried for a distance before she finally slowed down. Looking all around, she listened before continuing on, but signaled him to silence. They walked for almost an hour before she relaxed.

"When you make a kill, you place yourself in peril," she explained. "There can be dangerous beasts very nearby, near enough to attack before you can get away to safety. Even when we're away from the kill site, the smell of the blood in the meat we carry can draw notice also."

"That's reassuring," said Dave.

"You must be vigilant always," she replied.

They made their way back to her camp.

"Do we make a fire and cook some meat for lunch?" he asked.

Again she looked at him like he was an idiot.

"This is no place for a fire."

Suddenly she froze, staring at something behind him. Dave felt a cold chill run down his spine. He slowly turned his head and saw a young woman standing casually just outside of the tree line watching them. Dressed in a white cloak, she had jet black hair streaked with white and carried a staff that was heavily carved with markings and symbols. Her eyes sparkled with potency. She was an intimidating sight and began to walk toward them; Dave's new friend drew her sword.

The stranger moved right into their camp with no sign of fear.

She glanced at Dave curiously looking at him and his garb from top to bottom, and then she turned her attention to his friend.

"I know what you are," said his friend in a frightened hiss. She held her sword pointed at the stranger defensively, just as she had when she first met Dave.

"And I know what you are also," the stranger replied in a soft melodic voice.

"Why are you here?" asked his friend.

"I was drawn here," the stranger replied. "There was some event of great portent that happened in this area. I'm here to discover the truth of that occurrence."

"That was probably me arriving," said Dave.

The stranger looked at him skeptically.

"You're definitely strange," she said, "but you're merely a man."

"He appeared out of thin air in a burst of light and sound," said his friend. "He's more than a man, though what he is, I do not know."

She looked deeply at Dave and reached out a hand.

"Stop…!" shouted his friend.

"What's wrong?" asked Dave.

"She's a witch," said his friend. "They leave men dead in their wake."

"I'm a white witch," said the woman, "and you're talking from superstition and ignorance. We're the guardians who safeguard the lands."

"You're vile and misguided predators that travel the land searching out the weak and helpless to perpetrate your evil designs."

"That statement is based on what?" asked the stranger. "You know nothing of our ways."

"I know that you always travel in pairs."

"I travel alone."

"I don't believe you. Be wary Dave for there's another of them nearby in hiding. They bear ill will toward men."

"I don't make judgments based on wild tales and prejudice," said the stranger. "I don't know this man to be able to judge his story, but I know you mistress. Your name is Jenna and you're prima virga of the Warlen nation. You're the first maiden. Your mate becomes the High Chieftain of the Warlen tribes. How is it you're so far away from your home in such a hostile place? You're in peril every minute you stay here. It's only through pure luck you've avoided danger and death in the jaws of a myriad of fearsome hunters, or even worse, capture by the savage people who live here. Your people would never have let you simply stroll away alone for a walk in the woods. You're warded every minute of every day. If I'm not incorrect, the tribes each sent their champions to compete for your hand in brutal combat. I would say that your choice for a mate did not win that fight."

Jenna's face clouded at the memory. "He would have been the best chieftain our people have ever had. He was not only brave and skilled, he was smart. He would have led the peoples to a better life. He was killed by Ragar who is a soulless butcher and a brute that is the worst of our people in every way. I would never submit to a life with such a monster. So what! What business is that of yours?"

"Every atrocity is the business of the sisterhood," said the stranger.

"Sisterhood, pah," said Jenna. "You hide in your keep and practice your unwholesome rites and call it a sisterhood. It's an abomination."

"You have no idea what you're talking about. These are stories made up by the ignorant to frighten their people into the very deeds that you have just described. We work for the day when such barbaric rites occur no more anywhere in the land. We offer enlightenment. We offer you another way along the path to serenity. If you could experience the communion of the sisters, you would understand what I'm saying."

"What I understand is that witches always go in pairs. They never go alone. If you're truly here without a partner, I think that you have a tale of your own to share. You've revealed my secret. Are you willing to reveal your own? What's your name?"

The stranger smiled wryly. "It was said that you're an exceptional woman, without peer actually. As I talk with you, I'm inclined to agree with that assessment. To show you that I'm without guile, I'll tell you my name is Selane. As you know, sisters give their names to a precious few, and only when there is a bond of trust, and we never give our names to men. See, I've given my trust to you, Jenna. Will you do the same?"

"I know that name. I think you're a prima virga of your own. You don't have a mate. Your order would never let you roam freely either. I think we're both loose abroad on a fool's errand. What do you say about that?"

Selane shrugged her shoulders.

"It's true I'll have some explaining to do when I return to the keep. I was being wooed by those who wished for me to be their mate. I wasn't favorably disposed toward any of them. I thought it best to take some time alone to clear my head and consider my options."

"Hah!" said Jenna triumphantly. "You ran away just as I did. Don't try to make it sound like some noble quest on your part. You don't fool me."

"Think what you want," said Selane dismissively. "Take out some meat for our meal. I'm hungry."

"Don't think that you can join us," Jenna huffed. "I will not suffer any longer the affront of your presence."

"There's nothing you can do to send me away and you're but one voice out of three of us."

"He will not abide your presence either. You'll kill him in his sleep."

"Is this your belief, interloper?"

"My name is Dave," he replied. "I don't know you, your order, or any of these things you two are talking about. All that I can go on is to look you both in the eyes and make up my mind. To tell you the truth, you're both really beautiful women and I don't feel endangered by either of you. Maybe you're a great peril to me, Selane, but I don't see it. I choose to trust you. I've got nothing to lose."

Selane looked at him in pleased surprise.

"I've not spoken with any man such as you ever before. You've the courage to extend your trust to a stranger when others would shy away in fear and prejudice. I'm greatly moved by your gesture. I'll tell you this. I name you friend to me and worthy of my trust. No man has ever received such a gift. To you Jenna I say, I'll dwell with you and provide my protection. That's no small thing. With me, you can live in safety. I can cloak us from the search of man or beast. The sisterhood studies the old ways and we have the power of the ancients to wield."

Jenna was quiet.

"If that's the truth, I welcome your protection," she said finally.

Selane took some meat out of their pouch and placed it in one of Jenna's pans. She whispered words and her hands began to glow. It reminded Dave of the glow around his uncle. The meat began to sizzle and cook. Before long the three of them dined on the steaks until they sated their hunger.

"This is a good place for a camp for a single night," Selane observed, "but it's fortunate for you that I'm here. You would have been discovered here before long. What was your plan? You cannot have chosen to make this spot your new home."

"I was running away," Jenna explained. "I wasn't going to a place, I was leaving one. I have no idea what I would have done next. Honestly, I didn't think I would survive this long alone."

"We can stay here for a time, but we should decide a place to go," said Selane.

"What do you say, Dave?" asked Jenna.

"I guess I'd like to find my uncle," he replied. "I have no idea how we would go about doing that. In the meantime, I don't mind hanging out with you guys."

The women looked at him curiously.

"What does that mean?" asked Selane.

"He often speaks like a fool," said Jenna.

"I see," said Selane. "Tomorrow we can move out of this deadly forest and farther away from the Warlen tribes."

"That works for me," said Dave. "Can you do anything about getting warm clothes for me? Walking around with Jenna's blanket wrapped around me is getting old."

That evening when they prepared to sleep, Selane looked at Jenna with surprise when she bedded down with Dave under the same blanket.

"You've made him your mate, Jenna?"

"Of course not," snapped Jenna angrily.

"We're just sharing the warmth," said Dave. "I had nothing to cover myself. She saved me."

25

Selane had a strange enigmatic look, which Dave didn't understand, as she considered his explanation.

"Have you told him the significance of your purity?" asked Selane.

"It's not an issue," Jenna replied dismissively.

"Oh, but it is," Selane insisted. "If a prima virga gives herself to anyone other than the champion of their contests, she is forfeit of her life, along with her consort. Any Warlen from any tribe is obliged to slay them on sight. Think carefully about how you conduct yourself with her, Dave. Her people will not take kindly to your dalliances."

"That's good to know, Selane," Dave replied curtly. "For your information, I'm a decent guy. I don't do that stuff. Good night."

He rolled onto his side facing away from Jenna.

"I'll watch over you and set wards to protect us in the night," Selane explained. She closed her eyes and began a soft chant. Her body shimmered with a soft blue glow while she worked. Later, when her magical construct was in place she glided over and knelt down by Jenna. She stared at her closely. After a few minutes she started a new chant. She created a floating glowing ball of energy, which she gently guided onto Jenna's head. Jenna stirred in her sleep, but she didn't wake up.

After watching the energy ball seep into Jenna, Selane laid out her own bedroll beside Jenna and dozed off to sleep.

In the morning when Dave opened his eyes into sunlight he saw Selane sitting beside Jenna staring into her sleeping face.

"What's up, Selane?" It startled Selane and it awoke Jenna.

"What're you doing?" asked Jenna angrily.

"I'm merely safe guarding you," she replied.

"Get back," said Jenna, pulling out her dagger.

"You've nothing to fear from me," said Selane, chuckling lightly.

"Don't think that your lies will keep me from seeing the truth of you," said Jenna. "I had very strange dreams last night. I think you had a hand in that."

"You think I can control your dreams?" asked Selane, scornfully. "Your thoughts are your own. You're too taken with your superstitious beliefs."

"Give her some space, Selane," said Dave. "Let's all try to get along. We've got troubles enough without you annoying each other."

After they ate a quick breakfast, they packed up their things and started to trek westward.

"Why are we going this direction?" asked Dave.

"To the south you go down into the flatlands and into the realm of Jenna's people, the Warlen," said Selane. "That wouldn't be a good choice in the best of times. With their prima virga missing, they'll kill first and ask questions later. To the east lie more of this forest, foothills of the mountains and similar perils from predators and bands of hunters. Northward the trek into the mountains is treacherous, and often deadly. The mountains that way are inhabited by horrible creatures that will capture you in snares of ice and magic. They drag you away to their ice caves to store you until they're ready to feed. It's a terrible way to die. The peoples that live there in that frozen waste are worse than the beasts of the mountains. It's said they also feed on captives for their meat, but they delight in tormenting their prey before the end."

"Let's skip that way," said Dave. "I'm not much on being an entrée."

"Entrée?" asked the women.

"The meal, the food," Dave explained.

They looked at him wryly.

Dark clouds roiled over the peaks of the mountains as they walked and soon it started to snow again, this time heavier. Dave glanced at Selane.

"You're not cold?" he asked.

"The fire of the sisterhood burns within me," she replied. "It warms me."

"Every time you do something, liking glowing, or working your magic, I feel kind of a tingle."

"That's impossible," she replied. "Men do not carry the flame."

"I don't know about that. My uncle traveled to another universe and brought me here and he's from this world."

Selane was taken aback and walked in silence, her facial expression furrowed with deep thought.

"So if he can do that, do you think I can start my own inner fire? I'm getting tired of wearing this blanket."

"The fire is a sacred trust given to the sisterhood. I've read that in the dawn times there were men who walked about wielding great powers. I always doubted that could be true. I've never seen a man who warranted such…"

She looked at Dave abashedly.

"Hey, no problem, you have your own prejudices too, don't you Selane?"

"I meant no offense."

"None taken..."

The witches hold all men in great contempt," Jenna added. "That's well known to all."

"Why do you hate men?" asked Dave.

"We don't hate them. You don't understand. Men aren't the equal of women. Their natures are to war, to feed, and to spawn. They don't have the faculties for the higher planes of reason, reflection, and introspection. They could never grasp the principles of the sisterhood, or the blessed bond we share. It's rapture unlike any other experience."

"I see," said Dave, sarcastically nodding while glancing at Jenna. He winked at her and she smiled. "I'm glad you clarified that for me, Selane, what a dolt that I am."

"Do you mock me?" she asked, incredulous, glancing between them. Anger crossed her face, but before she could rebuke David sounds of struggle rose just ahead.

They stood still and listened closely.

"There's a terrible fight up ahead," whispered Selane, as roars and yelps of pain erupted. "We should go around this place."

"No," said Dave. "I don't know why, but I feel like we need to go there, and quickly."

The women were apprehensive and it showed. Dave hurried away and they reluctantly followed. Climbing a small hill, they looked downward to see a massive being roaring in rage swinging a huge war club bashing at a pack of snarling creatures resembling oversized wolves. Behind the pack stood band of squat, thick bodied, dull featured warriors that looked like Neanderthals to Dave. They were tossing spears and hurling clubs at the huge figure.

"What are they?" asked Dave. "That big one has got to be at least twelve feet tall."

"A giant mountain troll," said Selane. "It looks to be caught in a trap of the Agia men who live in these woods. You're fortunate, Jenna, that you weren't captured by them. Your fate at their hands would have been an abomination, as you say. The trolls are ferocious, and they also eat their victims. This is no concern of ours."

"Wait a minute," said Dave. "This isn't fair leaving the big guy unable to fight back."

"Dave, you cannot interfere," said Selane. "The Agia men kill without conscience or thought. You would just be more meat in their cook pots tonight. The troll would offer you no better fate."

"Something isn't right. I feel like we need to save him."

"What!" both women exclaimed in horror.

Dave grabbed Jenna's bow out of her hands and notched an arrow.

"Don't do this," said Selane, but he fired before she could stop him. He hit one of the wolves and it dropped to the ground. The wolves looked up and started to bay in his direction. The troll used the respite to slam a savage blow with his club, felling three more of the creatures in a single mighty swipe. The Agia men milled around in confusion. Dave launched another shot and dropped one of them. They jumped back gesturing toward him and bellowing, but they didn't attack. The troll nailed the two remaining wolves and Dave dropped another of the Agia men. They lost heart and raced off with the wolves disappearing into the woods.

The women sat transfixed.

"We're not attacked," said Selane in shocked surprise.

"We just did what was right," said Dave. "Now let's go down there and help that big dude. I think he's hurt."

"No!" shouted both women, but Dave ignored them and hurried down the hill.

When he got to the small clearing he walked up to the troll. It bellowed defiantly and brandished the mighty club.

"Hey," yelled Dave, "cool off, we just saved your life."

The troll eyed him cautiously. The two women eased up behind Dave looking at the troll with fear.

Dave stepped forward. The troll growled and gripped his club.

"It will kill you," said Selane.

"I don't think so," said Dave.

He eased close and looked at the left leg of the troll. It was covered in blood and Dave could see that his lower leg bone was broken.

"Selane, come here," he said.

"I fear to do so," she replied.

"Look, you accused Jenna of being misinformed and prejudicial. I'm standing right here and this injured troll hasn't attacked me. Come over here and help me. He's hurt badly."

Both women edged forward slowly gazing in terror at the troll who was clearly in great pain.

"His leg is broken," no wonder he couldn't escape.

A large tree had been sawed and fashioned into a massive log and tied up suspended in the trees. The troll had hit the trip wire and the log had swung down and smashed into his leg shattering his bone.

Selane eased close eyeing the troll fearfully the whole way.

"Can we make a splint, or something?" asked Dave.

Selane examined the damaged leg and closed her eyes. She began a soft chant and began to glow brightly then put her hands onto the broken leg of the troll who cried out in pain. Crackling sounds of the bone moving back into place with splinters and shards being collected and realigned. As she finished the interior repairs of the bone and torn muscles, she then began healing the outer wounds of the skin. A half an hour passed before she completed the task.

When she was done she stepped back and the glow faded from his leg and her body.

"That was amazing, Selane," said Dave. Completely spent, she looked at him with vacant eyes, and collapsed unconscious into his arms.

Dave grabbed her and Jenna hurried over to help. They carried her to a nearby flat spot and laid her there.

The troll start to move behind them, took a step to test his repaired leg, turned and started toward them.

Jenna cringed in fear.

"The leg seems to be working fine," said Dave.

The troll stopped and looked at him curiously.

"I'm Dave. You don't need to thank us."

"It doesn't understand you," said Jenna. "They don't speak. I think it's going to kill us now."

"Kra'ac," said the troll.

"What's that?" asked Dave.

"My name," said the troll. He looked directly at Jenna. "Yes, tiny female, we do speak."

"I'm sorry, I didn't know," she said.

"That other one," said Kra'ac, nodding toward Selane. "Will she recover?"

"I have no idea," said Dave. "Her name is Selane, she's a white witch and this is Jenna, the prima virga of the Warlen's."

"Dave, you shouldn't be so free with this information," said Jenna.

"You think Kra'ac is going to go tell everybody in the area?" asked Dave.

"Nonetheless, we must use caution. We cannot be trusting of strangers."

"I'm a stranger. I turned out pretty good."

"That remains to be seen," said Jenna wryly.

"Hey," Dave objected.

"We must leave," said Kra'ac. "The Agia men will soon return in force. We must not be here when they arrive."

He picked up Selane like she was weightless and cradled her in his arms.

"We were going west," said Dave. Kra'ac nodded and they hurried off in that direction.

They traveled quickly. Dave and Jenna had trouble keeping up with Kra'ac who covered a great deal of ground with each step. It was particularly difficult because they were on the side of a hill walking on an angle and the detritus of the forest floor made for treacherous footing. Kra'ac took the lead by virtue of the fact that neither Jenna nor Dave could manage to get in front of him.

He led them to a small rock formation that was overgrown by a thicket far away from the site of his battle with the Agia men. He spread the tangle apart so they could all climb inside. Kra'ac put Selane down on a blanket that Jenna laid out and sat down protectively beside her.

Dave and Jenna sat down and shared some beef jerky and water. He offered a stick to Kra'ac.

"I've eaten," his voice sounding like a rumble of deep thunder.

When Kra'ac looked down at Selane, his face actually looked gentle.

"Sleep," said Kra'ac, looking back at Dave. "I will guard you."

"Thank you, and thanks for not killing us."

"Thanks for saving my life. Your kind doesn't show kindness to trolls. I'm beholding to you."

"I'm not my kind," said Dave, and then he grinned. "That came out wrong. I am my kind, but I'm different."

31

Dave crawled under the blanket with Jenna. Without thinking, he pushed against her back and put an arm over her realizing too late his impulsive act could be misconstrued; he didn't want to make the matter into an incident. Her body tensed up initially, but then she relaxed and snuggled back against him. Dave smiled.

"She finally trusts me," he thought to himself with satisfaction.

Strange Friendships

When Dave woke up, Jenna was already preparing a meal. Selane was still unconscious with Kra'ac watching her closely. Dave crawled over.

"Any change?" he asked.

Kra'ac shrugged.

Selane suddenly took a very deep breath and started to move, like she was fighting to come out of a coma. Dave grabbed her when she started to shudder and thrash about.

"Selane!" he yelled. She opened her eyes and stared wildly at him, like she was stuck in a nightmare.

"Selane," he said again. "You're okay. We're all right here. You're safe."

She blinked her eyes and focused on his face. Dave smiled at her and she returned the gesture. She glanced over and saw Kra'ac beside her. She jolted and tried to sit up and move. Dave grabbed her in his arms.

"That's Kra'ac, remember? You fixed his leg. He's very grateful and he's guarded you ever since. He's a good guy."

Selane looked at him in disbelief and then she looked at Kra'ac.

"I'm in your debt for my life, maiden," he said. "It's a life bond between us. I'll protect you for as long as I still draw breath."

"You're speaking," said Selane.

"Of course I am. How else would we communicate?"

"Apparently this is a day for busting myths," said Dave. "Can you be open minded, Selane?"

"I'm sorry I was a burden. The healing was far beyond anything I've ever attempted before. I'm fortunate I wasn't permanently injured in the attempt. I'm still weakened, but at least I can function now."

"Fortunate indeed," Dave noted. "That was amazing what you did. It's like Kra'ac was never injured."

Selane inspected his leg to be sure. Kra'ac sat patiently, unmoving under her touch.

Jenna came over and fed Selane by hand. Selane smiled at her warmly with mischievous eyes.

"Do not do that," said Jenna sourly.

"I'm grateful for your help," said Selane, with a look of innocence.

"We're fellow travelers, Selene, nothing more."

"I said nothing," said Selane, smiling and chuckling.

"You didn't need to," said Jenna reproachfully.

"I'm not following this conversation," said Dave. "What are we talking about?"

"Nothing," said Jenna gruffly. Selane started to laugh, but then coughed weakly.

* * * *

They left their lair and resumed their journey west. The day was grey with heavy clouds filling the sky and the air was slightly warmer, but not warm. Trees were thinning out a bit and they were able to find an animal trail that went in their direction, which made travel easier. They were able to cover considerable ground and by the end of the day, they were out of the forest and the realm of the Agia men.

Selane objected to being carried by Kra'ac, but while walking, she became fatigued very quickly, so grudgingly she acceded to riding again in his powerful arms.

"I feel like a little child," she complained.

"There's no other choice," said Jenna. "Be thankful he is here to carry you because I would not."

They continued through low hills paralleling the mountain range to their right. As the sun sunk on the horizon and the light started to fade they began to look for a campsite for the night. Kra'ac led them up a hill.

"It's the highest point of elevation," Kra'ac said, "the most defensible position that I can see."

As they crested the hill they saw a lone figure sitting with his back toward them facing a campfire, seemingly oblivious to their arrival.

"I guess I should introduce myself," said Dave. He started toward the camp, but suddenly felt danger and dropped instinctively to the ground. Instantly, the stranger whirled and launched a dagger toward where Dave had been standing. The dagger barely missed him and imbedded in a tree behind Dave. He looked at the man who looked back at him curiously.

"We don't want any trouble," said Dave.

"You're alive, how is that possible? No one can evade my attack."

"I just got this weird feeling to dive out of the way."

The man seemed to notice Dave's companions for the first time. Kra'ac had his war club at the ready. Both of the women were on guard, Jenna had drawn her sword and Selane appeared to be trying to draw forth her power, with little success.

"Relax everybody," Dave directed. "This is just a misunderstanding. We're fellow travelers, friend. This seemed like a good spot to camp for the night."

The man didn't seem to be concerned with the aggressive stance of the others.

"What sort of band is this? I see a woman of mystery who, if I'm not wrong, is a Warlen woman, an unmarried one without a Warlen escort. I see a witch, a white witch at that, a part of this company. White witches are never allowed out of the convent and I don't see your scarlet ribbon, child. You're not yet mated, and you're alone? That would never be allowed."

"How do you know so much about our secret customs?" asked Selane.

"I travel extensively and I'm a good listener."

"We don't speak of our ways outside of the sisterhood," said Selane haughtily.

"Nonetheless, secrets have a way of being revealed. I'm further interested that you travel with a mountain troll renowned for their ferocity and hermitic ways. As far as you, my talkative friend, you're the biggest puzzle of all. I cannot place you in any group I've ever seen, and I've seen them all."

"Apparently you haven't seen them all. My name is Dave, that's Jenna, Selane, and he's Kra'ac. What's your name?"

"I'm called many names," said the stranger. "You may call me Graile."

"The blade master?" asked Selane. "I find it hard to imagine you would be here alone in the wilderness."

"As it happens, I needed to make a hasty exit from my last employer. We didn't see eye-to-eye regarding the matter of his…well, I guess it's better left unsaid. Therefore, since I'm between engagements, I'm free to join your odd little band of rule breakers. I'm curious how you have a name for the troll?"

"He told us his name," said Dave.

"I didn't know that trolls talked," said Graile.

"We speak when we have something to say," Kra'ac replied.

Graile laughed heartily.

"This is a fateful day indeed. How is it, Kra'ac, that you're so far away from your mountains? It's a very great journey from your country."

"I had a disagreement with others of my people. They had strong feelings about their viewpoint. I had equally strong feelings about mine. I chose to leave them to their ignorance. I had a sense I needed to come here. I didn't understand it, but I came anyway."

"That's somewhat akin to what I felt," said Graile with a puzzled look. "I came to this barren place with the idea I would meet someone here, and now I have."

"It would be a great boon to have you with us," Jenna volunteered. "There are many dangers for a band of so few as us."

"I don't think that a great many would chose to attack a mountain troll," said Graile. "Where are you going?"

"West," said Dave.

"What do you seek?"

Dave looked at the others sheepishly.

"Perfect," said Graile, "a directionless and pointless quest for no good reason at all. That's my kind of adventure. I think I would like to spend some time with this band of fools."

Graile walked over to the tree and pulled out his dagger.

"You should be dead," he said as he walked past Dave.

"Sorry to disappoint you, Graile. By the way, if you're a blade master, do you have a spare sword I can borrow, and would you teach me to use it?"

Graile laughed and turned to Dave. "You're a bold one. My blades are perfect, like my skills. They were crafted by masters. Some of them are imbued with power. They aren't toys for the untrained."

"How do I get trained? I'm out here helpless. I don't think that's a good state to be in with the hazards of this world. Who better to teach me than the best, if you are the best that is?"

He saw Graile grimace.

"Do you doubt my skill?" he hissed.

"I have no basis to judge anything," Dave replied. "Is it too frightening for you to consider teaching me?"

Graile drew his sword in a blur and pressed it against Dave's neck.

"That's a good move, Graile. Is that my first lesson?"

Graile smiled and put down the blade. "You've piqued my curiosity, stranger. I've never instructed another so you'll be my first apprentice. We'll spar tomorrow."

"Excellent," said Dave happily. "Thanks Graile."

"We'll see how much you thank me after we begin to train. What sort of name is Dave? Who are your people?"

"I'm not from around here."

"Do your people wear blankets in your land?"

"I arrived here a little unprepared. I need to get some warm clothes." They all sat down and ate a meal cooked on Graile's campfire. When Dave prepared to sleep under the blanket with Jenna, Graile eyed them closely.

"You're Jenna, the missing prime virga of the Warlen," Graile said.

"She's letting me share the blanket so I don't freeze," said Dave. "I seem to be explaining that a lot."

Graile watched Selane place her bedding beside Jenna and then Kra'ac sat down beside Selane."

"A white witch sleeping with a troll," said Graile, "you're indeed a bizarre group."

"He's chosen to ward me, though I don't need his protection," said Selane. "Don't concern yourself, blade master."

Next morning, after making trips to a nearby stream, they started moving. Dave's attempt to bathe in the ice cold water had been punishing. The other men didn't complain, so he held his tongue as best he could, although he did groan a great deal at the shock of the freezing water. It did feel good to be clean, though, once he was done. They met the women, who went to a different spot in the stream for their bathing, back at the camp. Resuming a westward trek, they walked for most of the day before entering another heavily wooded area.

Graile led the way as they slowly navigated through the dense vegetation. Suddenly Graile held up a fist and all the travelers dropped to the ground - a rustling sound in a nearby thicket, followed by a shout and the sound of battle ensued. Edging forward, they drew their weapons. A squat burly bearded combatant rolled out of the woods pursued by a tall slender opponent in a hood. They were about to attack each other when they noticed Dave and his band.

They backed up and turned to face each other while they watched the others.

"Greetings dwarf," said Graile.

The dwarf scowled. "Why are you gawking at us?"

"Why not?" asked Graile.

"Greetings, elf," he said.

The elf nodded. "Greetings, blade master," she said.

"What?" asked the dwarf, "you're a female?"

"Very observant," she replied scornfully.

"Why didn't you say anything?" he asked. "This is not an honorable fight if you're a woman."

"You attacked me," she replied.

"The dwarves and the elves have been enemies for centuries," said the dwarf.

"I'm happy to eliminate one dwarf," she replied sternly.

"Why don't we suspend the hostilities," said Graile. "I'm curious how you knew me, elf mistress? What's your name?"

"Lissette," she replied. "Elves keep themselves informed about all of the other peoples. It's a prudent thing to do."

"True," said Graile. "Who are you, dwarf...?"

"I'm Angus," he replied.

"Why is either of you here?" asked Graile.

"I was moved to visit this place," Angus explained. "It was a feeling in my gut."

"Did you have a feeling in your gut, Lissette?" asked Graile.

"No," she replied. "There was a slight disagreement in my village."

"You made yourself scarce," said Graile mirthfully.

They looked at the companions.

"You travel with a mountain troll?" asked Angus. "I thought they were deadly."

"I can squash you like a bug if you like," said Kra'ac.

Everybody chuckled. But Angus had a worried look on his face.

"I think you were destined to join our merry band," said Graile. "What do you say? Is it not better than a meaningless death alone in the wilderness?"

Angus shrugged.

"I'll join you," said Lissette. "I've always been curious about the witches."

She gazed at an impassive Selane.

Lissette looked at Angus. "I will not slay you while we travel with this band, but know that our quarrel is not over. You assaulted me without cause and I will settle that score."

"I don't war with women," said Angus, contemptuously. "I'm not surprised that an elf is filled with pride. It's one of the many flaws of the elf race."

"The list of your flaws has no end," she retorted angrily.

"Perhaps we should get moving," said Dave.

They started out walking in a single file. Lissette walked directly behind Selane, who was directly behind Jenna. Graile took the lead. Dave stepped into line behind Lissette, followed by Angus and then Kra'ac was in the rear of the column.

"The air here seems really fresh," said Dave. "There must be more oxygen in your atmosphere than in mine."

Lissette glanced back at him.

"What is it you say?" she asked.

"Your air is richer than where I come from," he replied, "maybe because you don't have pollutants."

"I don't understand you," said Lissette.

"That's fine," said Dave with a grin. "I was just making conversation."

Then, without a sound for a time, they walked silently

"Your planet is more scenic too," Dave said, breaking the forest silence. "Those mountains are a spectacular sight, but it's a lot scarier than at home with the dangerous animals you've got roaming around freely."

"Do you always talk so much?" asked Lissette.

"Pretty much," Dave answered.

He heard her mutter something.

"Do all of your people have blond hair?" he continued. "You look pretty cute with that pixie hair cut."

She turned abruptly toward him and stepped in close. He couldn't tell if she was angry, but she was provoked. Staring intently, she pointed a finger in his face and started to speak, but became contemplative.

"Elves have a strict ritual about conduct between males and females," said Graile. "I think she doesn't understand your intentions."

"I don't have any," said Dave innocently. He shrugged his shoulders. "I think she's really nice looking. Is that a crime here?"

He saw the slightest hint of a smile from Lissette.

"You're a stranger," she said, "so I'll take no offense to your boldness."

"You don't think you're cute?" asked Dave.

"Of course I am," she replied with a sly smile.

The others chuckled, relaxed and resumed their trek. Selane gazed at Lissette thoughtfully before she turned and walked away.

They trekked to the lower flatlands and made their way toward the closest town a busy and prosperous center for travelers at a crossroads to major travel routes. The buildings were well constructed from wood with stone fireplaces instead of the hovels and huts made from crude mud bricks, or animal skins stretched over wood frames in the poorer villages in the surrounding area. A level of craftsmanship to the construction set the town far above the nearby villages, with wrought iron implements and other signs of greater affluence and a variety of shops offering goods for vanity rather than just items of necessity and survival. A high protective wood stockade constructed of thick logs sharpened on the high ends, surrounded the town, but the city gates were open and the local guards didn't challenge them when they entered. The guard's curious gaze revealed none of them had seen trolls, or witches, this close up before.

"Is this Warlen country?" asked Dave.

"We're west of the Warlen," Graile explained. "This is territory of the confederation, a loosely organized collection of towns and small cities who have banded together under mutual defense agreements. They have their own small armies to protect their towns and in the event of a war, they would contribute a levy of troops for a mutual single army to defend the region. It works well for them and commerce has been good, so they're prosperous. The mass of the Warlen hordes could sweep them away, but they've never organized for such large scale operations, and they're content to dwell in their own lands. The Warlen have never been motivated to war on their neighbors. They have fighting enough between their own tribes to keep them occupied. This Ragar, though, is a cause for concern. He has designs for mischief that could threaten all of their neighbors in all directions. The confederation has frequent councils to assess the threat and recently have started to patrol their eastern borders."

When the diverse group got into the outskirts of the settlement, they caused a stir. Women and children screamed and ran when they saw a troll and a witch approaching.

"You're really popular, Selane," said Dave.

She glanced at him dourly.

The first trip was to a clothier and at last Dave was able to dress appropriately for the climate. He crammed his Terran clothes into a pack and donned white fur lined cold weather apparel.

"That's better," he said. "Now I look like one of you."

They all looked at him doubtfully.

Next stop was a large inn. The dining room cleared out when they came in the door Selane and Kra'ac's appearance causing the most anxiety. A terrified waitress eased over to the table, staring at Selane and Kra'ac in fear.

"Hi," said Dave. "What's the special today?"

"What?" asked the waitress, not comprehending him.

"We'll have your meat and vegetable stew for the table, and fresh bread," said Graile, "and ample ale."

"I'll have wine," said Lissette.

"As will I," said Selane.

"I also," said Jenna. Both Jenna and Lissette pulled back their hoods. Dave hadn't seen Jenna's full bodied lustrous long brown hair before. She saw him staring at her.

"It's clear that your world has no manners," she said. "It's rude to stare at a woman."

"Sorry," said Dave.

"Do you truly come from another world?" asked Angus.

"Yes," Dave replied.

"That seems impossible. I'm not calling you a liar, but I have trouble believing it."

"I didn't believe it either until my long lost uncle showed up and whisked me away. I don't know what I expected here, but this isn't it. It feels like real life, but at the same time everything also feels weird. Everything is starker, sharp, and vivid, even feelings, especially feelings."

The innkeeper came to the table with the waitress to serve them. He was a fat, short, balding and flabby man.

"Does this food meet with your approval?" he asked, with a worried look.

"I'm sure it's fine," said Graile, smiling warmly. "I'm sorry that we've chased away your other customers. It wasn't our intention."

"We've not seen a troll before, close up, or a witch."

"We don't bite," said Dave.

Everybody looked at him.

"Do not listen to him," said Graile. "His mind is gone."

"I see," said the innkeeper. "If you need anything else…"

He didn't finish his statement. He scurried away with the young waitress. She looked back at them the whole way.

"Thanks Graile," said Dave wryly, "I like being slammed."

"I'm sorry, my friend," he replied, "I meant no offense, but it's easier than trying to explain your senseless babbling."

They dined on the meal hungrily. Kra'ac ate a prodigious amount of food. The innkeeper had to bring three additional helpings before they finished eating.

He came back when they were done as if he expected them to bolt without paying the bill.

"Allow me, my friends," said Graile. He produced a money pouch and paid in gold. The innkeeper's eyes went wide.

"This is too much," he said.

"I don't agree," said Graile. "I think it's just enough. It's hard enough to make an honest living these days. People like you should prosper. May we request a room? We must prepare for a long journey."

"Certainly," said the innkeeper, "but I have no beds to accommodate him. He's too big."

"We'll make do," said Graile. "Give us the biggest room you have."

"I can give you side by side rooms," he said. "We have no rooms large enough for seven."

"Thank you," said Graile.

After leaving the dining room they went outside.

"I'll go to procure supplies," said Graile. "I'd suggest that Kra'ac stay at the inn."

"I'll accompany Selane," said Kra'ac.

"That's not necessary," she said.

"Nonetheless, I will accompany you," he said.

She shrugged.

"Will you accompany me, ladies?" she asked. "I need some supplies of my own."

Lissette nodded her head. Jenna looked doubtful, but she also acceded. Dave watched them walk away. As he was turning away, something caught his attention, a furtive movement in an alley, but there was nothing to see. An image of a dark cloak appeared in his mind, disappearing in an instant.

"It must be my imagination," he muttered.

"I'm going for more ale," said Angus.

"I'm not thirsty, but I'll sit with you," said Dave. "I'm not much of a drinker."

They walked back into the inn. Dave glanced back at the alley, but whatever had been there was gone.

When Graile returned a few hours later, he was leading several pack animals loaded with supplies. The women returned soon afterward. It was easy to see Kra'ac in the distance towering over them as they walked. The townsfolk were adjusting to Kra'ac when they saw he didn't devour the people around him. They still gave him a wide berth, but they no longer screamed and ran away.

After another large meal for their supper, Graile arose.

"Come Dave, it's time that we begin your training," he said.

"I'm ready," said Dave.

"Somehow, I doubt that," Graile replied, smirking at the others.

They went to the nearby barn followed by all of their companions.

"Have you ever wielded a sword?"

"No, but I've seen movies of sword fights."

Graile shook his head. "Whatever that means, I'll assume you know nothing."

"That would be wise."

Graile unrolled a thick pouch. Inside were a number of swords in cloth slots. He removed one and handed it to Dave. Dave took a couple of practice swings. Graile watched him skeptically.

"Let me tell you that what we're about is deadly serious. You must be perfect every time. One mistake is all it takes to be slain. Do you understand?"

"Sure," said Dave excitedly. "Let's do this."

Graile glanced at the others and shook his head like this would be a useless waste of his time.

"Bring your sword up to a high position. It's easier to strike down to block an attack than to try to bring your sword up too late to deflect death. These are the basic strokes."

They went through numerous moves. Dave paid very close attention to what he said, but he focused on watching his hands, his grip, how he rotated between poses and how he struck.

They squared off and started to spar.

Dave felt surreal, like he was looking down on himself as a separate entity. He felt strong, and potent. Graile began a basic series of attacks, which Dave handled easily. Graile attacked again, but with more speed and power. Dave continued to counter the moves. Suddenly, Graile began a real foray meant to knock Dave back and intimidate. Graile struck with blinding speed, but Dave blocked everything. Before Graile had begun, Dave had focused his mind and his concentration. It was like he could read Graile's moves beforehand.

Graile stepped back, silently stared and struck again with the same result. Dave defended himself perfectly.

"Come at me now," said Graile.

Dave took a deep breath and attacked wildly. Graile parried his swings easily and tripped up Dave's off balanced lunge landing him sprawling on the floor.

"Strange," Graile said, as he pulled Dave to his feet. "You have perfect defense, far beyond the level of skilled and seasoned fighters, yet your attack is hopeless, just the type of incompetence I would expect from a beginner. That's very strange dichotomy."

"When you were coming at me, I felt sort of a tingle. I could read what you were going to do. It was like the sword had a mind of its own, but when I attacked, I didn't feel anything. I was out there on my own."

"I can teach you that side of it. It's good that you can defend yourself. That will keep you alive. You're a strange man indeed, an enigma. Let us try something."

Graile took Dave's sword, put it away and pulled out a different wrap containing a single weapon, sparkling with a jeweled hilt. A sound resonated throughout Dave's body, like a deep metallic hum. Angus and Lissette gasped and came over to closely examine the sword.

"I know this blade, its named Gloin," said Angus in awe. "This is the work of the master Barac, the greatest craftsman in the history of the dwarves. See his mark at the top of the blade. It's been lost since the dawn times."

"The elfin legend Tilian touched this weapon and imbued it with power," said Lissette. "She gave it sentience. It has the power to kill if the wielder is of poor character and has ill goals. Evil is repugnant and it will react forcefully to it."

"So, should I try it?" asked Dave cautiously.

They stared at him. Dave carefully took the hilt of the sword and took a fighting position. Where he had felt a tingle before, with this blade he felt a surge throughout his body. His vision was suddenly sharpened to incredible clarity.

Graile attacked without hesitation, coming at Dave with full skill and determination. Dave easily deflected the attack, as if Graile was now the beginner. Each of the combatants wove a web of blinding strokes too quick for the eye to follow. Graile didn't relent, but it didn't matter to Dave who felt like he could fight all night."

Graile stepped back.

"Attack me," he said.

Dave thought about his first attempt at offense. Instead of wildly swinging, he took a guarded probe, reacting only to Graile's moves and battled to a stalemate until he felt he had a handle on the fight. Dave pressed, forcing Graile increasingly to the defensive. Dave kept attacking and forced Graile back, sensing a slight opening. The sword reacted faster than Dave could command his muscles to move. With a blinding flourish, Grail's blade was knocked out of his hand and fell harmlessly to the ground. The inhabitants of the room were stunned.

"How is this possible?" asked Angus. "You're without peer, master Graile."

"I'm without mortal peers," he said. "I think there's more at work here than I can explain. This legendary sword has claimed you, my friend."

"Amazing," said Dave, "that was amazing," and walked over to the others who were seated, staring in shock.

"Am I still an infant, Jenna?" he asked.

That broke the spell of awe and the others started to chuckle.

"In some ways, you will always be an infant," said Jenna, smirking. "If you think this display and your pride have changed my opinion of you, you're sadly mistaken."

"Wow," said Dave, "I thought maybe I scored some points with you, but instead I get torched. What's that about, Jenna? You're a mighty tough customer."

"I don't know what that means," she answered, "but I think I like it."

The friends laughed again.

"Hey guys, I'm offended," said Dave, but nobody offered him any sympathy.

"I perform like Zorro, and you could care less," he added, but the others were already filing out of the barn and heading to the inn.

Graile smiled and handed him a sheath for the sword.

"Ward this sword with your life, Dave. It's a priceless and iconic relic, and a powerful talisman."

"I got it," said Dave sourly.

"Did you think to win the favor of the prima virga so easily?" asked Graile.

"I thought maybe I could take a step in the right direction,"

"Come, we need to get some rest."

"Women are kind of frustrating."

Graile chuckled.

"Is it so obvious that I like Jenna?"

"Yes," said Graile.

"That's great, I step in it even when I'm trying to do well."

"Each day brings new opportunities, my friend. Let's see what tomorrow holds."

They went up the inn's stairs to the rooms. The doors were open to the two rooms, but everyone was standing awkwardly in the hallway.

"What's up?" asked Dave.

"Kra'ac intends to stay near Selane, in the women's room," said Lissette.

"She's right next door, big guy," said Dave.

Kra'ac glowered at him and then looked at Selane. She looked back at him with a neutral expression.

"I'll be here if you have need of me," Kra'ac growled in defeat.

"Thank you, Kra'ac," said Selane. "I'm comforted and gratified by your diligence regarding my safety. I'm not without defense."

Kra'ac muttered, but it sounded like two massive boulders grinding together.

The parties went into their separate rooms for the night.

Kra'ac put his bedding onto the floor and stretched out, covering most of the room. Angus and Graile laid down onto the king sized bed. Dave curled up in a large soft chair and dozed off after a time, but in the night he awakened. The tingle he felt earlier, extenuated by contact with the power of the sword, had grown into a smoldering flame in his body, but he sensed it was not him. Rather he was sensing power from others. Closing his eyes, he focused on the energy. In his mind he got a hint of that power, which had a feminine feel and realized he could now "feel" Selane's nearness. Her aura was strong and getting stronger. He tried to extend his touch, but had no idea how to do that and lay curious about the new phenomenon for half an hour. Suddenly her aura receded, like snuffing out a candle. Dave fell back to sleep.

The Journey

Dave awoke in the morning, stiff and sore from his night cramped in the chair, when he heard Kra'ac get up off the floor and grumble. Pausing, Dave tried to sense the aura next door again. He could not, but heard them moving around.

"Morning," he said as Graile sat up and put his feet on the floor. "I want to go talk to the girls about something."

Graile gave him a wry smile.

"I really do have a question," said Dave defensively.

He went out the door and Kra'ac followed him. Dave tapped on the door and Lissette opened it.

"Hi," said Dave. "Did you guys have a good night?"

Lissette eye him strangely, as if his question was flawed.

"Can I come in?" he asked. "I've got a couple of questions."

She looked back. Selane nodded.

Dave went in. Kra'ac followed and made the room seem very small. The giant looked directly at Selane. She was all that mattered to him in that room.

"Can I ask you something, Selane?" asked Dave.

"What?" she asked.

"This power you've got, what does it feel like for you?"

"Well, it's not something we talk about with men, but I long ago lost proper decorum with you. It feels something like a warm glow, an excitement, a feeling of rapture. Perhaps it varies from person to person, I don't know about that. That's how it is for me."

"I understand. These tingles, they're getting stronger for me. When I took that sword, it knocked me for a loop. Can you tell if it's some sort of power in me causing this?"

She looked at him skeptically.

"I don't think that it's power. Perhaps it's a misery afflicting you. Maybe your supper didn't sit well."

The girls all chuckled.

"Real funny, Selane, I'm serious, is there a way for you to check?"

"You don't understand what you ask of me. There are strict rules about such things. Among the sisters there are prescribed protocols for such intrusive contacts. They don't include protocols for contacts with men."

"I don't care about your stodgy dogma. I only want to know what's happening to me. You saw me fight Graile. I've never touched a sword in my life. Will you check me out please?"

Selane looked very uncomfortable.

"If I do this, all of you must swear that word of it never leaves this room. I would be subject to the severest of penalties for such a blasphemous breech of our rules. Such a thing has never been done before."

"Yeah, yeah," said Dave dismissively. "So what do we do?"

"Sit here on the bed," she said. "You must clear any thoughts and open your mind. I must attempt to touch your consciousness. It's a very intimate connection between us. We must let down our barriers to each other completely. You must trust me."

"No problem. Go for it."

She eyed him hesitantly.

"Close your eyes."

Selane's hands gently touched the sides of his head. They felt very warm. That warmth seeped into his skull just like what his uncle had done, although much less powerful. It was a strange sensation, neither pleasant nor unpleasant, merely a foreign intrusion.

The sensation of femininity returned again as she probed his thoughts and feelings. He tried to be still, but he was drawn to her, especially when he felt her near an area of potency within him. She paused at the brink of that pool before she took a tentative plunge forward which evoked a powerful surge within him that he couldn't control. For a time they intermingled in a joyous communion of shared power and awakening, as he touched her essence. He knew Selane as he'd known no other person - her history, all of her experiences, her choices, impulses, and feelings at what had been put upon her by the sisters. And she knew him, every step of his painful path, the absence of a father from his life, shame at the ridicule from classmates - every secret was revealed. Each other's weaknesses and darkest impulses, as well as their noblest aspirations, were exposed and realized. He knew Selane's secret plans and goals and she knew his.

He would have been content to stay in that union with Selane, but suddenly she ripped away their connection, leaving an overwhelming feeling of inconsolable loss. He blinked his eyes. Selane was shuddering, her arms wrapped around her looking away.

"Selane?" he rasped.

Sobbing, she took a deep breath.

"Are you okay, Selane?"

Lissette looked like a raptor about to strike. Jenna, eyeing Selane with worry, sat down and embraced her sympathetically.

Trying to compose herself, she looked at Dave.

"I'm sorry. I wasn't prepared for you. I've shared with sisters in this manner before, but it wasn't the same. It was gentle and enlightening, a mutual union. With you it was a cataclysm. You're filled with a vast pool of roiling potency. I've never seen such power. It was overwhelming and seductive. I was barely able to escape the pull of that vortex. Your life force is wound within your innate strength. I was terrified and I was awed."

"So I have power, Selane?" '

"I cannot believe I'm saying this to a man, but yes, you have power within you the like of which I've never seen."

"Can you teach me to use it like you do?"

"I'm not qualified for such a daunting task. I'd only the briefest contact with you and you nearly swallowed me up. I've never before been frightened by the power I've seen in another, but I was frightened by you."

"Help me to control and use it. I have a feeling I need to do this, and quickly. I can't explain it, but these feelings and premonitions I'm getting haven't been wrong so far. You're the only one here able to handle the job."

"That isn't entirely true," said Lissette. "We elves don't reveal this outside of our own people, but we too wield power. With my help, I think that Selane will be able to teach you, as can I. With knowledge, I think that you'll be less of a hazard to us."

"That works for me," said Dave.

Selane was doubtful, but didn't reject the idea.

"I suspected you had power, Lissette. When I picked up on Selane's gift, I felt something about you too."

"I started to believe you truly are a man from another world," said Lissette thoughtfully.

Selane suddenly turned to Dave. "We must talk," she said urgently.

"After we eat breakfast we can take a walk," he replied. "We can stroll around the town and chat."

Selane started to say something further, but looked away instead. They joined the men to go downstairs to eat. She was relatively silent during the meal and after they finished Dave stood up.

"I'm going for a walk with Selane. We have some things to talk about. We'll be back later."

Selane stood up and followed. Kra'ac stood up also. Selane turned to him.

"I'm in no danger. I wish to speak privately with Dave."

Kra'ac scowled, but didn't argue.

They walked outside into a bright sunny day, though it was still winter and the air was cold. There was no wind blowing so it was crisp, but bearable. Dave glanced at the mountains, which stretched along the entire northern horizon.

"That's a heck of a sight."

"Yes," said Selane dismissively. "I fear I've made a terrible mistake. I shouldn't have melded with you. It was beyond my abilities and in so doing I've revealed secrets of the sisterhood that should not be known outside of the order."

"I disagree. First, it was a two way street. You saw all of my secrets too. Secondly, I saw your life with different eyes. I can give you an impartial view you couldn't get anywhere else, and I think there are a number of important things for us to consider. These precepts you live by, there's nothing wrong with having standards in your life, but somebody needs to take a look at your rules."

"This is so wrong. There's a reason that the sisters guard our secrets."

"I know that. It depends on your point of view, though. You ascribe nobility and great purpose to the sisterhood, but that isn't what I saw. These sisters travel the lands taking little girls and young women away from their families, because those families have no power to stop them. That's how they replenish their ranks. They sense power in the girls and take them into the fold, but that isn't all Selane. If they sense power in little boys, they will take them too, but the boys never make it to training at the keep. They're enslaved, sold off, or flat out killed because the sisters want to control who uses power. There's nothing noble about that, it's self serving and diabolical. They created their dogma to cover their crimes. I know why you covet Jenna. She would be a priceless gem and a huge coup to bag from the Warlen nation, stealing their first maiden. They warped you as a child with no protection from their falsehoods. They gave you a version of life that's unnatural and arbitrary. You know this to be true. You questioned it throughout your whole life there, and you saw all of my life to see the difference, and how things should be."

"I did see your life," Selane said. "I could never have imagined such a world. Those strange devices were mystifying."

"In my universe we have technology. My uncle told me that. Here you have magic. That's as strange to me as the cars and televisions are to you, Selane."

"I saw the pain you endured as a child, Dave. I saw the cruelty of those children and I saw how deeply it marked you."

"That was tough, but I got through it."

"Your personal experiences when you were older with your women friends, I shouldn't have seen those private things. Your ways are so much different with what is permissible on your world. I didn't know of it or perhaps I wouldn't have agreed to the melding."

"It's no big deal to me. It was no more revealing of me than your secrets. I don't hide behind a façade of perfection to mask my fallibility like the sisters teach. I admit I make mistakes. You should too."

Selane flushed red.

"You can see why I told you this was such a mistake."

"Listen Selane, none of the past really matters. I need to learn about this gift you say I have. I need to be able to use it and control it. I have a feeling that before we're all done, we'll need every defense we can muster, from all of us."

"Although I know with my head I should part from you and the others, I find I'm drawn, compelled actually, to follow this quest to the end. I fear that I'll pay a terrible price for what I'm doing."

"I like to think of us like a family, the brothers and sisters I never had. One of my brothers happens to be a really big dude."

Selane laughed heartily.

"Are we good?"

"Yes, we're good."

"I've got to say one more thing, though. I know that you're using your power on Jenna. I picked up on it in the night. I'm not going to interfere with your goals. I'll leave it to Jenna to decide if she wants to become a witch and live with you, but I'm not going to allow you the advantage of masking the truth, tampering with her mind and feelings, misleading her like you were misled. I like her, so guess I'm saying I'm going to compete for her too, which you already know. Is that a problem for you?"

"I accept your honesty and will honor your request. I will compete, as you say, on an equal footing, and have decided I will assist with your seeking your power, although I tell you I'm a poor choice for a teacher."

"You'll do. I feel really close to you, Selane. Maybe you don't like that, but I do."

Dave stopped her, embraced her, and then he impulsively kissed her.

Selane blinked and looked at him in wonder, her cheeks flushed again.

"Oh my," she said.

"You're a really nice looking woman, Selane."

"Thank you," she replied, distractedly.

"Let's go back to the inn," said Dave.

Kra'ac was outside watching anxiously for them when they walked up.

"See Kra'ac, I am unharmed."

He grumbled and eyed Dave sourly.

"I think he's jealous," Dave whispered to Selane.

"Don't be silly," she replied, with a smile.

They went up to the bedrooms to talk. It was very cramped trying to fit all of them into one room.

"We have no plan," said Graile, "but I think we all feel the pull to move on, and to move rapidly. I have no explanation for it. My thought is that there's a legend of a great mystic that dwells in the mountains named Raja Kai. I cannot say if there is such a person, but his legend is everywhere, so I think there's some truth to the legend. Perhaps he can

53

enlighten us and offer some guidance about where we should go and what we should do."

"Isn't that dangerous?" asked Dave. "What about the deadly things that supposedly lurk up there?"

"There are dangers wherever we choose to go," said Graile reflectively. "If it's our fate to end up as a meal for monsters, I would say, let's get to it, but I don't think that's our fate."

"Aye…!" Angus shouted.

Graile looked around at them.

"Do you know the way?" asked Lissette.

"Not exactly," said Graile, "but I have an idea. So who's with me?"

Angus nodded quickly. Lissette paused before she nodded too. Graile looked at Jenna.

"I will come," she said.

"As will I," Selane added.

"I guess I'm in too," said Dave. "I really like hanging with you guys."

The group looked at him, uncomprehending of his jargon.

They looked at Kra'ac. "If Selane is going, I will accompany her."

"It's settled then," said Graile. "We'll gather provisions and leave tomorrow. Perhaps we can go out and tip a few mugs this evening."

That afternoon Dave was sitting in the women's room with Selane and Lissette attempting a first lesson with his power. Jenna was snoozing on the bed when there was a rap on the door.

As Dave went to open it, he was knocked backwards by a group of armed warriors who burst into the room and spotted Jenna on the bed. She sat up in surprise.

"Are you harmed, Jenna?" asked the leader of the band pointedly.

"I'm not harmed in that way or any other way…"

The leader of the troupe eyed Dave grimly.

Suddenly Kra'ac forced his way into the room, knocking the warriors down like bowling pins.

"Stop!" shouted Jenna. "These are Warlen warriors from my tribe concerned for my safety."

The Warlen were torn between their desire to rescue Jenna and their fear of a troll.

"Andron," said Jenna, "it's good to see you again. I'm in no peril. Put away your weapons. These are my friends."

"When you disappeared, the tribes were thrown into pandemonium. A search was begun immediately, but when no sign of you could be found, Ragar tried to claim control of the nation as champion of the contest. Most wouldn't support him, so skirmishes broke out and turned into open conflict. Now each tribe guards their own people, and trust has disappeared between tribes. What are you doing with these strange people?"

"We're on a quest, I know that you're duty bound to determine my fate. Tell Ragar you've found me and I'm untainted, and I reject him still. I'll be going away on a dangerous journey, and I trust my friends regarding my safety. Please tell my parents I love them and miss them terribly, but this is my fated path."

Andron stood open mouthed. "I cannot permit this," he said.

"There's nothing you can do to prevent it. See, I have the finest of companions, the mighty mountain troll warrior Kra'ac, Selane, a white witch of the sisterhood, the warrior maiden Lissette of the elves, next door is the sword master Graile, and the dwarf warrior Angus, and here stands Dave, traveler from another world who has powers too fearful to contemplate."

The Warlens eyed him fearfully.

"Return in peace to our village," said Jenna. "You've fulfilled your charge."

Andron stood indecisively. Finally, he turned to leave.

"Come back to us safely, Jenna," he said. "You're more than just a Warlen maiden, you're the symbol for the nation. I fear we need you back for us to endure as a unified people."

They filed out, eyeing Kra'ac nervously. After they were gone Dave looked at Jenna.

"Powers too fearsome to contemplate...?" asked Dave. They all laughed, even Kra'ac.

"I had to say something momentous," Jenna answered, chuckling.

"You should have gone with them, Jenna," said Dave. "This quest could be real trouble."

"I'm no less brave than the rest of you. It's what I choose to do."

Graile and Angus came over as the Warlens were leaving.

"What was that about?" asked Graile.

"Her countrymen have discovered her whereabouts," said Lissette. "They weren't happy to leave the inn without her. I think we must use caution from now on. The warring factions of the Warlen may get ideas regarding their prima virga. We may not have seen the last of Warlen war parties."

"We'll leave for the mountains at first light," said Graile, "if that's agreeable with you, Dave."

"Sure," said Dave. "I'm happy to let you lead us, Graile."

"I'll act as a guide and a companion," Graile answered, "but the consensus of the group is you're our leader."

"Me?" asked Dave, incredulous. "I'm the least qualified of anybody here to be the leader. I'm nothing."

"I would hardly say that," Graile replied. "You fought the greatest swordsman in the world to a standstill when you say you've never had training. You've frightened a white witch of the order who has verified you have a vast pool of power upon which to draw. I would say you're much more than nothing. You may be a champion without equal for this world."

An uncomfortable half grin grew on Dave's face.

"I don't believe it, but Selane, Lissette, maybe we better have an intense session with my gift if we're going to be out in the field. We may never get a safer place than here."

The women grudgingly acceded and Jenna went next door with the men.

Dave sat down and closed his eyes.

"Don't fear, Selane," said Lissette. "Allow me to join with you and we'll enter Dave together. It will be much better this time for you."

Selane nodded. Dave felt their presence in his mind moments later as they went straight to his center of power. This time he found they could communicate with each other with thoughts. A mental image formed in his mind of a glowing stag.

"*Touch your power*," a mental instruction transmitted, "*and then touch the stag*."

Moving into the glowing pool, he extended his reach toward the stag, but it moved away. He reached out more firmly, but it moved again to evade him.

He made an awkward surge toward the stag.

"Control the power, guide it," they advised him. "Don't try to overpower your prey."

He tried again, without frenzy this time, and was surprised he could exert a measure of control. He reached again toward the stag, this time mirroring its evasive moves by staying very near to it and sent a flow of molten power surrounding the stag - cutting off any escape. Something warned him not to grasp the creature. He simply kept it at bay.

"How did you know to do that?" they asked him.

"It seemed the right thing to do."

The stag disappeared from his vision, which blurred a moment, and then he felt a strong feeling of urgency replaced by a vivid forest scene. In the middle of a clearing was a series of arches in a circle radiating light into the darkness. Inside the circle was a great glowing orb. Out of the orb a stream of flickering light ascended into the dark sky. With a thought, he moved to the edge of the circle in an instant and paused to examine the arches. There was a clear path inside, but he sensed an invisible barrier. A tentative touch of his hand exploring the obstacle and a tone sounded as he felt resistance against his probe like stings of insects. Pushing harder, the resistance increased to match his effort, along with increased pain. Levitating now, he tested the entire structure on the sides and over the top. It was fully encased, but the golden stream flowed through the barrier unimpeded.

He touched the stream, which felt like warm water flowing over his glowing limb and was a pleasant fragrance to his consciousness.

He eased down to ponder the puzzle and tried a forceful assault to crack the encasement, but control of his power was unsure. Instead of the firm bump he intended, he unleashed a withering blast that struck the barrier and the concussion bounced back towards him. A bright flash accompanied the impact and a booming sound echoed away in all directions like a thunderclap.

"No!" someone yelled in alarm.

Dave wasn't injured by the eruption, but the dark sky reflected a colored aurora that rippled for a time before receding and dying away. The golden flow stopped coming out of the circle, which had a menacing alternating tone and haze around it that blinked with ominous warning tones.

"Desist," they pleaded, but Dave didn't like failing this challenge. Tapping into a vast pool of energy, he cloaked himself in a dazzling aura of blazing power. He moved back to the barrier, which beckoned, to his spirit beyond his understanding.

On his next try Dave didn't assault the circle, but instead touched the hazy barrier, which brought the tones to a loud steady note. He ignored the pain of the contact; intuition guided him to respond with a tone created with his power. The barrier began a musical joust with varying notes, which he countered with a tonal response. Dave began to master the contest and changed his approach, deepening his sounds, adding overtones and resonance. He split his tones to form chords and then complex rhythms. Because Dave had unlimited reserves to draw upon, the barrier couldn't match his output and began to succumb. Suddenly the barrier was gone and Dave glided inside the circle to the great orb that pulsed like a heart beat when he drew near.

He reached out with limbs of glowing might and touched the orb. Instantly he was filled with awesome power flooding him like a tidal wave. Through molten eyes of fire, he saw the universe laid out before him - the plan and the purpose of all things. Beings of majesty daunted him to tears. They sensed him at once and looked upon him with compassion and love beyond the grasp of mere mortals. A mere meaningless speck to such divine creatures, they showed him only all encompassing love. One of the entities reached out to him.

"It's not your time brave little mortal. You have tasks you must yet perform."

He felt himself being returned from that serene place back to the planet, but just before he was gone completely, he got a strong feeling of his mother nearby.

"No!" he cried in agony and pain, like he had lost her a second time. His searing torment rocked Lissette and Selane breaking the meld as they all opened their eyes devastated. Both women were crying wretchedly.

"She's gone," said Dave hopelessly. "I couldn't do anything about it. She was right there."

He looked at the women in his abiding grief, but was moved to compassion for them above his own torment. He put his arms around them in comfort. They gradually calmed down from their shared pain and returned his embrace in a gesture of union.

At last they sat back from their shared emotions and compelling experience.

"If every lesson is like this, I don't know if I can endure it," said Dave.

"You exceeded any possible lesson," said Selane. "We gave you the stag image, but when we attempted the next illusion, you formed the thought of that glade within yourself and your own nature. It was a thing far beyond us. We were mere witnesses and tried to aid and anchor you, but you cast us aside like straw. That ritual was on a plane and on a scale far beyond me both in power and understanding."

"I got a glimpse of that holy place, we call heaven," he said.

"Your pain when you were cast out was beyond bearing. The memory of it haunts me still," said Lissette compassionately.

"I sensed my dead mother," he whispered. "I know that can't be, but she was very clear to me. I felt that anguish again."

"I don't know how to teach you, Dave," said Selane. "You're far beyond us, so I fear that you must learn control by your own doing. It's dangerous beyond belief. I have never beheld such power in any other person I've touched."

"My uncle seemed to think my mixed heritage was a big plus. Maybe that's it. I think my father was some kind of wizard."

"I don't know what that would mean," said Selane. "I have no explanation. Perhaps you're right that your heritage makes you unique."

"I'm sorry if I scared you guys. I got a little carried away with that barrier thing. I should have listened to you."

"You said you feel close to me," said Selane gently. "I understand that now. I cry for the loss of your mother as you do, as does Lissette. You've made me a new person since I've known you. I don't know if that's a good thing, but I cherish your friendship like no other I've ever known."

"Thanks," said Dave. "I appreciate that."

"Let's join the others for our final night of safety," said Lissette.

"Good idea," Dave replied.

They got up later than intended the following morning after imbibing of the local spirits; a celebration that gained momentum the more they drank as they all felt they were on the verge of something momentous.

After loading up the pack animals, they headed out the gate on the opposite end of the town. The townsfolk waved and smiled, as they had gained some notoriety during their visit, and started a new legend for the ages.

Dave was glad for the warm clothes he had, because it was a cold and windy day, but the wind still cut through and chilled him anyway. Their footsteps crunched in the frozen snow and their breath billowed out in little clouds in the crisp air as they walked along. The landscape was pristine as Dave glanced about, a perfect picture for a painting, and was hard to imagine deathly hazards lurked about waiting for the careless or unwary.

Traveling was easy in the flat lands. The mountains ahead of them seemed very near to the eye, but Dave knew they were a very long way off.

"I went to the Rockies once back home," he said to Lissette. "They were big, but nothing like these mountains. They look like they go all of the way up into space."

Lissette looked at him curiously.

"Your atmosphere only goes up so far and then stops," said Dave.

"I'd not thought about that," said Lissette, looking upward.

"I saw his former life," said Selane. "He speaks the truth. His world is very much different than ours. They fly through the air in vessels, air ships."

"That's hard to conceive," said Lissette.

"Believe me, I've been in them," said Dave. He saw Jenna look back as she listened to them. "What's wrong, Jenna?"

"Of all of the companions, I'm the least fit to be amongst us," she said. "Each of you has rare talents and skills. You're singularly able to defend yourselves. I'm the most vulnerable. I must depend on you for my safety."

"None of us would see you leave us," said Selane. "You're a vital part of the fellowship in so many ways. You're precious to us all."

Jenna looked unconvinced.

"I hope I'm not a fatal flaw in our group and lead us to some tragedy through my weaknesses."

"No," said Dave.

They waited expecting him to elaborate. After a few moments everybody chuckled when he said nothing further.

"See Jenna," said Selane, "Dave has resolved your worries."

Jenna muttered something, but she did smile.

They stopped early to make camp at the beginning of the foothills in a gully behind a hill blocking the view from the road.

"I will take first watch," said Graile. "Since word of Jenna is out, we should watch for signs of pursuit. I suspect we may have other eyes watching too. The order will not rest without finding you Selane you know that. Even the dwarves and the elves will seek their own."

"I'll take a watch," said Dave.

They looked at him doubtfully.

"You're not familiar with the land," Graile clarified. "It's better if we others man the watch. We know when something is amiss."

Dave shrugged his shoulders.

"I want to pull my weight," he said.

"There will be other tasks for which you're better suited. Be at peace, my friend. None of us doubts you in any way."

Dave continued his habit that night of sleeping beside Jenna. She didn't resist his companionship any longer and even was starting to show a level of affection for him.

He stared up into the alien sky before dozing off. It was strange that the usual constellations were not there. The big and little dippers, the North Star, the hunter, none were there to reassure him. The stars here were much more luminescent, with no ambient light coming from large cities to dim the view. This planet had no moon and the roar of predators on the hunt in the woods, split the night. Glancing up at Graile sitting on the hilltop was comforting to see that someone was vigilantly safeguarding them. He rolled over and fell asleep.

In search of a Legend

With no idea where in the mountains to find the legendary figure, and the span of the mountains endless - from horizon to horizon - Dave had doubts.

"What are the chances we're going to find this guy," asked Dave, "assuming that he exists?"

"I think we're generally in the right area," said Graile.

Dave looked at him skeptically.

"You have no idea, do you Graile?"

"Don't tell the others," Graile replied with a sly smile. "If I seem confident, they'll feel confident too. I learned long ago that if you project authority, people will assume that you warrant it."

Dave laughed. "You wily old dog, you're just slinging around a bunch of bull. You've got these guys thinking that you've got all of the answers."

"Maybe I have the answers and don't realize it yet, or perhaps you have the answers."

"That is so weak, dude. I hope that it doesn't end up costing us. How sure are you that there is a mystic in the mountains?"

"Of that I'm more confident."

"Somehow, I don't feel reassured."

"A wise choice my friend," said Graile, chuckling.

Dave just shook his head.

Dave glanced back at the others plodding along behind them. Selane looked up. She furled her eyebrows questioningly, like she could read his thoughts.

"You're going to get busted, Graile," said Dave. "They're not stupid."

"I'll worry about that if it happens," he replied evenly. "In truth, I do believe there is such a being. There are too many stories in this region, especially when a particular area is taboo."

They traveled all day toward the mountains. Toward the end of the day the land became steeper and trees began to dominant the landscape.

"We're less in the open to be spotted from a distance," said Graile, "but on the other hand the trees give cover for those wishing to prey upon us. We'll make camp here."

They set up the camp quickly and ate stew and loaves warmed by Selane's power that evening. They watched Dave use his power to melt some cheese onto his stew, questioning his sanity.

"It's good this way, you should try it."

No one tried his suggestion.

As they traveled, Dave practiced an hour each night fighting Graile, then Angus, and then he battled against Kra'ac to see what it's like against a much bigger and stronger foe. His inner connection and communion with the empowered sword made him a daunting challenge even for Kra'ac. His reflexes and agility and his ability to anticipate the actions of an opponent made him near to invincible. When he finished with those physical exercises, he sat with Selane and Lissette where they communed together. He honed his control over his power and learned to use it in many different ways. The mental interplay with the women was particularly instructive to him in learning about minds and their complex structure. It fascinated Dave who was avid to learn and loathe to end the sessions.

"We must rest, Dave," Selane had to say every night.

He even improved to the point that the others would allow him a turn at nighttime guard duty.

"I've made it," he said proudly on his first night to stand on duty.

The others smiled wryly.

"Enjoy your loss of sleep," said Angus scornfully. The others chuckled, but Dave was undeterred with pride of accomplishment he was finally becoming a worthy companion.

Dave sat in a tree watching all about in the darkness with bow ready in case of a problem. It was a clear cloudless night and an area where there was distance between trees, so he could see if anything came near. The end of his shift was near and he was getting heavy eyelids when his inner sense snapped him back to alertness. Scanning the area for trouble, he didn't immediately see anything and sat motionless waiting and watching. Then he noticed movement coming up from behind them - dark shapes stealthily creeping toward the camp. Reaching out with his power, he "touched" Lissette and Selane and they sat up abruptly.

"Trouble is coming," he warned as they reached out and awakened the others. Grabbing their arms, they set their bedrolls as if they were still asleep there, then fanned out into hiding and waited.

A scout crept up to the tree Dave was hiding in, pausing to assess the camp and signal to his mates. Twenty of them in total suddenly rushed into the camp, attacked the bedrolls and realized they had been duped. Dave fired an arrow, which started the counterattack. Climbing out of the tree quickly, he loosened his sword. He was the last one to get to the camp. His friends were already engaged in the fighting. Although they were outnumbered, it was not a fair fight. Kra'ac alone could hold off half of the attackers. Selane was like a scythe in a wheat field with her power. Graile was a blur of deadly sword strokes. The fight was over quickly and most of the attackers were slain.

"These are Warlen warriors," said Jenna. "They're from Ragar's tribe."

"Why did you attack us?" she asked one of the survivors. "I'm still the prima virga and I'm still pure."

"You've abandoned your people," he said. "Ragar has decided you should die for your crime."

"What crime?" Jenna said contemptuously, "The crime of rejecting an animal such as him? He would lead the peoples to ruin."

"He will have his revenge for the shame you've brought upon him," said the man. "Never before has a prima virga done such an insult to a champion."

"He's no champion," said Jenna angrily, "he's a shedder of blood and nothing more. Go back to him and say that I too have a score to settle with him. I'm on a vital quest now, but there will come a time when he'll see me again."

"I'll be there on that day when he brings you low," said the man. "We'll see if you're still proud and arrogant lying at his feet in chains."

Kra'ac suddenly picked up the man off the ground as if he weighed nothing. He cried out in terror.

"Kra'ac, let him go please," said Jenna. "See, I give you back your life although you don't deserve it. Now go away and don't come back, because if I see you again you will not survive it."

The man looked truly frightened and hurried away into the night.

"You did very well, Dave," said Graile. "You've proven worthy of our trust."

"Thanks," said Dave, smiling smugly at Jenna. She rolled her eyes and shook her head, and then went to her bedroll, closely followed by a playful Dave.

"Jenna," he whispered.

"Do not speak to me," she replied, holding up her hand toward him shaking her head dismissively.

Kra'ac collected the bodies and disposed of them down the hill. They heard scavengers dragging the bodies away moments later.

The following day they moved into steeper territory on the foothills of the mountain range, causing travel to slow down considerably.

Dave sensed they were being stalked. He looked around, but saw nothing.

"I think something is trailing us," he mentioned to Selane who was walking beside him.

"I feel something also, Dave..."

"Do you have any ideas, Selane? Do you think it's more of Jenna's people?"

"I don't. It's a cold, cunning creature that hunts us. We must be wary."

They climbed up a steep incline and were about to walk past a large boulder. Suddenly Dave's hackles rose in fear. Selane and the others stopped, staring up in terror. Dave slowly looked up to see a massive beast sitting on the boulder preparing to spring. The creature looked like a cross between a cat and a bear with a shaggy mane and thickly furred body, thick shoulder muscles, large paws with menacing claws, long sharp teeth, and a look of imminent death.

In a leap of intuition, Dave, with his power, projected his mind into the beast. The raw killing lust of the animal shocked and overwhelmed him. Exerting strength and control, Dave drove back the animal hatreds, and then sifted through the monster's brain as he'd learned to do with Lissette and Selane. The animal had a rudimentary level of sentience, which he cultivated and enhanced. With his power he made the beast

65

into a new creature, while he held it suspended in his control. The beast gained self-awareness and began to commune with Dave though only on the most basic level, but beyond anything the animal could ever have evolved. It learned about reasoning, and all about Dave's "pack." Now the beast was a part of the pack.

They all stood in shock watching the standoff. Only Lissette and Selane were able to observe the inner battle and the incredible change Dave had wrought. The great beast relaxed suddenly and stared at Dave.

Dave turned to the others.

"We have a new friend…"

They were speechless.

"It's a Death cat," said Graile in wonder. "They're the most fearsome hunters in the land. This is not their territory. None go to their territories. They're instant death."

"Well," said Dave, "now he's our companion."

"How can this be?" asked Graile in total disbelief.

"He was pretty mad," Dave explained, "but I reasoned with him. Once he understood, he was okay. I just had to get his attention."

The others looked at Dave like he was talking gibberish.

"You're truly an avatar," said Graile. "There are none who could do such as this. I saw it with my own eyes and I still don't believe it."

"I can sort of see through his eyes, feel what he feels and I can understand his impressions," Dave added.

"I have a sense of it too," said Selane, glancing at Lisette.

"I also," said Lissette.

Dave started to walk. The deathcat jumped off the boulder and fell into step beside him. Dave petted the creature benignly.

The others looked at each other, shrugged and then followed Dave and his new pet as if the impossible were a matter of routine.

That evening, when they stopped to make camp, they ate their meal. The cat disappeared and wasn't long before they heard a yelp in the woods. The cat came back a little later licking its reddened muzzle. Instead of going to Dave, it went straight over to Jenna. She cringed in fear, but it simply lapped her cheek and then lay down beside her.

"Sorry," said Dave. "I think it picked up that I like you, so I guess it likes you too now."

"Could you like me a little less, Dave? I'm frightened with it so close. These creatures are consummate hunters and killers."

"Look at it this way, Jenna," said Graile, smirking. "Nothing would ever challenge a deathcat, so with it nearby, you can never be in peril."

"See there," said Dave, smiling hopefully.

Jenna glowered at the both of them.

"By the way, I named it Bear," said Dave. The cat opened its eyes and looked at him when he said the name. "Everybody say the name so he knows you all."

They all said, "Bear," in unison.

He put his head back down and lay against Jenna.

She looked at the predator and then Dave. The look on her face was not encouraging.

The presence of Bear became accepted and routine much quicker than Dave would have thought possible. The women especially, once they were satisfied it wasn't going to turn wild on them, began to pamper and spoil it, often petting and talking to him.

Dave continued to work with its mind, bringing in Selane and Lissette as they attempted to increase Bear's connection with them and to an extent to try to increase his mental capacity. That growing sentience, though still rudimentary, gave it a unique place in the world. Now it could outthink animals and recognize human hazards.

Bear was a huge boon for their trek into the mountains. Bear's animal perceptions helped them avoid dangerous predators that feared the death cats and thus avoided the quest party.

Up to the time they entered the foothills, the weather remained neutral, but as they started to climb to higher elevations, the temperature dropped noticeably. The snow was deeper so it became much more difficult to drive forward and required more frequent rest stops. Bear needed no stops, but waited patiently for the travelers when they stopped.

They climbed for a week into steeper and more challenging areas.

"I hope we aren't off course for this seer of yours," Dave huffed to Graile when they stopped for a night. They were both panting from exertion.

"The air is thinner up here," Dave noted.

Graile simply looked at him.

Huddled together that night for warmth, Bear lay in the middle of them all. He didn't mind that they laid against him and each other for warmth. Even Kra'ac who was always near to Selane, but usually with some separation, on this night crawled against the mass of bodies. When they awoke in the morning, light snowfall blanketed them. After breaking camp their climb was difficult as they maneuvered around jagged boulders and much steeper paths. The footing was treacherous.

Kra'ac positioned himself directly behind Selane. Once she slipped backward into his waiting arms.

"I will not let you fall," said Kra'ac.

"Thank you," she replied.

They made their way to a flat area, which was an ideal place for a camp and decided to stop early as a storm was rapidly approaching.

"I don't think we want to fight that storm," said Dave. "We can wait it out here."

With plenty of room on the ledge, they treated themselves to cooked meat. Dave had progressed to the point he could help Selane cook the meat with his power.

Dave sat beside Jenna as they munched on the sizzling strips of steak. Jenna ate her share, but fed pieces to Bear who had his massive head on her lap. He sighed contentedly.

"Being up this high, that's a spectacular view out there," Dave commented.

"Yes," said Jenna while petting Bear who was attempting to purr, but was emitting a deep rumble sounding more like a growl.

"I cannot believe the things you do, Dave," she said. "They're impossible and yet routine for you. Here's the most feared creature in the world resting peacefully on my lap. How is that possible? Do you even have any idea of all of the things you're capable of?"

"Not really. I don't know how I do this stuff, it just happens. I can't seem to do what matters the most to me though."

"What's that, Dave?"

"Impress you, Jenna."

She stared silently out at the panorama for a short time.

"Dave, you don't understand. You have impressed me, and all of us beyond words. I know you favor me, and I'm not unmoved. I don't really have a choice about my mate. Although I make a great show about Ragar, I'm still the prima virga for all of my people. I'm not free to simply choose who I will. If Ragar is eliminated from the picture, I have a duty to consider the choice of my people for who will be their next leader. That person must be my husband. Do you understand? Do you not have obligations and responsibilities in your world?"

"Not like this," said Dave, clearly upset.

"I'm sorry to vex you, Dave. It was not my intention. I cherish your friendship above all other things."

"Friendship? No problem," said Dave sullenly. "I think I'll let you get some sleep. You've got Bear right here and Selane."

Dave, hurt and embarrassed, got up and went over to lie down on the far side of Lissette - the first time he would not share the blanket with Jenna - who sadly watched him go.

The storm blew in rapidly and pelted them with a strong wind, heavy hail and blinding snow. They curled under wraps against the onslaught.

Dave had difficulty falling asleep at first, but suddenly felt calmed and serene. His mind was strangely numbed, although something deep within was amiss and nagged him in the midst of complacency. He tried to dismiss the impulse, but it was stubborn, gaining strength to the point he started to pay attention. Something was fighting that little red flag of danger waving wildly within him. He started to reach for the red flag with his power but he felt like he was immersed in syrup and he couldn't move. He struggled harder against the malaise instinctively searching out his might. The instant he touched it his mind became a great conflagration and he snapped away the constraints sapping him. His eyes flew opened in time to see a great maw about to bite his face. Throwing out his power like a giant fist, he knocked the large creature back. In an instant, Gloin was in his hand. The creature snarled and lunged forward. In that instant, Dave saw intelligence and calculation in those eyes and felt a wave of paralysis circle his body. But he was an inferno of power and shrugged off the attack easily. The creature, surprised and shocked, tried to back away, but was too late, and too close to Dave. Gloin hummed a menacing tone as Dave struck down at the creature in an arc of glowing power and caught it flush - unable to escape his fury. In an instant, the beast lay lifeless at Dave's feet; then he looked around the camp. Kra'ac was fighting fiercely against several of the creatures. Selane and Lissette were standing back-to-back using their powers to fight off the creatures. Angus was on the ground, but was moving. A creature was crawling onto a prostrate and unconscious Bear. Dave surged into his mind and snapped the constraints. Bear roared to life and threw off the creature, attacking ferociously. The mysterious creatures fell back when they saw one of their own had been slain. Regrouping, they rushed toward Dave, but they merely claimed the fallen member and dragged it away, scrambling up the path and quickly disappearing into the storm.

Dave looked around.

"Is anybody hurt?" he yelled.

"I can fight," said Lissette.

"I'm unharmed," said Selane.

Angus stood up wobbly.

"Careful master dwarf," said Lissette. "Do not fall off this ledge. We still have our disagreement to resolve."

She grabbed the dwarf and sat him down.

Kra'ac came over and looked at Selane.

"You saved me, Kra'ac. That thing took control of my mind. If you hadn't knocked it away, I fear that it might have devoured me."

"They were Konocks, Selane. They dwell in the high mountains and are a curse to the living. Even trolls must be wary of them. They encroach on our lands more and more seeking us as their food. They're deadly predators and are why few come up into the mountains, and why none ever leave."

"It would have been nice to know before we came up here," said Dave.

"I couldn't know if they're everywhere," said Kra'ac. "If our quest requires for us to come here, we had no choice."

"Where's Graile?" asked Dave.

"I'm here," yelled Graile, coming down from the path. "They've taken away Jenna."

"What?" shouted Dave, as he raced up the path.

"Wait," said Selane. The others grabbed Dave to restrain him.

"What do they do with their captives, Kra'ac?" Selane asked.

"They don't take captives. We're prey, we're their food. Any who are dragged away are taken to their lairs and consumed. They don't pause about doing that. I fear that Jenna is already dead and eaten, from our experiences with the Konocks."

"NO!" screamed Dave in rage. "If they've killed her, I will wipe out every last one of them."

"Dave no," said Selane. "I share your pain, but that would be suicide to chase them into their lair and face the mass of their numbers. We were lucky to survive their attack."

Dave turned slowly and looked fiercely at the group.

"You came with me of your own free choice," he said grimly. "You may leave me just as freely. I'm going up there and I'm going to avenge Jenna if need be. You may come with me, or not. Gloin hummed loudly and glowed brightly with his rage and power. Bear jumped ahead and started up the path. He started his climb as fast as he could. The others silently followed.

The footing was incredibly treacherous, but he was driven and had no thought of the hazard. Only one grim thought filled his mind.

Bear climbed steadily and it was difficult for Dave to match the pace, but eventually he saw Bear disappear into a cave and quickly come back out to look for him. Dave hurried to the entrance, stepped into the semidarkness and looked back at his companions. They weren't far behind. Once they were all gathered in the cave, Dave looked at them deadly serious.

"No mercy," he hissed starting forward using Gloin to light the way.

"Flammis," said Selane and the walls of the cave began to glow. They hurried deeper into the cave and reached a fork. Dave reached out with his power.

"This way," he said.

Jogging down the tunnel, they saw a glow in the distance. Dave "felt" something ahead like an itch.

"Selane, I think there's power here."

"I feel it too, Dave."

Slowing their pace around a curve, they entered a chamber with a solid glow from the walls lighting the entire room. A heavy table cut from stone stood near the far wall. On the table laid Jenna's exposed body her skin pale and face ashen. Neatly folded and stacked in a corner, lay her clothes. It struck Dave that she had the same serene look as his dead mother's face in her casket. Jenna was surrounded by a number of the shaggy beasts of different sizes who were gazing at Jenna and all chanting in unison.

"Somehow they're using power," said Selane. "I don't understand it."

"Damn them," said Dave in rage, charging into the room brandishing Gloin as it hummed menacingly.

He collected his power and reached out with his mind to link with Selane and Lissette, rage building like an electric charge.

As he was about to unleash his fury a loud voice rumbled.

"Hold your attack!"

Dave looked around in confusion as a dark figure came out of an adjacent tunnel.

A tall, wiry wizened, white haired man stepped into the light. He looked ancient, but moved about easily, with great vitality. His eyes were sharp, glance piercing and filled with potency; his great power was ubiquitous.

"Why do you attack the Konocks?" asked the old man. "Why have you come into their home?"

"They attacked us," said Dave, shaking with hatred. "They're animals who tried to kill us and killed Jenna. They took the life of the person I loved and now I'll take their lives in return."

"The Konock meant no offense to you," said the man. "It was you that killed Manag."

He eyed Dave thoughtfully.

"Manag was our greatest hunter. You're the first to kill a Konock since their transition."

"It was kill or be killed," said Dave. "I didn't have time to do anything except react."

"The Konock hunt only for food and must feed, as all of you feed. Do you concern yourselves about the lives you take? You have no thought about your food at all. The Konocks are not like that and revere their prey for what they give to our family. Listen to them, they worship your Jenna's great beauty, compassionate spirit, her mind and all of her attributes. When a person or an animal is taken into the tribe, we gain from that consumption. First the life essence is prepared and taken by the flock. We've gained sentience, we've gained power, strength, and cunning. The body is then consumed to nourish the bodies of the tribe. We save choice parts like the brain and heart for the young ones so they may most benefit from the sharing. The Konocks were once mere beasts, but with sufficient time they've progressed remarkably. Yes, little witch they've eaten your sisters before. We've eaten wizards in the distant past. This is where they gained the ability to ensorcle the prey. It's rare

72

for any to escape that snare. You're the first in a very long time. Your kinds are seen with great reverence by the Konocks. It's a holy thing that you donate your lives, spirits and bodies to advance them. I've lived amongst men. You're callous, thoughtless, and heartless, filled with greed, lust, and ill intentions. Here I live amongst beings that are pure in their motives and aims."

"You're a shape shifter," said Dave as reality dawned on him.

The man smiled.

"You make me think of the last man who stood before me decades ago," the wizard said. "He also had great power."

"That's all a great story," said Dave. "It doesn't change the facts they killed Jenna. She didn't volunteer to be dinner."

"They didn't kill her," said the wizard. "She's not dead."

"What?" Dave asked.

"She's begun her journey. She's between planes of existence."

"Call her back," said Dave.

"That's not possible," said the man.

"I don't accept that," said Dave harshly. "If you won't help us, stand back out of the way."

Dave marched forward. The Konocks turned and started to growl and howl at him. Dave waved a hand and they fell down like dominos, crawling back against the wall, fearful of his power.

He entered Jenna's psyche linked with Lissette and Selane. Jenna's mind was a blank wasteland. The trio surged throughout Jenna's brain searching for some sign of her former self, but Dave, now frantic, thought it was too late. On impulse he sent a surge of power into her brain and Jenna's body convulsed in response. Dave stimulated the autonomic area of her brain as her heart beat wildly and color returned to her skin, but he still couldn't find her essence.

They went through her mind again. Dave sensed something and moved them toward it in an instant. A faint glow of light appeared and he tried to move to it, but was prevented. He pushed harder, frightening Lissette and Selane, but his efforts caused the faint glow to brighten. He pushed out a powerful sending with his mind toward the glow. Within that glimmer there was movement and then a form. Reaching into his reserve of power, he tried the barrier again. This time, with an immense effort, he breeched it and raced toward the distant form. A strange exhilaration overcame him and he began to get the sense of that holy place again until he was abruptly stopped.

He was in the presence of one of the divine beings.

"You can go no farther," she said with her thoughts.

"Mother?" asked Dave in wonder. "Is that you?"

"I'm no longer that person," she said, "but I was she who bore you. You cannot join me, my son. It's not your time."

"I came for Jenna, I love her, Mom."

Suddenly Jenna was brought before him.

"Return to your life, my son. Beware the snares of the enemy for he is powerful."

"Mom, I love you," he cried. The force of his love affected the divine being and her aura changed, love and concern appeared on her face, replacing the imperious countenance.

"I love you too, Davey, I'm with you always." she said while fading away.

Suddenly the trio was violently thrust out of the limbo. Dave and the other women fell down to the floor, but quickly stood up as Kra'ac hurried over to help Selane. Jenna's eyes fluttered and then opened.

"Dave," she rasped.

Selane and Lissette quickly dressed Jenna who was semi-coherent, but back amongst the living.

"Incredible," said the wizard moving close. "Why did you say you were in the mountains?"

"We came here to find the mystic, Raja Kai," said Graile.

"That's a name I have used," the old man replied.

Raja Kai

"You're the mystic?" asked Dave skeptically.

He chuckled. "Am I more or less than you expected?"

"You're different than I expected."

"Come with me, my quarters are this way. You're frightening the Konocks and this is their space and home."

They followed him on a convoluted downward path through numerous tunnels until reaching a large cavern. It was surprisingly luxurious with comfortable furniture, running water facilities built in, storage areas filled with food stocks and multiple adjacent rooms carved into stone to make sleeping areas with comfortable beds. Underground aquifers provided fresh clean drinking water. A deep volcanic vent tube funneled hot spring water for bathing into stone-carved bathtubs. Other volcanic tubing ran to the surface to vent the chamber and helped circulate fresh air.

"It was difficult hauling this furniture up the mountain, but I like my comforts," said Raja Kai pleasantly, "and I'm well prepared for the infrequent times I entertain guests."

"Let me see if I've got this right," said Dave, curiously. "You're a man, or at least you were a man. You choose to live up here virtually cut off from civilization. Somehow, you learned to shape shift and you've become a member of this tribe of Konocks?"

"Essentially that's correct. Dinner?" he asked, as some Konocks carried in large trays filled with meats, cheeses, fruits and berry wine.

They all looked at the meat suspiciously.

Raja Kai laughed.

"It's elk," he said. "I don't eat human flesh in this form. The food is delicious. Fill your need. Who knows when you'll get another good meal?"

They cautiously sampled the food before eating hungrily.

"When you're one of them, do you share their meals?" asked Dave pointedly.

"Have I eaten humans? Yes, I have. It's delicious, the best meal imaginable."

They looked at him in horror.

"It's the truth. It doesn't take long before your aversion to human flesh goes away. You judge me, but you do so without a basis to make a judgment. I have the benefit of living in both worlds. There's much more I would be ashamed of as a human than in my life as a Konock. I learned about purity here. Konocks have no guile in their natures, would never torture others for pleasure as humans do and do not war against their own kind. They have reverence for life that's missing in humans, recognize growth their in intellect and power and despair it comes at the cost of other living creatures, but there's no other way."

He paused and looked at them to gauge their reactions before continuing.

"Also, I've anointed all of you as honorary members of this tribe. You'll never again be set upon by my people or any other Konock anywhere and this includes your pet. Although rarely caught, they're a great delicacy for us. Gaining their considerable attributes into the family is a more than a worthy goal. Deathcats are much revered, second only to tender young women."

Jenna shuddered.

Dave looked dourly at Raja Kai who laughed heartily.

"I fear that my humor suffers with these long absences from human companionship. I find that I'm happy that you've joined me this evening, my friends. Drink the berry wine, it's a very good year for wine."

"We came here with the hope that perhaps you could give us enlightenment and guidance," said Graile.

"What is it you seek?' asked Raja Kai, "riches and wealth, fame, power, control over your peers, the secrets of the universe?"

"I can't speak for the others," said Dave. "As for me, I don't appreciate your sarcasm. It's obvious you have a bone to pick with humanity in general. I don't care about that. That's your problem. I was

76

brought here from another world by my uncle, but something happened in transit and I got separated. I want to find him to be sure he's okay. He implied this world has real troubles and seemed to think I could help. Since I've come here and started to develop these powers and abilities, maybe he's right. I know so little about this world. I don't know where to start."

Raja Kai got a contemplative look.

"This explains a great deal and is why I couldn't place you with any group of this world. I sense considerable strength within you. Certainly, I've never seen any accomplish such as what you did in melding with the witch and the elf to become a single combined psychic entity. To go to the brink of death and past to pull back your loved one, I didn't know that was possible. What you've done to change the deathcat defies belief. It inspires me in my own efforts to advance the Konock. I haven't dwelled on the travails of this world in a long time, but I'm not unaware. The threat you refer to is indeed dire. When last I spoke of this, it was the wizard who asked me these questions. He had the same taste I sense in you. Perhaps he was this father you say was lost to you. He was traveling to a site of great evil, Mortus, but it wasn't for me to deter his ill thought plan. Going alone to confront what awaited him there was courageous, though foolhardy and suicidal."

"Fools rush in where angels fear to tread," said Dave.

"That's exactly right," said Raja Kai. "I don't know that saying, but it's very telling."

"It's from my world," Dave replied, "from my religion."

Raja Kai eyed him closely. Dave could feel a tentative probe of his mind.

"There's much I would like to learn about you. Your mind is alien and familiar all at the same time.

"I have a feeling we don't have a great deal of time," said Dave.

"There's much you don't know. Where we're located here is a mere 'back water' on this world. Across the mountains is a great empire where hope is dimmed, despair is the norm and life hard. The Emperor is a dark being filled with malice. His vast imperial army enforces iron will and cruelty on the helpless masses of its subjects. The capital city is a center for his depravity and taste for torment. Those few so foolish as to try to rise up in rebellion were crushed mercilessly, suffering hideously before their painful ends. Their priesthood conducts blood rites that are nothing more than butchery to sate their lust for pain and death. They're not a real religion, just excess to give total freedom. They're an abomination demanding redress, but no force on this world is capable of overcoming them. We avoid their wrath because the mountains protect us, but I fear soon they will turn their designs in our direction. In the past, we were too paltry to warrant interest, but I'm afraid that is changing. Imperial forces now patrol mountain foothills and their army would overwhelm any force we could throw up against them."

The group sat soberly listening to Raja Kai.

"We have no unity here," he continued. "Your people war among themselves, Jenna. The other races are no better. Elves and Dwarves are bitter rivals. The witches choose their own path of ritual culling the very men who could become a force for good, along with warping young girls into their twisted beliefs and practices. You alone, Selane, can see them for what they are only because you've joined your mind with Dave and have gained true enlightenment. I've ignored this scourge for too long burying my human side, but I fear that's no longer a path I can pursue. If it's your intention to go to that evil place, I must tell you that the horrors of the capital city are by no means the worst of what you'll find. Mortus is an ancient and a hidden city. What dwells there defies description and poses a threat I fear none could ever defeat alone or in concert. Your father went to that awful place and met his end. I would counsel you against it. At the same time perhaps it's a journey you cannot avoid and you're meant to confront this evil. You have a unique blend of companions and possibly will have the wherewithal all others didn't have. Also, I must tell you I have a twin brother. You may see me as deviant and perverse because of how I choose to live my life, but I'm the good twin. My brother sought out the dark places and tainted knowledge that's abhorrent and vile. I fear he dwells in the midst of wickedness. If you encounter him, he will be no less a daunting challenge as me. You've not seen what I can do so you don't understand the severity of this threat. He's equally capable, but has no conscience and no qualms about inflicting suffering and death upon any who come within his reach. There he has found brotherhood with those as dark as himself. They're the foundation and the strength of the emperor and give him the power to maintain his rule. In return he allows them any excess they desire. There's no lack of helpless victims available to them for their dark pursuits."

"That's really bad," said Dave. "Is your brother stronger than you?"

Raja Kai sat and thought a moment.

"It's not a matter of who's stronger, for we're equals. The case is I have compassion where he does not and would never hold back a killing blow. He would revel in it and delight in seeing life drained out of a living being. A fight against him could only be ruthless, as he would give no quarter. It's hard for me to conceive we sprang from the same loins. No being could be more different from me than he in every substantive way."

Dave looked around at the others who were all consumed by what they were hearing. Jenna especially, fresh from a trip to deaths door, had a haunted expression.

"My brother sees me as weak for the pity I show to lesser creatures," said Raja Kai. "His name is Raja Dul, by the way. Pray that you never meet him. It would be best if you dwelled here in safety."

"As you said," Dave replied, "we may not have that option. I'm sure that wizard, if he was my father, had no desire to die. If he went anyway, there had to have been a very compelling reason."

"True," Raja Kai agreed contemplatively.

"Can you tell us anything else that we should know? I'm just has frightened about this as everyone else. I don't want to die either, and I really care about my friends. They truly are my family now."

Raja Kai eyed him steadily.

"To travel across the empire is a daunting enough task to stop any foolish enough to try. If you succeeded and could manage to get past the capital city of the emperor, approaching Mortus, if you could find it, is truly attempting the impossible. It's warded by all manner of protections, seen and unseen. It doesn't need protections for in truth it's intended as a lure, a trap, to snare unique and skilled prey such as you. There are special horrors waiting those few worthy of the attention of Mortus."

They sat in silence trying to digest the grim prospects laid out by Raja Kai.

Selane turned to Jenna.

"This is too much for me to absorb. Can I ask you about your experience? To my knowledge, none have ever been so close to death and returned to the embrace of the living."

Jenna thought a moment.

"It wasn't unpleasant at all. I felt no fear or foreboding, quite the opposite. I felt divine and abiding love and I felt at peace in a way I've never felt before. I saw a great light ahead, which called to me. It was alluring beyond measure, because it was flawless purity at the center. I had no question about wanting to go there and was on my way when I felt the desperate call behind me. I knew Dave was coming for me. It was difficult for me to stop my journey into the light, but Dave's call was so compelling. I felt his love and it moved me greatly. There was a moment where I could have chosen to go either way. Knowing his pain over losing me was a terrible agony that stopped me and I turned back to this world. I felt terrible loss because I could have had eternal bliss with but a single step. At the same time, I couldn't cause Dave such torment, so I allowed him to embrace me in his power, and suddenly I was lying on the cold stone table, returned to this world. I will no longer fear death for it's merely a passage to a better place."

"Amazing," said Dave.

"I hold no malice for the Konocks," Jenna continued. "What they did was in their nature and as Raja Kai has said, there was no malice. If one is to die anyway, perhaps dying in such a manner and advancing their species is a worthy and a noble goal."

Dave looked at Jenna surprised.

"I think your ordeal rattled your cage. Getting eaten alive isn't a good end for anybody. You better stick close to me until you get back to normal."

His friends smiled at his self-serving statement. Jenna appeared to be lost in her thoughts and didn't react to David's suggestion.

"A day does not go by," said Selane, "when I don't marvel at each new wonder that Dave reveals."

"You're welcome," said Dave dismissively. He was focused on Jenna.

Bear came trotting into the cavern accompanying by a phalanx of jittery Konocks.

"Bear!" they exclaimed, wrapping arms around his massive body.

"Are you okay?" asked Dave.

"See, he's been well cared for," said Raja Kai. "I should ask for compensation from you for the cost of the prodigious amounts of food needed to feed this bottomless cat and our hungry troll friend. We'll need to hunt for months to restock our provisions and supplies."

"Poor baby," said Dave, mockingly. Nobody comprehended his jest.

"Rest here in my home for as long as you like," said Raja Kai, eyeing Dave wryly. "I'm afraid there's no one who can give you any insight about travel in the empire, or the pitfalls to watch for. Any who have gone there have not returned."

"Thank you," said Dave. He looked at the others. They simply looked back at him.

"Maybe the fact that we're a small group will work to our advantage. We won't draw notice like we would if we took an army with us."

"Perhaps," said Graile, unconvinced.

"I'm with you," said Angus.

Dave smiled. "I like your optimism, Angus…"

They spent several days resting and talking about future plans. The Konocks were never far away from them, but they didn't cause any trouble. Bear, however, didn't "forgive" the Konock, and if any of them came near, he growled loudly. The Konock kept sharp eyes on Bear at all times, though they made no aggressive moves.

"I think that we need to travel back down out of the mountains on our side," said Graile. "We should travel further west, because there's a great pass through the mountains we can travel through. The confederation stations a garrison on our side. I don't know what we'll find on the imperial side. There's virtually no travel there. That will give us that much more time to think about this plan. It seems a fool's errand."

"I can't disagree," said Dave, "but I don't have a safer plan. Unfortunately, this intuition that's guiding me points toward going across the mountains, regardless of the danger."

"So be it," said Graile, resignedly.

They left the protection of Raja Kai's lair filled with trepidation and marched right into another bitter snowstorm. Travel was very slow going down the dangerous trail with swirling snow and stiff winds blurring vision during the day and frigid nights spent sleeping in poorly protected nooks in the rock face. It took them twice as long to descend as it had taken to make the climb. By the time the temperature moderated and the steepness of the terrain leveled out somewhat, they were exhausted from the effort.

81

Later the following morning they left, taking their time walking single file into an area of increased trees and hills. Graile was in the lead, although Bear had jogged ahead to go hunting. Each day the usual routine was Bear would leave to seek out his food and sometimes would be gone for protracted time periods.

They walked through a notch between two huge boulders and into a group of trees. The path made a sharp right turn just out of the notch. Each person disappeared into the dense stand of trees. On this day Angus was behind Graile, followed by Dave, the three women and then Kra'ac. When Dave stepped through the trees he was surprised to see Graile and Angus lying unconscious on the ground. Suddenly, he felt a jolt to his mind, like he was electrocuted, and fell down.

When he managed to open his eyes, he was tied up lying beside the other men, including Kra'ac with two grim faced women staring at them. He hadn't seen the women as he stepped through the trees into their ambush. He glanced at the other men. Only Kra'ac was conscious.

"Who are you?" asked Dave.

"Silence!" snapped one of the women and smacked Dave across the face. It stung and did no physical damage, but did ignite his anger. He eyed her darkly.

"Do not gaze upon us, dog," said the woman who struck Dave.

Dave was riled, but didn't look away. The woman stepped forward to strike him again, but the other woman stopped her. They turned as Selane came around a tree with Jenna and Lissette.

"Well young Selane," said Dave's attacker, "what mischief are you about here?"

"What I do is my own affair, Lascia," said Selane curtly. "Why are you and Aylan here?"

"We have the same concern for you, Selane, as do all of the sisters. When you disappeared without a trace we all feared you'd fallen victim to foul play. Though you're a white witch, you're young and don't have all of the strength of experienced and senior witches. You still have much to learn, dearest. We're here to ward you and to return you safely to the keep, but I see there's also other business here to tend to. This is truly a strange collection of miscreant creatures. A dwarf and an elf so far from home and working together no less, and a mountain troll even farther from home. You have the elusive prima virga of the Warlen, whose capture is excellent work on your part, and most strange of all is this other man. I sense something percolating within him, something dangerous and forbidden. It's a good thing that we happened upon you as alone you were in danger. With three witches together, we can stand against any threat they might pose. I must ask you, have you been touched in any way by these vile males?"

"Of course not," said Selane angrily.

"The holy mother will be well pleased with your work, Selane, perhaps enough to forgive your youthful inattention that allowed you to be spirited away," said Aylan. "You're missed by the long list of your suitors who were greatly distressed when you were reported to be missing. They long for your return to their sweet affections in hopes you'll make your choice of a life mate soon."

Selane stood stone faced at the thought.

Graile awoke and looked up. Angus awakened moments later.

"These males show a great deal of rebellion," said Lascia. "I think that they're in need of a harsh lesson."

She reared back her hand again. All of the men glared at her.

"See Aylan, my darling," she said, "this is what happens if you don't keep a tight leash on the lower species. They're mere males, but are capable of great mischief."

"Selane, have you examined the women?" asked Aylan. "My impression is they're fine candidates for the sisterhood. The elf is especially endowed with the gift, the most powerful I've ever felt outside of the order. Has she given you trouble?"

"No," said Selane, her eyes focused on the ground.

Lascia leaned close to Dave.

"You disgust me," she said. "We shall see if you continue to stare at your betters once I've had a chance to administer retribution for the affront of your insolence."

"Bring it on," Dave replied.

"What?" she asked. She turned and looked at Selane. "Is he addled in the head?"

"He speaks as a fool," said Selane.

"Hah," said Lascia. "So you're less than a man."

She smacked him again.

Aylan took Lissette's face in both of her hands. Lissette's eyes hardened into defiance. Aylan's hands began to glow as she tried to pry into Lissette's mind. Dave closed his eyes and linked with Lissette and with Selane. They supplied Lissette with virtually limitless power to deflect Aylan's probe.

"What?" asked Aylan, stumbling backwards while holding her head.

"What's wrong?" asked Lascia hurrying over to her. "What happened?"

"This elf, she has some defense against my probe," said Aylan. "The strength I encountered was immense and daunting."

"That cannot be," said Lascia angrily. Glaring, she grabbed Lissette's face and tried to assault her with a powerful sending, but her potent weapon was feeble against the mighty barrier that was the combined entity of the three. She fell to the ground dazed.

"Lascia!" cried Aylan in surprise. They both looked at Lissette with fear.

"What are you?" asked Aylan.

Lisette merely smiled.

"Come Selane," said Lascia, "we need the three of us to attack her simultaneously."

Selane looked into their eyes and they saw she was not one of them.

"What's happened here?" asked Aylan.

"You were planning to kill the men," said Selane grimly. "They've done nothing to you, yet you require their lives. These women, you've not consulted with them as to whether they wish to join the order, yet you would take them regardless. You've no thought about any other beings but yourselves. I'm shamed I once subscribed to your beliefs and practices. Thankfully, I've met these friends of mine who've opened my eyes to the truth. If you wish to examine someone, I invite you to examine me."

Selane stepped forward toward the cowering witches. They threw out an aggressive attack with their power, which Selane brushed aside as if it was nothing. With the joint power of the three, she was a titan against them.

"Selane no!" cried Aylan, shielding her face.

"What mercy have you shown?" asked Selane in a hiss.

Suddenly Kra'ac snapped the bonds holding him and got to his feet.

"I ward Selane for I owe her a life bond," he growled. "None may threaten her and live."

He started to raise his massive club. The witches attempted to attack him, but Selane prevented them.

"Enough!" she shouted. She released the bonds on Lissette, and then on the other men.

"What's happened here?" asked Aylan.

"I've changed, and I've been changed," said Selane. "I see with new eyes. I'm no longer a slave to the sisters."

"That's blasphemy," said Lascia in a hiss, "it's beyond blasphemy, its heresy. Don't think you're no longer subject to the power of the order. There will be an accounting for your sins and I'll be there to see it."

"I think if I were you," said Dave, "I'd shut my mouth."

"I can take care of that," a quiet voice spoke behind them.

They turned to see Raja Kai.

"What are you doing here?" asked Dave in surprise.

"I had a feeling you might need me. I alone have the answer to this problem. These witches will hasten back to their keep and will set the entire sisterhood after you, Selane. You'll be declared a heretic and an outcast subject to death on sight. As a group they can be a real force. It's not what you need to happen, in light of the more important issues of our joint situation. These witches cannot be trusted to be set free. You all know that. I can offer them a home living with me."

Selane looked horrified.

"I cannot agree to that," she said, in horror.

"They'll be quite comfortable," said Raja Kai with a grin.

"Although I know the error of their way, to condemn them to such a horror," said Selane, "please Raja Kai, is there no other way?"

"You know the answer to that question. You know this pair. They've left a path of death and destruction in their wake with no concern for those whom they trample. Their own victims cry out from the grave for justice. These two have their own price to pay for their sins."

Selane started to weep and turned her back.

"What's this about, Selane?" asked Aylan in panic when Konocks appeared from the forest and took them. They tried to use their power to fight back, but were contesting against empowered Konocks and the great mystic - a hopeless fight. Realizing they were doomed, they cried out in terror; but their cries were quickly silenced.

"We'll leave you now," said Raja Kai, "safe journey to you, my friends."

Selane was distraught.

85

"How could I allow that to happen," she wailed. "They were misguided, but they were my sisters."

"I'm afraid that Raja Kai was right," said Graile patiently. "If the sisterhood was warned about you they would pose a very serious threat, one we possibly may not have survived. And what they would have done to you, Selane, I'm sure would have been terrible. You would have been treated hideously as a warning to any others who questioned their ways. It was a terrible thing, but necessary."

Jenna and Lissette stayed close with Selane that night. None wanted to think about the fate of the captured sisters. Dave sat apart watching them talk softly.

He looked at Graile, Angus, and Kra'ac.

"Were we wrong to give up those sisters to the Konocks? I'm feeling pretty guilty right about now."

"There are harsh realities and harsh choices to make," said Angus soberly. "That's the nature of life here. Set loose, that pair would continue to kill, and would have made Selane outcast. For the time being, it's what we had to do. Perhaps Raja Kai has some powers of prescience and knew this was what was required at that moment, grisly though it may be."

"I feel like I'm at fault somehow," Dave said. "It wasn't like the fight with Warlens where everything happened so fast you didn't have time to think about killing people. You just tried to survive."

"This is just another facet of that same situation," said Graile. "We're just trying to survive. Those witches would have had no qualms about killing us. They were going to do exactly that to us. Whether we killed them in self-defense, or they're food for the Konocks, dead is still dead. There's no difference."

"That sounds logical," Dave observed, "but somehow doesn't make me feel any better. Seeing Jenna stretched out and pale on that slab will haunt me to the day I die. It's tough to hand them over for such a death sentence."

"I think you're bothered because they were women," said Angus. "Women can be as brutal and sadistic as any man. They're no less a threat. Those women preyed on the weak. They will not be missed in this world."

"Someday, I might need to do something about that keep of theirs," said Dave. "We can't just ignore them. They're the ones to blame here."

"We have plenty on our plate already," Graile replied. "If we survive this quest and there's a future for us, we can consider such matters then."

Dave went over to the women. Selane wouldn't look at him. Jenna and Lissette were seated on each side of her.

"I know this is tough for you, Selane," he said. "With time, you'll realize you're not at fault for anything. They made their choices in this life. We're going to need to get back on the road. Is that going to be a problem for you?"

"No," she whispered.

"We'll take a day to get ready," he said. "If you want to talk, or anything, I'm always available, if I can help."

Selane looked up at him. Her face was haunted and tired.

"Also, Kra'ac offered to counsel you," said Dave. He hadn't meant to be funny, but the women smiled.

"Counsel from a troll," said Lissette. "That's something I would like to hear."

They chuckled softly. Selane smiled weakly.

"I guess I'll be going," said Dave.

He went back and sat down beside Angus.

"You were wasting your time, Dave."

"I had to try, Angus. She feels guilty. I do too."

They went to sleep early that night. The three women slept side by side away from the men.

When Dave woke in the morning the women were already up and away from the camp.

"They have gone to the stream," Angus explained.

"I should do the same thing," said Dave. "You get ripe pretty quickly on the move in the field. I don't know how you guys can stand that ice cold water to bathe."

"You do what you must," Angus replied.

Dave focused his mind on Bear.

"*Stay here in the woods, hunt and feed,*" he said with thoughts. "*We must go across the flatlands before we go through the pass. It would be better if you weren't exposed down there.*"

87

Detour

Once the women returned, Dave took a quick turn at the stream. They ate their meal and resumed their journey soon afterward. Descending further down the mountains heights and gradually through the foothills, the temperature became tolerable and travel much easier. It was not yet spring, but wasn't too far away either.

When reaching the lowlands, they weren't that far away from where they'd begun their ascent.

"There's a small town not far from here," said Graile. "It's in the same direction we're going. We can spend the night there."

They plodded westward as the sun climbed directly over head and warmed the day. Dave peeled off heavier clothes, as did the others. They traveled for most of the day before the town ahead came into view.

"We will be there before dark," said Graile. "It's probably only an hour's walk."

Dave had edged to the front and was walking beside Graile. Angus was actually walking beside Lissette talking with her, their personal feud long forgotten with their adventures together and their growing relationship.

Selane and Jenna were behind them talking. As always, Kra'ac was at the rear not far from Selane.

As they walked past a thick stand of trees, suddenly, behind them, loud war cries erupted and a large band of Warlen horsemen charged. Hugely outnumbered, the raiders were on them fast and the fighting started so quickly Dave didn't have time to do anything but react. Gloin was in his hand humming loudly as he fought off numerous attackers. Leading the raid was the Warlen man from Ragar's tribe, Cral, who they'd released from the earlier ambush.

Cral smirked at Dave and as suddenly as they had appeared, the attackers raced off after a brief skirmish.

"Is anybody hurt?" yelled Dave.

"Where's Jenna?" asked Selane, in panic.

"They've stolen her away," said Graile.

Dave started to run after them.

"No," said the others, grabbing him. "We cannot pursue them on foot."

"We're not going to give her up to them," said Dave angrily.

"We must go to the town, Dave. We can get horses there."

"What about Kra'ac?"

"There are very large chargers capable of carrying a troll," Graile explained. "I doubt we'll find any in this town, but once we get mounts for the rest of us, I know a place we can go to get a beast for Kra'ac."

Dave started a brisk and determined trot toward the town. The troop followed and they got there in about half an hour. While Graile procured the horses, Selane and Lissette got food to eat on the move.

They rode out of the town going southward and it took them several hours before coming upon an outpost and supply store. The garrison consisted of twenty rough looking, unrefined, but very competent men.

"Retainers of the proprietor…" said Graile as they rode in.

"They look like a band of highwaymen," Angus commented.

"They probably have experience there too," Graile reflected wryly. "Don't concern yourself with them here. Their employer takes good care of business; his men are well paid and satisfied. Although, if you met them in the field, keep a hand on your sword. This isn't the sort of place that would cater to trained soldiers. He needs enough of a force to deter bands of robbers who roam freely about the area. We're in the confederation here, so there's no federal force to protect citizens. They must fend for themselves."

"Graile, my friend," said the rugged looking proprietor coming out of the building smiling warmly.

"Arga," Graile answered. "I think you've gotten fat sitting around and filling your face in your little store. How do you stay in business eating up your profits?"

He laughed. "I can still give you all the fight you could handle. I'm surprised to see you and more surprised at your new friends, but what is it you need?"

"Kra'ac needs a mount," said Graile.

"A troll, riding?" asked Arga. "That would be a sight to see."

"Can you help us?" asked Graile. "We're on a matter of urgency and time is short."

"It just so happens I do have a great beast that will serve your purpose," Arga stated. "It will work out well for both of us as it takes all of my profits just to feed the cursed animal. There's no market for them."

"We need to get going," said Dave anxiously.

"Patience Dave, we'll spend the night here," Graile explained. "We cannot ride blindly in the dark. Our adversaries will have stopped for the night too."

Dave grimaced with frustration and muttered.

"Let's see this animal," said Graile. "Come Kra'ac."

Dave stayed in the building with Lissette, Angus, and Selane. They were all grim faced.

"If they touch her, I'll put every last one of them in the ground," said Dave in frustration.

"They will not touch her," said Selane. "She's still their prima virga and they would be killed if they tampered with the first maiden. They'll conduct her back to their lands and into the control of Ragar. He'll use her to try to gain the control of the tribes he covets."

"These ritual fights they have, are they open to all comers?" asked Dave.

"No outsider has ever presented a challenge," said Selane.

"Then I'll be the first."

"I don't know if they'll allow you to approach or enter the great council. It's holy ground in their religion and outsiders are banned. Very little travel across their lands is allowed and only by trading caravans accompanied by Warlen escort parties. If the six of us tried to ride across their country, we would be fallen upon and attacked."

"We better think of a plan then," said Dave irritably, "if we have to fight our way in, so be it."

Graile, Kra'ac, and Arga walked in.

"That's not a plan," said Arga. "If you ride into their midst, you will die."

"What do you suggest?" asked Dave curtly.

"The only way that you could cross that territory is in a Warlen column," Arga explained.

"Wait a minute, remember those guys from Jenna's tribe? Wasn't that guy named Andron?"

"You know Andron?"

"Sort of," Dave replied.

"I know him. They come to this post periodically."

"We don't have time to wait around."

"I can try to get a message to Andron. They'll not be pleased to hear Ragar has captured the prime virga, a woman of their tribe."

"So you expect us to sit around here in the meantime?" asked Dave hotly. "Right now they're out there within riding distance. I don't plan to let them get away with her."

"Why does this matter to you what they do with her?" asked Arga curiously. "She's their prima virga. They wouldn't allow her to marry an outsider. Surely you know that. They would kill her themselves before they would let that happen."

Dave stood glaring at Arga, simmering with rage. He was very close to becoming an unwarranted outlet for Dave's wrath.

"Thank you for your insight," he said softly but his eyes snapped with his ire. "Regardless, I don't intend to allow them to sacrifice her to such a horrible life with that Ragar dude."

Arga wrinkled his face in confusion and then looked at Graile. "Can he be serious about challenging the entire Warlen nation?"

"Yes," said Graile. "Don't underestimate what he can do for he's much more than he appears. Look at the friends that have gathered and pledged to him."

Arga looked around at them all.

"I'll send for Andron, though I fear you're signing your own death warrants," he said. "It's your funerals."

* * * *

Dave paced around, muttered and stewed as they were forced to wait for a week before they saw riders on the horizon.

He recognized Andron as he dismounted and came cautiously into the outpost.

"Do you remember us?" asked Selane.

"I do," he said, eyeing them suspiciously.

"We were ambushed by Ragar's people on the road," Selane explained. "They stole away with Jenna. We propose to ride into Warlen to rescue her. Will you help us?"

"You ask me to betray my people and bring outsiders onto our land?"

"Would you prefer seeing Jenna forced to marry Ragar?" asked Dave hotly. "Would you prefer giving your allegiance to Ragar? Would you prefer seeing him start wars with all of your neighbors and seeing your country torn apart?"

Andron's face clouded.

"That would be a dire outcome. I think there would be open rebellion amongst the tribes. Never has one so foul prevailed in the fights and become qualified to claim the prima virga."

"My idea is that we ride in as a part of your tribe into the great council of yours. I'm going to challenge Ragar to combat. You say he's a killer. He won't be able to deny me, or the combined tribes will call him a coward," Dave said angrily.

"That has never been done, Dave. The people may turn on us immediately for our deception and slay us before you could issue any such challenge."

"Slaying us may not be so easy a task as you might think, Andron. We've got a potent group."

Andron eyed them thoughtfully.

"Were it any other person, I wouldn't even consider this. Ragar killed my best friend. He would have been a great leader. Perhaps I'm a fool, but for a chance to see Ragar brought low and to save Jenna, I'll risk my life in your cause. I cannot speak for my tribe though."

"Bring them in and let's ask them, Andron," Dave replied impatiently.

Andron went to the door, motioned for his people and they began filing in eyeing the intimidating group suspiciously. They gathered behind Andron at the ready in case of trouble.

"Hi, fellas. My name is Dave. I want to start by telling you that Jenna was a part of our group and a part of our quest. We were ambushed by Ragar's men and they carried her away."

Andron's men's expressions turned grim.

"You can blame us for allowing that to happen, but what's important is right now she's being held by Ragar's tribe of the Warlen that I'll bet you despise. I'll have to take your word they won't mess with her in their custody. I don't know if I believe that in light of what I saw of them. Regardless, every minute we delay here is another minute they have her. For me, that's unacceptable, and intolerable. I will not allow that to go on. She's from your tribe, you all know her and she doesn't deserve this. We're here to ask you to help us do something about it. I know this breaks some kind of tribal rules, but we need you to sneak us into the great council so I can challenge Ragar to combat. You have the choice to stay mired in your silly beliefs about outsiders, or you can make a bold move toward making a better life for all of the tribes."

They looked amongst each other and then at Andron.

"I've chosen to aid them," he said. "I couldn't speak for you about such a radical path. You know our people will be very angry if we manage to get to the council with these outsiders. We may never get the chance to confront Ragar. I'm taking that risk."

Andron's men glanced back at Dave and his friends doubtfully.

"It isn't as if we're helpless," said Dave. "How many of you would choose to go up against a mountain troll?"

Kra'ac stood impassive, but flexed his massive muscles.

"Have you ever battled against a white witch?" asked Dave. "How about Graile, the greatest blade master in the world? That's not even talking about Lissette, supreme elf huntress, or Master Angus, dwarf warrior. As for me, I'm not without abilities. I'm not bragging, I'm just telling you we're valuable friends and allies. I'm hoping you can move past your prejudices and give us your best support to help Jenna, and the Warlen peoples, including all of those women and children who will suffer and die if Ragar gets control."

They gathered and put their heads together; whispering amongst themselves before Andron turned to speak.

"My people will support you. They still don't trust that the troll will not eat them, or that the witch would turn them into mindless animals."

"Let our enemies think those things," said Dave. "We're all friends now. We'll defend each other to the death."

"That they understand," said Andron, smiling broadly.

* * * *

The following morning Dave and the others were shocked when Arga brought out Kra'ac's mount.

"Is that a horse?" asked Dave.

93

"I think perhaps they're like cousins to horses," said Graile, "very big cousins."

"That thing looks like it could do some damage."

"It's a savage beast in the wilds. Kra'ac was very resistant to riding, but once he saw this magnificent creature, he was pleased."

"Can he ride?"

"That will be an interesting question to answer."

Kra'ac was uncharacteristically anxious as he grasped the reins of the massive horse.

"A frightened troll," said Angus. "Will wonders never cease?"

Kra'ac growled angrily at Angus who simply laughed. Angus got onto his horse.

"Are we to wait all day for you, troll?"

Everyone else mounted up and finally Kra'ac took a deep breath and climbed onto the beast that snorted and cantered about nervously.

"You must control it," said Arga, "and you must become one with it. These beasts are loyal to the death once they pick their master."

Kra'ac ran his hand down the side of its neck and then gently patted it. The horse calmed down and they tried a brief stroll around the paddock. Kra'ac was unsteady and nervous, but determined. They practiced for a little longer until he looked less awkward in the saddle. Finally Kra'ac nodded to them.

"Okay then," said Dave. "Let's do this."

"We'll go to my village," said Andron. "There will we travel with the tribe to the great council. We can disguise you in our garb, but the troll will stand out for his size."

"Keep him dressed as a troll," said Dave. "You can tell them you captured him and he's your slave."

Andron chuckled.

"No one would believe that…"

"Well, if you have him in your midst and he isn't fighting you, they'll have to believe your explanation," said Dave.

"I think I've lost my mind to believe we can prevail with this plan, but it's too late now," Andron said shrugging his shoulders.

"Jenna needs us, Andron. That's the thing to think about. Without us, she has nothing and is at the mercy of Ragar. I know you care about her. I saw it in your eyes back at the inn. Well, I care about her too."

Mounting up, they rode toward the east.

"Goodbye my friends," said Arga, waving his arm. "You'll always have a friend here at the outpost."

They rode steadily and got to Andron's village in the afternoon. The entire village gathered and stared at the strangers. Some of the looks were curious, others concerned and some hostile.

"What have you done, Andron?" asked the village elder.

Andron explained everything, including their plan. Most of the villagers were resistant to the idea. Dave could tell which two were Jenna's parents and he approached them.

"We're not here to disrupt your way of life," said Dave, looking into Jenna's mother's sad eyes. "You know what awaits your daughter in the tent of Ragar. I will not allow that to happen. We're not Warlens, but if we're willing to stand up for Jenna, why can't the rest of you?"

"We would be slain before we ever got to the council," said a male villager.

"It's forbidden for outsiders to attend the holy council," said a woman villager.

"I don't need to hear your dogma," said Dave. "That won't protect you when Ragar starts his reign of terror. You all know it will destroy your nation."

He walked over to a little girl and picked her up into his arms.

"Does she deserve that?" Do you think Ragar will care about her future when he starts warring on your neighbors and other tribes of the Warlen?"

The villagers stood silently pondering the difficult decision.

"It's true none would have Ragar become the High Chief," said the elder. "He's cruel, but we're but a single village. We cannot stand alone against the entire nation."

Dave stood in the center of the crowd and motioned to Selane and Lissette to join him. The trio linked hands forming a triangle and closed their eyes. After a moment, they began to glow. With no tricks at the ready to dazzle the village, Dave let Selane control the meld.

Selane began a chant. Dave felt her psychic surge and her draw on his and Lissette's power. Radiating in all directions, their glow brightened to a blinding beacon. Selane's chant grew in strength and evolved into an illusion, similar to the stag deception used on Dave. A great flaming dragon appeared in the skies bellowing challenge then turned and swooped down over the villager's heads. The villagers screamed and dropped to the ground as the glowing dragon arose high into the sky and trumpeted another mighty roar then quickly disappeared in an explosion of light and sound. The concussion echoed across the flatlands like thunder.

The villagers were cowed.

"What was that?" asked the elder in terror.

"It looked like a dragon," said Dave. "Do you have dragons here?"

"I have not seen such a creature, or heard tell of it," said the elder.

"It's a mystical creature from my world," said Dave. "Do you see what we mean when we say we're not going to this council in weakness?"

"With such power to wield," said the elder. "I fear you more than I fear Ragar."

"Like I told my friends, I see you as family now," said Dave. "We'll defend you to the death."

He turned back to Jenna's parents and led them aside.

"I don't know if this will come out right, but I want to tell you I've never met a girl like Jenna before. I know you already know how fantastic she is, but I'm not from this planet and I'm really taken with her. I know that she's supposed to marry the next big cheese for your tribe, but I've got feelings for her. I want to stake my claim, just so you understand. My parents are gone, so I guess there's a possibility you guys might be my parents if we get married."

They looked at him wide eyed.

"I probably spoiled your lunch or something. I'm an honest guy. I don't hide things from people. Now you know where I stand. If it comes to a fight, I want you guys where I can see you, because I'm going to protect you like I would my own Mom and Dad."

They looked at each other.

"This is strange beyond our imagining," said her Mom. "My name is Talia and my husband is Hachen. We don't understand all you're saying, but we do understand you're honoring us. For that and for your protection, we're grateful. If you can save our daughter from Ragar, we'll owe you a life debt."

"You owe me nothing," Dave answered humbly.

"I believe you're a good young man," said Hachen. "What you propose may not be possible, but we'll not stand in your way. Jenna is more than just our daughter. She's a symbol for all of the Warlen peoples. That's not a thing that's easily dismissed. Your honorable intentions may not suffice for the peoples of the nation."

"Well, I guess I better come up with a plan for that."

Dave put out his hand to Hachen. Hachen stared at it curiously.

"It's a gesture of mutual trust and respect in my people."

Hachen shook his hand firmly. Dave took Talia into his arms and hugged her. He heard a gasp from the villagers and turned to them.

"These are gestures in my people," he explained. "It's different from your ways, but it's not wrong. We can learn from each other."

"What have we done?" asked the village elder shaking his head. People started to chuckle.

The entire tribe packed up every piece of material down to the smallest stick and started eastward for their long journey.

Dave put Talia onto his horse to ride while he walked beside Hachen. She smiled at the honor and the prestige that Dave was affording them.

"Tell me what happens with Jenna?" asked Dave. "Andron said the bad guys won't hassle her."

"It would be death for any who touched her in that way," said Hachen. "Ragar's tribe is low, but none would dare violate that rule. The prima virga must be pure before she is wed. As his bride, he could do with her whatever he wishes. We would be powerless at that point."

"Is he planning on marrying her at the council?"

"Certainly he is. My wife and I try not to think about it."

"I think you're seeing a perfect example of why you need to take a look your stodgy old rules. They need to be modernized."

"I don't understand your words," said Hachen, furrowing his brow.

"Regardless," said Dave. "We're going to get things turned around."

Hachen glanced up at a smiling Talia.

"How's the ride, Mom? By the way, I can see where Jenna got her good looks. You're a fine looking woman."

She laughed.

"It's not proper to say such things to a married woman."

"Nonetheless, it's true. Remember, I don't have your same rules. From where I come from, we appreciate beauty. Isn't that right, Dad?"

Hachen grinned as Dave smacked him on the shoulder.

"You're a strange person," Hachen replied.

"If his babbling becomes too bothersome, simply club him in the head," said Angus. "That's what I would do."

They traveled for weeks through the territories of neighboring tribes, all of whom were also making the trek to the great council.

Kra'ac drew stares and controversy, but simply walked along harmlessly, so the other tribes let him be.

Marching over the crest of a hill, they saw the massive encampment below. Tribes were arriving from every direction. Jenna's tribe made their way down the basin of the broad valley where the weather was warming to spring like temperatures and foliage was budding. Weaving around other tribes they found their assigned place near the center of the mass, because they were the tribe of the prima virga. Kra'ac got much more scrutiny as they drew near to the important people of the tribe. Tribal elders were housed centrally together, separate from their clan's, in the middle area of the council. Chevrons of fierce warriors stood guard nearby. Ragar's tribe was given a position of honor because he was the champion. Dave spotted them easily.

"They've always been the lowest of the tribes," said Talia, "and hunger for power to address their need for respect they've never earned or warranted. They happened to spawn a skilled killer in Ragar, so now they feel they can prevail and impose their will on the other tribes."

"Stay tuned," said Dave.

"What?" asked Talia. "You speak so strangely, I don't know what you say half of the time."

Dave simply smiled at her. "It wasn't important."

While Dave watched closely for any sign of Jenna, he bunked his pseudo-parents in the circle with his friends. They were pleased at the new status he accorded them.

"I want to check on her," Dave said impatiently after they settled in from the journey.

"You cannot," said Graile. "We're fortunate to have gotten this far undiscovered. Ragar would never leave Jenna unprotected. She's probably in the middle of their tents. You must wait patiently, Dave."

Dave scowled.

"You need to focus on the business at hand," Graile continued. "If we can manage to arrange this fight, you must be ready. You cannot discount Ragar. He's survived because he learned killing skills and perfected them. Don't think you're invincible, Dave. You must be careful, as you never have before, for this will truly be a fight to the death. If you don't prevail, none of us will survive. Ragar will wipe out Jenna's tribe, her family and Jenna will be a victim for all of her remaining tortured days. You cannot think about anything other than preparing for Ragar. Remember also that men like Ragar don't care about rules or good conduct. He will kill you in any way he can, so expect anything. Show him no quarter, because he will show you none."

"You're right, Graile," said Dave as he laid back and stared up at the stars that became partially obscured by a cloudbank rolling across the sky.

The following morning brought a steady drizzle. It dampened spirits in the camp and gained intensity turning into a full-fledged downpour. Dave stayed inside a large tent.

"She's right over there," he muttered, staring at Ragar's tents.

"Don't do anything foolish," said Graile. "You have no way to know which tent she's in, assuming they don't have her away at the back of the camp somewhere. Be patient my friend."

The rain continued for two more days before the clouds dissipated over the horizon and the sun climbed into a clear sky.

"Finally," said Dave. "What happens now?"

"A day full of ceremonies," Hachen explained. "Ragar will make his appearance after the evening meal, there will be a great bonfire and then you must present your challenge. It will be a delicate matter as there will be outrage when you make your appearance. How you will get the attention of the masses to hear your demand, I don't know. You can see what a vast throng of people are the Warlen nation."

"I've got just the thing to get their attention," said Dave.

"If you're speaking of magic, that's a great risk," said Hachen. "The people fear magic and fear those who wield it."

"Under the circumstances, that's exactly what I need," Dave replied. "Without that, I could never get my chance against Ragar. It's worth the risk I believe."

Hachen shrugged his shoulders. "One way or another, the Warlen nation will never be the same after this night."

"I want you and Talia to stay with my people, Hachen. If you can escape with Jenna, you'll have Kra'ac and Selane to frighten any attackers away while you get clear. Don't worry about me. If I go down, there's nothing you could do for me at that point anyway. I just care about Jenna's welfare."

"I thank you for caring about my family, Dave. We'll do as you say."

They stayed in the tent during the day, out of the sight of passersby, watching the various ceremonies.

Just before the great supper meal, Dave finally saw Jenna as she was escorted into the main area completely surrounded by Ragar's guards and seated at the place of honor to the right of Ragar. She wasn't close enough to see Dave. A blank look of hopelessness covered her face and she ignored any who spoke to her. The only time she reacted in any way was when Ragar's mother attempted to speak to her and when Jenna ignored her, Ragar smacked Jenna hard on the arm.

Kra'ac had to restrain Dave from sprinting out of the tent.

Dave panted with rage, glaring at Ragar with deadly intent.

"We must wait," said Kra'ac.

Dave finally stopped struggling.

"Bunch of cowards," Dave muttered. "They all saw what he did and none of them raised a finger to defend her. They don't deserve her."

Jenna's parents were allowed to come up and visit her. Jenna lost her composure and embraced them tightly as her body shuddered with sobs. Talia whispered in Jenna's ear and suddenly Dave could see Jenna's posture and demeanor changed. Jenna looked directly at Dave's tent and shook her head no. She looked frightened now.

"No way, darling," Dave whispered. "This guy is in for a rude awakening."

Tribal members brought food from the feast to the tent for the friends to eat. Dave gobbled down some food, but passed on the wine and drank only water.

Selane touched his arm.

"If you're determined to do this, we must talk this through. We're facing the entire Warlen nation. Lissette and I will perpetrate the illusions as we've discussed. We'll need to tap your power continuously, not only to maintain such a massive magical display, but also to maintain our own strength. I've never performed such a feat. No one has. I fear we could draw away precious reserves of power at the very time you'll need them in your fight with Ragar."

"That's a risk I'm willing to take, Selane. We've already looked at the alternatives remember? There were none. This is a 'do or die' situation."

"It's the dying part I would like to avoid, Dave."

"Likewise," he replied. "Kra'ac, this is the time that you have to be really diligent. We know that Ragar is a dirt bag. He'll try to cheat. I wouldn't be surprised if he tries to use his tribe to hit me from other angles. You've got to protect Selane and Lissette. They'll be vulnerable to weapon attacks while they're swept up in the magic. Graile will help, but he's going to be guarding me from outside attacks. That only leaves Angus with you and Jenna's people. If things go bad, we don't know how they'll react. They may turn on us."

"They will not," said Andron who walked into the tent at that moment. "We've all decided to follow you, even if it leads to our end. Living under Ragar's boot would be worse. It would be better to die here."

"I'm sorry to drag you into this," said Dave. "I wish there was another way."

"I must return to the table," said Andron. "Jenna has sent word for you to flee from this madness, as she says."

Ritual Battle

As anxious as he'd been for the showdown, Dave started to feel nervous as he watched the feast winding down. He thought about the safety of his former life on Earth and how quickly he'd discarded it. The violence of Faenum and quick death was now his reality. In his haste to save Jenna, he hadn't thought about the possibility of failure. Now that the moment was near, it dawned on Dave the people most depending on him would all suffer terrible fates if he failed. He'd never been tested in a fight to the death and had no idea how he would react.

Dave glanced at his new friends. Kra'ac was steady and strong, like granite, he never showed any fear or any hesitation. His decisions were swift and his actions consequential. Graile was supremely confident. Dave knew that came from his lifetime of successes. Graile smiled bravely at Dave, as if the night was already won. Selane was beautiful and sat with eyes closed preparing for the awesome task awaiting. To most she was frightening to behold, but to Dave she was a great comfort. He felt some confidence knowing she would be on his side. Lissette was a delight in her own right. An enigma, she was beautiful to a fault and yet at the same time incredibly dangerous. Angus was comedic to Dave, although that was due to his idiosyncrasies, like muttering, conversations with himself, badgering Kra'ac and his pretended animosity towards Lissette, to whom he was showing increasing affection. Angus the warrior was a deadly foe.

The sun was sinking quickly on the distant horizon. Dusk was transforming into the darkness of evening. Dave watched the head table closely. Ragar was drunk with perceived success and joked with his thug friends. It wasn't hard to tell what they were saying. He leered at Jenna and made vulgar comments after which he and his friends laughed disrespectfully. Jenna turned her head away from their vile talk.

"That's right dumb ass," whispered Dave. "You think you've got it made. We'll see about that."

At long last, Ragar arose, grabbed Jenna by the hair and pulled her to her feet. She was staring in fear at Dave's tent. Ragar dragged her to the center of the ceremonial clearing and threw her down to the ground at his feet in front of the assembled elders. Cral and a number of his friends followed and taunted Jenna.

"Is everybody ready?" asked Dave, "its show time."

Ragar bellowed demands to the council of elders, demanding Jenna be forced to marry him immediately and the council declare him the new High Chieftain.

Dave, followed by his friends, crawled smoothly out of the tent while the attention of the throng was directed at Ragar. Lissette and Selane flanked Dave a step behind and Kra'ac was directly behind the trio. Angus and Graile flanked Kra'ac followed by the rest of Jenna's tribe. They all marched directly into the sacred circle before Ragar noticed them and stopped talking, confused at the unexpected interruption. Jenna began crying.

"What is this?" asked Ragar, confused.

"They're the outlanders," Cral warned, but the surrounding masses of the people didn't hear him with the prevailing clamor of so many people close together.

"I demand the right to challenge Ragar," Dave shouted. "He sent his men like vermin to steal away Jenna after she rejected him, because he's unworthy to rule the nation. He'll lead the Warlen to destruction."

The uproar around them grew to deafening proportions.

"Now..." said Dave. He closed his eyes and gave free rein to Selane, who chanted loudly as the trio began to glow brightly. Cries of fear rose all around them. A piercing beacon of light shot straight up into the night sky coalescing into a roiling glowing ball of power. The orb gained in strength and size and then erupted with a massive detonation of blinding light and thunder. Warlen dropped to the ground shouting in terror.

"I will not allow Ragar to defile your prima virga," shouted Dave in a booming enhanced voice. "Your women and your children will pay the price for anointing him High Chieftain. You cannot allow this travesty. I will face him man to man."

"You will use magic," shouted Ragar in fear.

"I will not," said Dave. "Selane is wielding the power. She's the white witch. I will have a sword as my weapon."

"You lie!" shouted Ragar.

"Look upon your champion, Warlens," yelled Dave. "He quakes like a little child, yet he claims he should lead you. He brings nothing but shame on the bravery of your people."

Ragar's face transformed to rage.

"I will kill you, outlander," he shouted. "I will bathe my wife in your blood before I take her to my bed."

Dave edged forward. He was trying to concentrate on Ragar, but Jenna was so close to him now he couldn't resist glancing down at her. Ragar used that moment to strike, but he wasn't faster than Gloin, which deflected his surprise stroke. Dave blinked and instantly was into his zone weaving a complex series of sword strokes. Ragar was very good, but wasn't equal to Graile. Ragar won fights with brutality, clubbing down opponents after wearing them down with great stamina and had never fought an opponent like Dave. Dave fought efficiently and aggressively, gave Ragar no openings and pressed him so Ragar could not rest. Ragar roared and tried to overpower Dave with fierce heavy strokes. Dave simply deflected the blows, letting Ragar waste strength in ferocity.

Dave forced him back and away from Jenna. Ragar's men tried to claim her, but Angus, Graile, and Kra'ac easily knocked them back and pulled Jenna to the safety of her family tribal members.

Now that Dave didn't need to worry about Jenna, he went at Ragar, taking the fight to a new level. Ragar was immediately worried, fighting desperately to survive and knew Dave could win the fight. The background noise silenced as the transfixed Warlen watched the epic battle. Dave's combatant skill was a wonder to behold. Selane maintained the pyrotechnic display in the sky to be sure that no one would get brave and join Ragar in the fight against an outlander.

Time passed and they sparred steadily. Usually a long fight worked to Ragar's advantage, but Dave churned along undeterred, a constant hazard to Ragar. Ragar suddenly glanced to the side, nodding, and Dave was instantly on guard. He was aware of movement behind him and heard the clash of blades as Graile engaged three of Ragar's tribe who had slunk out of the shadows. Angus shouted something and more sounds of fighting broke out. Ragar backed up breathing heavily and watched the action behind Dave.

Dave suddenly turned and hurried into the fight with his friends. Graile was fighting ten warriors; Dave attacked and whittled down the enemy numbers quickly. He sensed Ragar's advance and turned to engage his next attack. Ragar was relentless, determined to end this fight while he felt he still could. Dave started to feel some fatigue; the vast magical workings were drawing on him, like a wound bleeding.

He hoped Ragar couldn't sense his fatigue. They battled on ferociously. Dave heard more fighting behind him and knew Graile was guarding his back from more treacherous assaults. Kra'ac roared, telling Dave that Ragar's people were trying to assault Selane and Lissette.

Dave made a decision at that moment. He needed to put an end to Ragar. Dave's fighting intensified. Ragar felt it and became frantic and fearful as Dave ground him relentlessly backward. Ragar dropped all offensive moves and could only manage a feeble defense. Dave forced him back until the Warlen champion was pressed up against the table of elders.

Dave saw an opening, but instead of killing Ragar, made a lightning move that knocked the sword out of Ragar's hand. Panting exhausted and surprised he'd been beaten, Ragar was helpless to defend himself.

"According to your rules," yelled Dave, "I should take his life right now, but I'm here to show you a different way. I come from a place where life is precious. We don't kill other men for whim. I don't need to kill Ragar to show you I'm the superior fighter. The Warlen have lost far too many good men over the ages for no good reason. If your men compete for the right to lead you, is it killing that separates them as the best leaders? That's foolish and it's time to stop. Do you want to die, Ragar?"

Ragar shook his head.

"Does this council demand that I kill him?" Dave asked looking directly at the elder from Jenna's village who smiled at Dave.

The elders looked at each other and Jenna's elder stood. "There is no rule that Ragar must die at your hands."

"Do you acknowledge you're not the High Chieftain?" Dave demanded, pointing his sword at Ragar.

"Yes…"

"Ragar, do you renounce any claim you had on Jenna?"

"Yes."

"Then I say go back to your tribe in peace."

Ragar looked at Dave, surprised, stood up and looked at the elders before claiming his sword from the ground and hurried away glancing about furtively at the Warlen citizens eyeing him contemptuously.

"I think you can relax now, Selane," said Dave.

She ended the magic abruptly and fell into the arms of Kra'ac.

"I'm afraid wielding that much magic is very taxing," said Dave to the elders.

"What is it that you wish outlander?" asked Jenna's elder.

"If I understand your customs, I'm now worthy to marry the prima virga. That's what I want."

"The prima virga's husband becomes our High Chieftain," said the elder. "Do you propose to rule the Warlen nation?"

"I would like to marry Jenna now, but my friends and I are about to embark on a dangerous quest beyond the mountains, so I must leave you. If I'm the new High Chieftain, I appoint Andron to act as regent in my stead until such time as I return."

The elders were speechless.

"Andron!" shouted Dave.

He came forward cautiously.

The elders looked warily at Andron, conferred among themselves and finally brought a ceremonial headdress over and placed it on Andron's head. Then they all looked at Dave.

"Good," Dave said. "Andron will do a good job for you. Here are my new rules. First, there will be no further fighting allowed between the Warlen tribes. You work with each other. If any tribe breaks that rule, you toss them out - exiled from the land. Secondly, there will no longer be prejudice against strangers. You make peace with all of your neighbors and start trading with them. I don't understand this rule against marrying outsiders, so my third rule is that now anybody can marry whomever they want, starting with me and Jenna. If I think of any other rules, I'll let you know. Unless you've got any questions, I'm going to go hug my fiancée. Are you okay with this, Andron?"

"I have no words for this," he said humbly. "I never thought to be…"

"You don't have to thank me," said Dave. "Let's go to the tent."

The elders were speechless along with the peoples of the nation, but it wasn't long before they began to talk excitedly about the mystifying traumatic events they'd witnessed, not the least of which was an outsider as their new High Chief.

* * * *

Jenna, kneeling down stroking Selane's hair, looked hopefully at Dave when he came into the tent. Selane was resting after the drain of the magical construct she'd perpetuated.

"I thought my life was over. Again you do the impossible, Dave. They tell me that you're now my betrothed."

"I hope that's okay with you, Jenna?"

"Do you even have to ask? Do you not know I prayed for this impossible day when I could pledge to you?"

She got up and grabbed Dave, full of emotion.

"Even when I was humiliated in Ragar's tent, I believed you would find a way to come for me. I never lost faith. I've loved you from the start, but I couldn't say it until now."

"You know how I feel." He kissed her tenderly before they turned back to Selane.

"Are you okay?" asked Dave.

"I will be fine, Dave. I just need some rest, you've made me stronger. When I exceeded myself healing Kra'ac leg, I was disabled for days. Tonight I sustained a much stronger magic for a far longer time, and I'm recovering much faster. I think I can share a little wine with all of you later."

"Are you up to a wedding?" asked Dave.

"Dave, I've had no time to prepare, to even think about it," said Jenna worriedly, "my dress, the arrangements, the preparation rituals, how can I do everything?"

"Your whole nation is right here. Let's do it now, because where we're going won't be a good place to get married."

Jenna turned to Selane. "I don't wish to easily dismiss your entreaties, darling," she said gently. "You're a dear person to me now, though I wouldn't have thought that could be the case in the beginning. I've thought deeply about your wishes and I wasn't unmoved by what you offer, I was honored that you would think of me."

Jenna looked intently at Selane who smiled weakly. They grasped hands and whispered to each other.

"You have my blessing," said Selane finally. "You weren't meant to be one of the sisters." Jenna kissed her on the cheek and then looked at Dave and smiled.

"I must go tell my mother," said Jenna excitedly and hurried out of the tent.

Selane looked at Dave who then sat down beside her.

"Sorry for messing up your plans, Selane."

"I'm happy she'll make her life with you, Dave."

"It isn't as if you can't still be friends. We'll be together. Maybe it's a good time for you to take a look at your others options, Selane."

"Other options?" she was confused.

"I think you can figure them out."

Andron came into the tent.

"We'll have the wedding tomorrow, as you've requested, Dave."

"How do the people feel about that, Andron?"

"There is much turmoil. We've never had such momentous events at a council meeting. I think it will take some time for most people to become comfortable with the changes you've wrought. Having an outlander as High Chief is, well, unprecedented."

"I didn't really have much chance to think it through. It will work out though. When the people see the good we do, they'll come around."

"I'm terrified at the responsibility put on my shoulders, Dave."

"You'll do fine. You're not someone with selfish motives. You think about what's best for the people."

Andron shrugged self-consciously.

"Listen Andron, there's something else I want you to do for me. Right now you're a nation, but you still function in your little tribes. I need you to create a central authority, a government unifying all the people. I know there will be a lot of resistance to breaking with old ways, but I need to consolidate control. Once again, emphasize the mutual benefits of what the tribes are gaining rather than their perceptions of losing something. I'd like to see the formation of a central army rather than these little militias riding around causing havoc. I don't know what's going to happen when we go into the empire. If we stir up a hornet's nest, that may spill over to here. Do you understand?"

"I'll do what I can, but I must tell you what you propose would seem to be beyond the efforts of any man."

"Use me as the bad guy. Threaten them with my wrath, if you need to. Collect trustworthy people around you and work hard at finding allies from the other tribes. If they think you're trying to make your tribe supreme that will lead to trouble. You need to populate the government from all the tribes."

Andron looked sickly.

"It will work out," said Dave reassuringly. "We'll sit down with the elders and have a talk. I'll outline how the new government will be structured."

"As you wish," said Andron, nodding.

* * * *

The following morning was a perfect spring day with a cloudless sky. Jenna had gone to stay in a separate tent with her parents for the night. Decorations and fancy clothing seemed to appear magically as the Warlen warmed to the idea of the marriage. A delegation of Warlen women came with Andron to "prepare" Dave for the ceremony. First, they described the ritual and the words he needed to speak. They spent considerable time helping Dave perfect his role. After deeming Dave marginally competent, they hauled him away to be consecrated in a sweat lodge. After he hooted painfully as they bathed him in ice cold water. The Warlen women laughed at his reaction.

They dressed him in the ceremonial garb of the High Chieftain, placed a headdress on his head and led him out on display leading him on a tour visiting numerous tribal camps for the people to see him. He nodded blithely, paying close attention to the mixed reactions of the crowd, which seemed split fifty-fifty of those for versus against him.

He felt foolish in the gaudy draping with feathers everywhere, the cumbersome headgear and the strange powder blue color choice.

Finishing his tour, they led him back to his tent to wait. Drums started up and then music of wind instruments fashioned from bone or wood.

"Where's the CSO when you need them," he muttered.

"What is a CSO?" asked Angus.

"The Chicago Symphony Orchestra," said Dave. "They're great, you'd really like them."

109

Angus smiled wryly. "Someday, I think I'll crack you on the side of the head to knock this craziness out."

"It's worth a try," said Dave.

The drone of their high shaman chanting a ritual song hummed along as Dave waited patiently until women dressed in finery came to the tent to retrieve him. He let them guide him to the center of the sacred circle, the place where he'd fought against Ragar. The land was covered with Warlen people as far as he could see in any direction.

The shaman finished his chant and eyed Dave coolly. The music started again as Jenna was led toward him. At least he assumed it was Jenna because she was heavily draped from head to toe. Led by a beaming Hachen and Talia, Jenna was dressed in pure white soft doeskin decorated with feathers and beads.

"Who stands with the prima virga?" bellowed the shaman.

"I do," said Hachen. "She is my daughter."

He placed Jenna's hand into Dave's and she squeezed slightly.

The shaman went through a long ordeal more like a speech about honoring the old ways before he got around to the marriage vows. Dave stood through the ceremony patiently, speaking all the pledges and attestations for Jenna and the Warlen nation.

The shaman pulled out a long knife and nicked them both so they could mingle blood before he pronounced them married.

Dave pulled back the wraps covering Jenna's head, took her face gently in his hands, kissed her exquisitely and broke tribal protocols in the process. The shaman was not pleased, but everyone else shouted and a vast celebration began lasting three days and nights.

Dave and Jenna's "honeymoon" was a white tent erected in the center of the camp. Each night after they retired they were serenaded by singing groups of women or by young men shouting and boasting of their own prowess - not the ideal setting for Dave to romance his new bride, but they made due.

Days later, when they rejoined their companions, Jenna pulled aside Selane and Lissette.

"Had I chosen to accompany you to become a sister, Selane, you would have begun preparing my mind, seeking out my power. I wish to travel that path with you and Lissette. I'll no longer tolerate being helpless. I wish to have the ability to wield magic as you do."

"That's not an easy thing," Selane explained. "I'm willing to walk that path with you, but realize it will not be like with Dave. He was unique to have power so close we could evoke it with the slightest of efforts. With you, I fear we would need to search deep within you and even then I cannot guarantee to what extent you will be functional."

"Whatever abilities I have, I wish to find them," said Jenna. She looked at Dave. "Do I have your permission to do this, husband?"

"Well honey. Maybe I should explain something else. When you married me, you married a man from Earth, and you're in an Earth type relationship. We're equals. You don't ask my permission for what you choose to do in your life. You command me as much as I command you. If you want to do this, you don't require my permission. I'll support you in whatever you do. Having some power of your own seems like a good idea to me. If I can connect with you like I connect with Lissette and Selane, it would be a very good thing."

"Thank you," said Jenna. She looked at her parents and smiled. Talia looked at Dave.

"You're a wonder, my new son…"

"So far, so good, Talia…"

"The tribe will be returning to our territory," said Hachen. "Do you plan to travel with us?"

"I do," said Dave. "Andron is going to have some work to do here, but we're going to stay with you while Jenna works on her powers."

Hachen smiled and hugged his daughter.

"It will be good to have you with us again, Jenna, even if it's but for a short time."

"I'm happy for this chance also, father."

* * * *

The vast gathering scattered and dissipated surprisingly fast as the tribes headed away in all directions. Semi-nomadic, they were very skilled at rapid movements of large numbers of people.

"Did you see Ragar and his people?" asked Dave as they rode away.

"After his defeat, they were shamed and left the gathering immediately," said Hachen. "I fear they'll continue to be troublesome. It has always been their way."

"I could have killed Ragar, but that just isn't me. I was hoping my mercy and sparing his life might give him a different perspective. Maybe he's one of those people who don't want to improve."

"For as long as there has been a Warlen nation, they've lived in a low way," said Hachen. "They don't desire change. Other tribes will be a problem too. They're not as bad as Ragar's people, but are not far away from that sorry path. I regret you cannot live with my tribe to learn what we can teach you about the peoples."

"Maybe when I get back, Hachen," said Dave as he glanced at mountains in the distance.

* * * *

The tribe returned to home grounds and set up camp. As spring took hold melting away the frozen grip of winter, the weather continued to improve. The air had a fresh smell as buds turned into blooms and birds filled the skies and trees.

Jenna spent considerable time alone with Selane and Lissette as they sought out her inner secrets.

"I want you to understand what we'll be doing," Selane explained. "It's very invasive so you must trust us completely. As Dave found out, there will be no secrets withheld between us. We'll know all of your thoughts, feelings, desires, and secret motives, and you'll know ours. We'll see your whole life, even those things which you wouldn't wish to be revealed."

"Is that how it was for you, Selane? When the sisters took you, is this what they did?"

"Yes and no. Our end result will be the same, probably better. The bond I have with Lissette and Dave exceeds anything I ever achieved with the sisters. With us there's no hazard. At first with the sisters, I felt violated and never felt fully trusting of them. They took by force, while amongst us we choose to share."

"I'm ready," said Jenna.

"The first probe will be the most difficult for you. Again, I can only tell you that you can trust us and know in your heart we wish only the best for you. Some things you learn about yourself and about us will be disturbing for you. None of us can hide our secret desires and that can be unnerving. Secrets can be galling revelations, but once the complete truth is known, it's the first step to enlightenment and will be true between you and your husband. Remember, he had a life in his world before he met you. Their ways are much different than ours. You cannot judge him based on our rules here. Before melding with Dave, I would never have thought it possible to be on such a footing with any man. He's shown me

112

a new and a better path for my life and for that I'm grateful. We'll get past this test and then we'll find your power."

Jenna looked at Lissette.

"For me," said Lissette, "I've been drawn into a new world. I can tell you that never has any elf wielded such power as have I. What I could do before is a pale shade of the power I have within me now. Our union has expanded my personal power beyond my belief. Now I could face a witch of the sisterhood without fear. In concert with Selane and Dave, I cannot imagine any power we couldn't defeat. Revealing my secrets and learning those of Selane and Dave haven't proven to be a problem for me. I'm as flawed a person as any other and I have more than my share of frailties, but I've come to terms with that side of me. I believe we all have."

"Good," said Jenna, "let's do it."

"You sound like your husband already," said Selane, chuckling and they all laughed.

Facing each other, they sat down inside the tent forming a triangle. Closing their eyes, they began the connection.

Jenna's anxiety rose. The initial feelings, of having others inside her head, were more disconcerting than expected. Her body and mind reacted with feelings of nausea and vertigo. Wobbling, she felt both other women grab her to keep her from falling over. Her first breakthrough came when she was able to communicate mentally with them.

"*The disorientation is temporary,*" they shared with her. "*Your discomforted feelings will recede quickly. There's nothing for you to fear. Move to us and accept us into your essence.*"

Jenna was surprised when she did just that, though she had no idea how.

"You control with your thoughts and your wishes," said Selane. "Do you see?"

"Yes," Jenna replied.

"*Now we'll reveal ourselves to each other. Put your trust in us for we're your sisters truly, closer than if we were born from the same mother.*"

Jenna felt them seep deep inside her, exploring every facet, thought, impulse and memory. While exposing her life to their scrutiny, at the same time she fully saw both of them in their own vulnerabilities. It was mortifying as her darkest secrets, and greatest humiliations were replayed, but the same thing was true for the other women too. Jenna was forced to sublimate shame and move past bruises from her past, but that was made easier as she saw how the other women had coped with their own mistakes.

Locked into the union with Selane and Lissette, Jenna had no conception of the passage of time. Dave came by the tent several times during the day to check on them, but the trio was totally oblivious to his presence. He saw them all glowing, their eyelids closed, but eyes moving rapidly like REM sleep states. At one point he tried to see if he could feed them, but they didn't respond to his attempt, their mouths staying shut.

It was late afternoon before the mental sharing and sifting concluded and Selane moved to Jenna's center. Jenna felt her come to the barrier and she felt a new wave of anxiety.

"We're with you," said Lissette, "do not fear."

Selane exerted force against Jenna's natural defenses and they reacted to the attempted intrusion instinctively. Jenna felt excitement, dread and fear simultaneously. Selane pushed again, but with more force. Jenna's defenses reacted, increasing correspondingly to Selane's level of power. Suddenly Selane sent a sharp jolt that pierced Jenna's barrier and for the first time Jenna experienced the mingling of essence Dave had felt - she was one with Selane and with Lissette. It was a rapturous feeling, unlike anything Jenna had ever experienced. She felt close, secure, and love for her new sisters, and she felt their emotions in return.

There was something else too, the tingle that Dave had described, now she tingled also. Selane provoked that power drawing it forth for the first time. She sculpted it into a ball, the roiling construct, and in so doing taught Jenna how to wield her newfound power.

Jenna reached out with her psychic self and embraced her strength and became empowered as a result - like opening a door, she "saw" like never before. Prior understandings morphed into a new view of her world. She felt her potency and it was exciting.

Worried the women were entranced for such a long time without a break, Dave visited the tent at dusk, thinking there might be a problem. Instead, he found the women open eyed and smiling blithely.

"Dave," said Jenna, lovingly.

"I'm glad you guys woke up, I wondered if I needed to step in…."

"We are well," said Selane. "Tomorrow you'll join the meld so your wife can become one with you."

"Sounds good, I just hope she doesn't kick my ass after she sees my former life."

The women looked at each other and chuckled.

"That will not be a problem," said Selane.

Before retiring, they ate a meal together. Kra'ac eyed them closely. His expressions were always difficult to interpret.

Dave nudged Selane.

"I keep telling you he's jealous," he whispered.

"You're a fool," Selane replied, but she eyed Kra'ac and smiled. Kra'ac relaxed visibly receiving attention from Selane.

The following day, Dave joined the women and established his mental link. It was strange that Jenna would be there too. Her psychic self wasn't the same to Dave as her physical self - neither bad, nor good, simply different.

This new Jenna was confident and potent - even a little cocky. The melding was a stark revelation for her to absorb seeing Dave's Earth life, and experiences. The world of technology was befuddling, but differences in social mores and practices were pieces she had the greatest problem coping with. Dave got to see Jenna's secrets too. Though her dark secrets were different than Dave's, they were equally challenging. He saw her in a new light and understood her prior actions and reactions more clearly.

With that task completed, the group turned back to the matter of the quest.

"Now I feel truly a worthy part of this great fellowship," said Jenna.

The Rajduk Empire

When they readied to depart for the mountains, it was a bittersweet day for Jenna. There were the good feelings from her marriage, acquiring power and new bonds with her husband, Selane, and Lissette. The flip side was she had to depart from her tribe, parents and the security of her old life.

She tried to put on a brave front, but while hugging her mother, she broke down.

"I'm so sorry, mother," she whispered. "If there were any other way, you know I would choose to stay here with you and father to make our life."

"I know that," said Talia. "Wherever you go, we'll be there with you in our thoughts. You have made us so proud, my daughter. Never has there been a prima virga such as you. Our whole people are blessed by the person you are. Your husband will lead us to a better life, I'm sure."

They mounted their horses. The villagers were secretly happy to see Kra'ac riding away on his gigantic mount, who ate nearly as much as the other horses combined.

"Goodbye Mom and Dad," said Dave. "When I come back, we can spend time together and you can get to know me better. I'm not a bad guy, I don't think."

They looked at him curiously.

"Be vigilant at all times," said Hachen. "You have precious charges to protect."

"I will," Dave replied solemnly.

Riding off, they headed west and then gradually turned northwest. On horses they were able to cover considerable more ground than on foot. Distant mountains grew each day as they closed the distance to the pass.

Each night they stopped in confederation towns.

Dave set a steady pace, but not one which would fatigue the horses. At night his wife was affectionate to a point.

Late in the night he embraced her.

She turned to him.

"You cannot put me with child, not with where we're going. I'm sorry, husband."

"Sure, you're right," he whispered. "I guess I wasn't thinking."

She kissed him sympathetically.

"That isn't helping Jenna."

She chuckled.

Again, they rode past the point where they'd gone up to meet Raja Kai, gazing upward at the peaks remembering their own versions of that traumatic adventure.

Paralleling the mountain chain for another week, they came upon the confederation border station. The guards eyed them curiously.

"Greetings," said Graile.

"Why are you here?" asked the guard captain.

"We're going to go through the pass into the empire."

The guards were stunned.

"Why would you do that? In my lifetime, that of my father and his father before him, we've never had travelers come back from the empire. Those few who went through from this side never returned. Do you have a death wish?"

"No," said Graile evenly. "We have pressing business there. Perhaps we'll establish trade with them once we've resolved our business."

The guards looked at him as if he was jesting.

"It's suicide to go through the pass, but if that's your intent, I wish you well. You realize if you have trouble over there, we will not be riding to your rescue."

"We understand. Thank you for your courtesy and your good wishes. We'll be on our way now."

"You should leave your women here. I don't think it will go well for them over there. The stories we heard were, well…"

"We'll be fine," said Selane.

Departing, they weaved their way along the rugged path. With no traffic the trail was choked, overgrown with foliage and the footfalls were obscured.

"Maybe we better walk the horses," warned Graile.

Travel became even slower and the farther they went the sharper was the angle of ascent. Each night when making camp they didn't make a fire, ate dried meat, chunks of cubed cheese and drank cold water from a nearby mountain stream. Several days passed before reaching the high point in the pass where they looked down at vast flatland to the horizon. Far away, at the opposite end of the flats, there appeared to be another mountain formation that didn't stretch across the entire landscape. They were a relatively concise formation, or at least appeared that way from a distance.

"What do you want to bet that's where we're going?" asked Dave, pointing at the distant peaks.

"It's logical," said Graile. "I think we must post a watch each night from this point on. We don't know what to expect down there."

Everyone agreed.

Dave glanced at Jenna who was communing with Selane and Lissette, so he lay down in his blanket alone. Jenna was spending increasing time with them trying to perfect her power with their constructs and practice methods. Dave felt a little disappointment even though he knew with his thoughts she wasn't ignoring him. He glanced at Kra'ac who was always close by Selane. Kra'ac had a look that made Dave feel Kra'ac felt the same way, like they were on the outside looking in.

"Suck it up, Dave," he muttered.

Descending toward the flatlands the next morning, greater caution was used.

"I see the post," Lissette exclaimed. She had the best eyesight of the group. "We should camp here tonight and approach them in the early morning."

"Okay," said Dave. "I'll take first watch tonight."

They set up camp. Jenna went straight to the women for her lessons. Dave climbed on a boulder and looked down, studying the post. There were no guards on this side of the station they were all facing inland. Men walking about were wearing scarlet and crimson uniforms with silver helmets. A large flag flapped in the breeze with scarlet background and emblazoned crimson crest.

From what Dave could see, the guards were very lax.

After dark Dave relaxed, leaning back against a big stone. Suddenly a deep tone broke out somewhere in the distant darkness. Unnerving, the sound was almost evil in some way. Someone had sounded a horn that could only mean trouble. He shivered and peered intently into the darkness to be sure no threat was creeping up the pass.

When Dave went to the camp for relief he shook Angus.

"Be very vigilant," he whispered. "There's something dire moving about out there."

"Aye," said Angus rising for his turn at lookout.

Sunrise came too quickly for Dave. He yawned and rinsed his face with some water to wake up.

They ate another cold meal and began their approach to the guard station.

"Ho!" yelled Graile as they came up to the rear of the buildings.

He startled the guards who jumped up and grabbed their weapons. Their officer ran out of the building, looked at the new arrivals and then at his men who were still forming up ranks.

Dave looked over the imperial soldiers who looked to be competent enough, but also crude, mean and disreputable.

"Who are you?" asked the officer.

"We're peaceful travelers come through the pass," said Graile.

"You came through the mountains?" asked the officer, incredulous.

"We've come to seek adventure in your country. In our land we hear only stories of the great empire. We've come to see it for ourselves."

The guards snorted derisively.

"If you seek adventure, you've come to the right place," said the officer, eyeing his men mirthfully. "We can give you adventures you'll never forget."

"Can you give us suggestions on where we should go?"

"Travel straight ahead. The imperial city is a wonder. I'm sure the Emperor would be well pleased to entertain guests from across the mountains. Is it true your land is backward and poor?"

"I'm afraid it is. We're hoping for a better life here. Do you accept strangers to live among you?"

"Yes, we have much to offer."

"Thank you sir, we'll be on our way."

"Watch for patrols on the highway. They'll safeguard your travels."

"Thank you," said Graile.

"Come out so we can see all of you."

Graile glanced back and all nodded approval. The women were at the rear and when they rode into sight the guards leered at the women.

"There's but one small thing," said the officer.

"What's that?"

"There's a toll for passage through the station payable in imperial tender."

"You know we don't have your money. I do have gold."

"That will not suffice. We'll only accept one of your women as payment."

Dave and the others reached for their weapons. The guards saw there could be a fight and drew their weapons.

"Wait!" said Selane. "I'll pay the price of admittance. Will I suffice?"

"No," said Dave anxiously.

"These are mere men," she whispered to him. "I'm in no danger. I'll meet you on the road. This will not occupy me long."

Kra'ac edged to her side.

"You must leave," she whispered to him. "I'm in no danger from these fools. Trust me, I'll join you soon."

"I don't like this," Kra'ac grumbled.

"Move along quickly before we arouse suspicion," said Selane. "Don't make me force you, Kra'ac."

Dave shrugged.

"I don't like this either."

"We agree," said Selane, with a crocodile smile. "Move along my friends, I have business to take care of with these handsome gentlemen."

Graile rode away at a gallop Dave reluctantly followed him.

They rode rapidly for a time.

"I think we should go back there," shouted Dave.

"Selane is a white witch," said Jenna. "They're not a threat to her."

Graile veered off of the road after a time and they rode into a sparsely wooded area.

"I don't think that meeting their patrols is a good idea," he said.

"Assuming that Selane gets away from those guards, how will she find us?" asked Dave.

"We're like beacons to her," said Lissette. "She can sense our power and we can sense hers."

"Am I the only one that's worried about her?" asked Dave.

"No," said Kra'ac. "She threatened me if I didn't depart, or I would have dealt with those soldiers."

"We couldn't cause an incident that would alert the countryside," said Graile. "I fear we'll have trouble enough with this journey."

Selane rode into their camp at dusk.

Dave hurried over to her, along with Kra'ac.

She had an amused look on her face.

"Did you fear for me?" she asked.

"What do you think?" asked Dave hotly.

Selane chuckled.

"They were infants, worse than infants," she said. "They'll awaken with poor recollection of our passing. As for their romantic intentions, I'm afraid their desires didn't work out as they'd hoped."

She laughed heartily.

"Selane," said Dave, shaking his fist. "You had me going there. I was worried."

Selane's expression softened.

"I'm gratified that you truly cared about me," she said warmly, her eyes sparkling. She kissed him on the cheek and started to walk over to the other women. She stopped, came back and pulled Kra'ac down and kissed his cheek too as the troll's face flushed red with embarrassment.

For their camp, they picked a spot obscured from sight of the highway. Horsemen rode by after dark while Graile was on watch. Dave crept out and knelt beside him.

"I counted twenty," whispered Graile. "They made no attempt to disguise their movement."

"There's nobody for them to fear out here," said Dave.

"Indeed."

"If they go to the border station, I wonder if they'll remember enough to alert the patrols about us."

"Selane was convinced that the guards wouldn't be a problem. We can only trust her judgment about the measures she took. Regardless, we're here and our situation is equally dangerous even if the border guards cannot identify us."

"You're right. I don't think I'll ever adjust to seeing women on the same war footing as men. Back on Earth, women can be in our military forces, but usually we don't put them into combat."

Suddenly, the loud deep blast of the strange horn echoed across the countryside - a chilling and very disturbing sound.

"That thing gives me the willies," said Dave.

"It is an ill sound," Graile agreed, "meant to terrify."

"It succeeds."

"You should get some rest."

Dave returned to the camp and slipped under the blanket with Jenna. She muttered and rolled over before falling back to sleep.

At dawn, they resumed their journey aiming toward the distant peaks paralleling the highway. Farms traversed were given a wide berth and once a small, run down village with the buildings decaying was passed. The few people moving around looked ill and unsteady on their feet.

"This isn't a good place to stop," said Graile. "There's plague here."

Quickly leaving the infected village behind, they kept moving. Next, they narrowly evaded a patrol that suddenly rode out of a wood. Fortunately, a nearby hill provided cover.

"That was close," said Dave.

"It's inevitable we'll be discovered at some point," said Lissette.

"We'll teach them the meaning of valor," said Angus.

"What do you know of valor, dwarf?" asked Lissette dismissively. "Your people skulk about and fall upon the weak and the injured if you outnumber them ten to one."

Angus scowled at her.

"I will not bandy words with an elf," he replied haughtily. "You're greatly taken with yourself, as are all elves. This is why elves don't make their camps beside water. They would all be at the bank staring at their reflections. I'm surprised an elf has not married itself, or have they?"

Dave started to chuckle.

"Do not listen to him," said Lissette. "Dwarves are known for having the brains of a stone."

"I see," said Dave.

Later they began to look for a campsite, but the area was open and flat, providing no concealment or protection.

Riding later in the day than they wanted to without any luck in finding a site, visibility became further obscured by ground fog that rolled in.

Graile was in the lead when suddenly out of the fog they came upon a lone man carrying a full knapsack. Yelping in fear, he dropped to his knees in fear.

"Please, I have a family," he pleaded.

"Do not fear," said Graile, "we mean no harm. Stand up citizen."

The man cowered in fear and disbelief.

"Come, my good man. We cannot stay here in this state. As you said, you have a family to take care of."

"What do you want from me?" asked the man, remaining on the ground.

"We want nothing at all. Perhaps you would be kind enough to invite us to supper so we can visit with you. We're new to this land."

The man eyed him unsurely. He didn't move.

"If you mean to take my life, get to it," said the man.

Kra'ac rode over. The stranger's face turned to sheer terror as he closed his eyes and waited for the killing blow. Kra'ac snorted aggravation, grabbed the man by the collar and hoisted him up onto the horse as if he was weightless.

"We don't want your life," said Graile, but we don't want to be out in the open any longer, now lead us to your home.

"I fear for my family."

"Would they do better without you?"

The man scowled.

"That way," he said, nodding forward.

Riding a short distance, they came upon his small farm; a wood frame covered with wood planks and wood shingles on the roof, but in poor condition - like every other building in the empire. There was a dull glow in the window.

They rode out back and went into a barn, similarly dilapidated on the outside, but neat, clean inside and well used. Domesticated animals grazed on straw, a stack of hay bales laid along the wall and various implements and tools were arrayed and neatly organized.

"Smart," said Graile glancing around, "nothing to draw attention on the outside, but functional on the inside."

The man was visibly upset strangers were in his secret reserve.

"Let's go to dinner," said Graile.

"I cannot feed all of you," said the farmer.

"That's not a problem. We'll treat you. We have ample supplies."

123

The farmer reluctantly went with them into his house. His entire family was sitting around a stone fireplace where a small fire burned. The wife's face went ashen with fright when she saw the friends walk in and the six children screamed and huddled around their mother.

"Good evening," said Graile. "I'm sorry that we arrived unannounced. My name is Graile, the dwarf is Angus, the elf is Lissette, Selane is a white witch, the troll is Kra'ac, this is Jenna, former prima virga of the Warlen, and this is Dave, her husband, and our leader. We're traveling through your lands on an important quest. We would appreciate your hospitality for an evening. We'll resume our trek tomorrow. What are your names?"

The farmer walked over to his wife and they looked at each other. "In the empire, there's no trust, especially for strangers. If you truly are from another land, you don't know the trouble you've stumbled into. Life here is a nightmare come to life. The people cower in fear and hide from the minions of the emperor and his vile priests. They drain all life out of the people. We have no power to stop them. We survive only if they don't find us. This farm has had many residents. Every prior family was stolen away by the imperial search. We moved in because they'll never be back. We know they'll come for us and are like timid rabbits anxious to race away at any sign they're near. If we're ever seen, they'll take us away to our doom."

Sadly, he continued.

"My name is Bashar, this is my wife Kela and these are our children. We love them desperately, but feel terrible we brought them into such a world."

"Well, for this night, you can rest in peace and security," said Graile. "We'll protect you."

"Against the search?" asked Kela skeptically.

"They have no power we cannot defeat."

"I'll work a magic that will protect this house," said Selane. "None can see it, can hear it, or approach it."

"Truly?" asked Kela. "That would be a blessing beyond measure."

"We have food," said Jenna. "Let's prepare a feast to celebrate our coming."

The children edged close and stared at their strange looking visitors. Kra'ac was surprisingly gentle with them. Selane went outside briefly and built her magical construct to obscure the farm. Coming back in she

124

smiled watching Kra'ac calmly sitting on the floor letting the children crawl unto his lap and hang on him. The smell of food cooking in the kitchen filled the air. Kela was beaming and talking as she helped make the food with Jenna and Lissette.

"Ladies," said Selane. "The magic is done."

"Good," said Jenna. "Come and talk with Kela. She has many questions."

"I've never had hope in my life," said Kela. "You make me think that we could have a different life."

Selane looked at the others sadly.

"Let's enjoy this night. I wish we could leave behind a permanent protection for your family, but sadly we cannot."

"Wherever you're going and whatever you'll do, perhaps it will mean a new day for people like us. It gives me something to hope for."

Dave sat down with Graile and Bashar to talk.

"I have no way to repay your kindness," said Bashar.

"You owe us nothing," said Dave.

"It's strange to feel safe, even if only for a night. It's something my family has never felt. I feel less than a man. I'm the father and the protector and yet I'm nothing against the scourge that rules this land. I've brought six children into this world to face hopelessness and desperation running in fear for our lives, how could I do that to them?"

"Don't think that way. Even in the darkest times, there's always hope."

"You're a mighty band, you have power, martial skills, strength. You don't know what it's like to be us. A lifetime of fear eats at people. It warps you into pathetic helpless shells."

"I don't agree," said Dave. "I think you have much more courage than me. To survive as you have in these circumstances is remarkable. Don't think because things are this way now they can never change."

"I would like to think there could be a good life for us, but for untold generations evil has ruled here. I don't doubt that you're a daunting group of heroes, but what you face is terrible beyond your imagining. My wife and I were born near the imperial city. Both of our families were taken away and given to the emperor. We escaped as youngsters because our parents hid us and we miraculously evaded capture. We ran away for months and months living off anything we could scavenge. We were nearly taken so many times, even the memory of that flight frightens me. We came to this region after numerous years squatting from place to place. We decided to become mates, though there was no formal bonding ceremony. There were none to perform it. We simply spoke words to pledge to each other. She and the children are the comfort of my life, the only reason for me to stay alive."

"Bashar, you've done a good job. We need to know about where we're going to and what to watch out for."

"I would warn you to avoid the imperial city. To go there is to die horribly. The Emperor is filled with blood lust and his priesthood is worse. They do unspeakable things in the name of their dark god. Any who resist in any way are publicly tortured and killed gruesomely to warn any others who might wish to fight them. I saw some things when I was young that would curdle your blood. I think they have power. I scc what your witch woman can do. I think they must have such powers also. For simple people like us, it was impossible to oppose them. For people like you, I cannot say. I don't understand magical power, so I cannot give you guidance in that area."

"Have you been inside that city?" asked Graile.

"I have not," said Bashar. "No one chooses to go in there."

"Have you seen the Emperor?" asked Dave. "What does he look like?"

"The Emperor doesn't leave the city. It's said that he's only partially human and the other part demon."

The women called them to dinner. It was satisfying to watch the children being happy, laughing and playing, secure for the first time in their lives and with full bellies to boot.

They had no more than finished eating when there was a scratching on the front door. Tensed, they looked at each other. Selane shook her head disbelieving anyone could pierce her magic spell.

Dave opened the door and was shocked to see Bear standing there. The children screamed at seeing the deathcat.

"Bear…!" Dave exclaimed. Bear sauntered in and the friends crowded around him.

"This beast is yours?" asked Bashar in amazement.

"He's a good cat," said Dave.

"It doesn't slay you?" asked Kela.

"He already ate," said Dave. "He does his hunting on his own. You're safe."

126

The children eased timidly up to Bear. After watching the women pet him, they began to stroke his furry hide. Bear purred and lay down covering much of the floor.

"Such unbelievable wonders that you bring," said Bashar, "this is truly a blessed day for my family."

"My husband does the impossible as a matter of routine," said Jenna, smiling at Dave.

"I don't know about that," he said. "I'm lucky more than anything else."

Selane sent power into the small fireplace and enhanced the fire to warm the house. It was relaxing and peaceful. When they curled up to sleep for the night half of the kids were draped on Kra'ac and the other half on Bear.

The following morning, it was difficult for Dave to see the sadness in the eyes of Bashar and Kela.

"You've given us a gift we'll never forget," said Bashar. "I pray that you remain safe and you succeed in your quest. Be wary at all times as the Emperor has eyes everywhere."

"Thank you," said Dave. The women all hugged Kela. She smiled bravely, but it was easy to see a feeling of hopelessness had returned.

"Please don't go," pleaded the children. "It was fun having you here."

"I wish we could stay," said Dave. "Maybe when we come back, you might consider coming with us back to our land."

"I would like that," said Bashar.

They went out to the barn to their mounts. The horses were always jittery around Bear, who eyed Bashar's livestock hungrily.

"No!" Dave commanded.

Bear gave out a whine, but meekly left the barn.

Mounting up, the friends started their journey.

"Stay safe," said Dave as they rode off. "I wish we could have done something to protect them."

"We couldn't take them with us," said Graile. "They've developed good survival skills. That must be enough for them. There were no other choices."

Once again, they traveled paralleling the highway. There was little traffic other than imperial patrols, which they avoided. Villages stumbled upon were equally run down, and small farms squalid. Deciding not to

Mortus ~Dennis K. Hausker

chance any further farm family hospitality, secluded areas were chosen for nightly camps.

One of those nights in the darkness the eerie horn blasted again.

"Something dire is afoot," said Angus.

The sound of hooves beat as a large mounted force rode down the highway. The force had been moving rapidly, but suddenly slowed down and stopped. Selane quickly worked a magic to conceal the friends. The unidentified horsemen waited a long time before riding away.

"What was that?" asked Dave.

"I think there was a being with power among them," whispered Selane. "I think we should move away from here."

"In the darkness?" asked Dave.

"Yes," said Selane.

They quickly packed up their things and led their horses away. Selane lagged back and hidden, kept watch on the site. Soon, a dark figure slunk into the former camp peering around extending a hand in all directions, like it was magically sniffing for their scent. Selane prepared for battle, building power behind her magical cloaking construct. Her enemy seemed tentative and unsure. Finally the being turned and left the way it had come.

Selane waited to be sure it wasn't a trick before rejoining her companions. They'd already started a new camp a few miles from the old one.

"What happened?" asked Dave as the others crowded around Selane.

"There was a person with power among them who crept to our camp, covered in a cloak so I never saw them. I don't think they face opponents here who also have power, so I think any hint of us confused them. I covered our signs and believe it worked, but Dave, Lissette, and Jenna, we must be very alert from now on for hints of power approaching us, because if we can sense them, they can also sense us. I'll need to teach you all cloaking spells to hide our magical scents. This will make our journey much more difficult."

First Blood

So far, their travels had gone surprisingly well, crossing at the border station without causing an alarm, evading the imperial patrols and disguising their presence from enemies who also had power but as they continued to journey, an edgy feeling developed, like their luck was about to run out. Even Bear seemed particularly vigilant loping ahead of them out of sight several times. Once, when he returned, his muzzle was red.

Selane created a magical construct to cloak them as they rode along. To be able to duplicate her work Dave, Lissette, and Jenna all worked through what Selane had taught them about cloaking spells. For most of the day they managed to travel without detection, but as the sun dropped to the horizon and darkness came, they relaxed and looked for a campsite.

Graile was in the lead as they rode around a small hill and headed for a stand of woods. Just as they neared the trees an imperial patrol burst out of the woods, swords drawn - a force more than double the number of the companions.

"Halt!" shouted their officer. "Off your horses and down on your knees."

Dave didn't make a conscious decision to fight, it just happened automatically. The friends sprang forward and attacked. Kra'ac was the first to hit the ranks of trained imperial soldiers, but they were no match for a mountain troll as he blasted three soldiers out of their saddles before they could react. Graile's sword was a blur scything down enemies like wheat. Lissette's arrows whistled past Dave picking off more enemy soldiers. Even Jenna whooped and charged forward waving her blade. Fear for her safety shocked Dave into motion and Gloin was in his hand in a second. The weapon hummed menacingly as he struck at the closest soldier. Beside him, Angus swung his war axe, savagely attacking, but stayed near to Lissette warding her.

The fight was over nearly as quickly as it had started. The friends looked around, panting from exertion and adrenaline.

"Is anybody hurt?" asked Dave.

"No," they replied.

"Sooner or later we were going to be spotted," he said. "We need to get rid of the bodies."

"We'll pile them together," said Selane. "I'll dispose of them."

They dragged the dead deep into the woods. There Selane began a grim chant and soon the bodies spontaneously combusted and burned away. The saddles were also burned and horses released into the wild.

Before resuming their travels, they decided to stay in the area for the night. Bear rejoined them gliding effortlessly loping along beside Dave. A week went by without further incident, but travel was more difficult. The villages were larger and there were more farms with less open land. Staying out of sight was virtually impossible now, and the number and size of the patrols increased sharply. Each day they traveled their hazards increased.

One day they stopped at a small stream to refill their water gourds. Bear paced about uneasily eyeing in the direction toward the highway.

"Something's up," said Dave.

"I feel it too," said Selane and quickly built a magic protection around them. Mounting up, they rode away from the road. Dave looked back and saw a troop of imperial soldiers ride up to where they had just been. The soldiers looked around, but Selane's magic hid them from view. The soldiers rode away quickly back toward the road.

"I think that we're being hunted now," said Selane.

Riding until it was nearly dark, they spotted some small hills strewn with a few trees.

"That's as good a place as we will find here," said Graile.

They rode over to the hills and made their camp.

Bear bounded away to hunt for his supper in the gloom.

The group huddled close together, each looking about in suspicion. The feeling of approaching danger was palpable.

Once it turned dark, they tried to fall asleep, but none slept. Lissette was sitting on the hill keeping watch.

Suddenly that terrible baleful horn sound wailed. They all sat up simultaneously and Selane stood.

"Lissette," she cried. "Come down here quickly."

Lissette looked toward the road before hustling down the hill. The sounds of hooves thundering on the gallop were coming toward them.

"We are found," said Selane.

Drawing weapons, they knew it was too late to get to the horses to flee. The enemy was already upon them.

Imperial soldiers whooped and charged around the hill led by a dark figure in a black cowl robe aiming a staff glowing menacing red, sparking with potency.

Selane began to chant and her body started to glow. The lone dark enemy loosed a searing crackling blast of red power. Selane aimed her own staff and launched a response - a bright blue ball of roiling power, striking the red line causing a loud concussion knocking everyone to the ground except Selane and the enemy. The dark opponent attacked again firing shot after shot at Selane, but she stood firm like granite rooted deep in the ground. Her responses appeared to be mostly defensive. The fight was very vivid for Dave as the forces evoked caused strong reactions within him and his own power. Compelled to join in the fight, Dave didn't know how - only Selane had the knowledge for this battle.

The dark figure paused and then started a chant of his own, but his chant was foul. It grated on Dave's psychic essence like the man was blaspheming all that is good. The dark enemy's new attack was an affront and Selane's expression turned murderous. She shouted a new chant of her own, drawing on powers deep from within her.

Selane's glowing blue aura blazed to incandescence like an exploding sun and she let loose a mighty blue ball of power. The dark man threw back a vicious red blast of hatred and bile. The two opposing forces struck and rose high into the sky gaining in strength until detonating in an eruption of sound and blinding light sweeping across the countryside, echoing loudly.

Selane remained solid and steady, her enemy shaken. He fired a quick deadly red lance of power, but Selane flicked it aside and reached out her glowing hands toward him. Dave could feel her psychic exertions as she grasped the man from afar in a cocoon of her might. He struggled desperately, fighting for his life, but Selane was too strong. The man made a final desperate strike from the depths of his essence in an attempt

131

to turn back the tide and for a time it appeared they were in a stalemate, but Selane was invincible. The dark man's defense cracked slightly and Selane burst it apart like shattering glass; he screamed and was consumed in a blue flame leaving nothing but ash.

The imperial soldiers stared at Selane in fear and disbelief. She was glowing brightly like the angel of death. Then the soldiers fled away to escape her wrath.

She did not slay them.

Some time passed before her aura dimmed and she sunk to the ground onto her knees, ashen faced.

Concerned, Jenna and Lissette grabbed her.

"Are you in distress?" they asked.

"I'm well," Selane whispered. "I've never faced an opponent set on killing me with their power before. It was frightening. That man had great power. None of the practice battles at the keep with the other sisters could have prepared me for this. The person I was before I met Dave would have been slain here. I've become so much more an entity with my communion in our group in both knowledge and in power. I feared for my life and for your lives the whole time, afraid that I couldn't win this fight, but what haunts me was at the end. I saw what this man has lived, the evil that warped and shaped him, and the evil that abides in the land. He saw his death before him and then I saw the truth in him. His goodness was still there buried and stunted, but he regretted his life and sought forgiveness from me for his evil when he saw the goodness in me. It was a pain I cannot describe to you. It was too late to restrain the dead blow. He was grateful to be released from this life, but I feel a terrible remorse."

"My god," said Dave.

"No person is fully good or fully evil," said Selane.

"I understand what you're saying. You can't dwell on that part of it. If you saw that small kernel of good, that means you must have seen all of the other part too, like what he would have done to you, and to us."

Selane shuddered. "The fate of those dragged into the imperial city is dire beyond words. What they do to women is, well, perhaps its better left unsaid. He gave me no choice but to take his life. I must begin to teach you to fight with magic Dave and you also Lissette and Jenna. You cannot be defenseless against what we'll face ahead of us. Fighting takes time and practice to perfect, so as difficult as it is in this dangerous land, we must do this each night. Defeat is simply not an option. They don't show mercy here. They exploit weakness. There's no room for error."

"Okay," said Dave, "we've learned what you taught us about everything else without any problems."

"This is different, Dave. Each person is unique, their habits, their relative strengths, their weaknesses, their skill level, their experience. This man I fought terrified me and I'm the most skilled and trained of us all. What if he's the least of his brethren? He'd experience killing with his power, a thing I'd never done. Part of my fight was learning from him in what he did, how he shaped and wielded his power. I was very lucky he didn't strike me dead with the first attack. I didn't know if my defense would protect me until after it worked. It was a guess on my part. When it comes to fighting, there's only so much I can teach you. The actual fight is the learning experience and you can only hope to survive initially. I hope that my experience gained here will mean I'll be more secure the next time. I cannot be certain of that though. None of the sisters have fought in a magical battle. Though sisters kill, they aren't personally threatened in the process."

"Are you saying we need to fight against you?"

"To an extent, yes I'm postulating, but if our other two participate by being connected in the fights, I think I can devise a way they can buffer our strikes enough to protect us from harming each other. Toothless feints would serve no purpose unfortunately, so we'll need to deal with the risk of injuring each other."

"But you aren't sure."

"It's the best that I can do, Dave."

"Watching you turn into a flaming star was pretty scary."

"I'm more than frightened of contesting with you, Dave. The deep well of your power is nearly boundless. If you evoke your strength from that molten pool without sufficient control, I fear the damage you could do. We've had too little time in helping you to wield your strength with proper control. You must be focused as never before if we're to attempt this."

"I understand," he replied soberly. "Do you think it's safe to stay here? That bomb you set off has got to have alerted everybody far and wide. They probably have the cavalry riding this way right now."

"How can we safely travel in the dark?" asked Graile.

As if on cue, Bear appeared out of the night.

"He can lead us," said Dave. "I'm getting that thought from him. He also says we need to move, trouble is on the way."

His cat eyesight was keen, like the night vision from back on Earth.

With that keen, cat eyesight Bear led them down a winding path through the forest trotting rapidly and steadily, undeterred by the poor visibility. Traveling for most of the night, he eventually led them to an abandoned farmhouse with a rickety barn where they could stable the horses out of sight. They huddled inside the eroding farmhouse. Bear stayed out on the porch to sleep lightly and maintain vigilance for what crept about in the night.

As if physical contact was affirmation of safety in the midst severe peril, they slept together backed up against each other. The sun came up too soon for them to be fully rested. They arose groggy and slow moving. Rather than race out into pursuit, they opted to stay put for a day. Selane used the opportunity to start her lessons in magical fighting. She started with Jenna who was the least potent threat. Lissette's lesson went smoothly also. At last it was Dave's turn to learn.

Dave was as worried as Selane. When tapped into his power, control had always been tenuous at best.

They made initial contact and established their link.

"I will initiate the first strike," she said. *"You will be in a defense posture until we can gauge your innate prowess as a fighter."*

As she ramped up her power, she began to glow. Knowing she didn't mean him harm, it was still intimidating and he felt his natural defenses come to life. She made a simple strike toward him and he instinctively surged to counter the move. The power she exerted was minimal compared to his response. A boom and flash of light knocked Selane backwards.

"Are you hurt?" he called, rushing to her.

"I'm uninjured. Your power is dangerous."

As they squared off again this time Dave had a better answer to her thrust. They battled for a time before she started to increase the level of the conflict. Dave fought keenly only to match her strength; for him it was similar to when he had first sparred with Graile - he seemed to know exactly what to do. Before long he was contesting with Selane forcing her to use her experience and her skills to match him as he gradually turned to the offensive. Their fight increased in speed and strength as power ominously crackled. Gloin was sheathed at Dave's side, but the raw power being exerted affected the sword and it hummed as if being wielded.

For Dave it was like another being had taken him over as he glided smoothly into greater complexion and strength in his attack and forced Selane to explore the fullest of her talents to compete. Neither exceeded the safe limit of power they brought into play. Although to the onlookers, it appeared they were involved in a fight to the death, with all of the menacing sound and scents of power in use, they were well in control of the conflict.

At a point they mutually stopped.

"I feared that this was out of control," said Jenna.

"Actually, the longer we fought, the more control we developed," said Selane. "This battle exceeded what I did against the dark enemy. I've learned as much as I taught here. I can better teach you and Lissette now and am not fatigued. My strength and endurance increase noticeably each time I compete and I feel better now about future fights. Dave has uncanny abilities already imbedded within him and it's simply a matter of drawing them forth."

The women went through subsequent sessions with Selane before squaring off against Dave. It was strange fighting them. They were a different "flavor" than his fight with Selane. Each was a unique challenge. In the case of Jenna especially, his wife, he couldn't evoke the emotional rage that accompanied true combat. It was too tame between them."

"You must help me to become a deadly fighter," she said reproachfully. "If I face an opponent set on harming me, I cannot be weak."

"You're right," said Dave. "I'll try again, but it's hard to fight against you. I don't feel like striking blows, I feel like kissing you."

She eyed him dourly and the other women chuckled.

They fought again, this time with force.

Bear left to hunt, so Graile and Angus decided to do the same and came back in the evening with a deer, which the group quickly prepared. Selane used power to cook the meat for supper. They filled the water gourds, collected some wild vegetables from an abandoned garden and spent a second night in the farmhouse. Bear returned late in the night to claim his place guarding the door.

The following morning as they prepared to leave, Dave turned to Selane.

"I've got a question for you," he said. "When we stopped at Bashar's farm, you put concealment over us, right?"

"Yes," she replied.

"How did Bear find us?"

"It's simple. Bear isn't subject to magic the way we are. My concealing spells would fool any humans, including others with power, but not Bear. He's attached to us in a different way. He would always know where we are, those of us in the group he has bonded with. He can walk through any spell."

"That's good to know," said Dave. "I wondered at the time, but never got a chance to ask you. By the way, I think he's getting smarter too. His thoughts were generalized before, more like I was sharing his feelings and instincts. Now, though, I'm picking up ideas when he ponders a problem and solutions he's working through. Does that make sense?"

"It's unprecedented," said Selane. "No one has any idea of what to expect from Bear. If he's mentally evolving to a higher plane, I don't know what would be the end point."

"I haven't really tried to share complex thoughts with him," said Dave, "like having a conversation or something. Maybe I should try."

"Perhaps, we have nothing to lose with such an attempt. Bear is a valuable ally on any level. Certainly his basic nature has been altered radically. For him to allow our constant presence, to tolerate children crawling on him, would never happen for a deathcat. They're solitary hunters and don't gather in packs except to mate."

"I know I'm wrong, but sometimes I think of him like a pet housecat. We don't have housecats on Earth that are ten feet long and almost as big as our horses."

"Indeed," said Selane. He realized she had no idea what he was talking about.

"You don't have housecats here, do you?"

"No, cats on Faenum are predators that kill humans, as well as any other prey they find."

They pulled out of the safety of the farmhouse and resumed their travels. Now the distant mountains, which were their destination, didn't seem so distant. It was a long way from the border crossing at the mountain pass, but didn't appear to be anywhere near halfway yet.

The countryside continued to be more densely populated, and mounted patrols became more numerous. Selane taught Lissette the concealing spell to protect the group. That magic hadn't come easily to Dave or to Jenna. They could form a small protection for themselves, but nothing for all of them. The fact that Lissette was able to do it was a great boon for Selane who carried the strain of providing nearly all of the magical services needed which was extremely taxing on her.

Earlier, most of the imperial patrols were without persons of power, now they were included in most of the patrols.

"We've been incredibly fortunate," said Lissette.

Campsites were far more difficult to find each evening.

"We may need to go farther away from the road," said Graile. "We've been using the highway as a beacon, but we can see where we're going. It's getting too congested out there to continue to stay so near to it."

"Okay," said Dave.

Angling away from the highway, the friends rode across farmland and past some villages, where they were spotted by villagers who quickly ran into their hovels to hide.

The campsite for the night was a rocky area on a hill. Dismounting, they started to unpack when suddenly a large group of horsemen rode out of a nearby stand of trees and surrounded them.

The friends formed a circle with weapons at the ready. Selane started to glow as she brought up her power.

"Hold," shouted the leader of the band - a woman. "We haven't come to fight you. We wish only to talk."

The group looked at Dave.

"Sure," he said.

The leader got down off of her horse, but her companions stayed mounted. She was tall, wore a wrap over her face and hair and had on a dress, but it was over pants. With a sword at her side and a bow, it was similar to how Lissette and Jenna arrayed themselves with weapons.

She walked slowly up to Dave.

"You speak for the group?"

"I guess I do," Dave replied.

She moved over in front of Selane.

"What are you?"

"That's none of your concern," Selane replied.

The woman chuckled.

"A woman after my own heart," she said and looked at her men, who relaxed.

"Will you speak with me?" she asked.

"What do you want to talk about?" asked Dave.

"Will you trust us enough to put away your weapons? I think that if it came to a fight, you could sweep us away with but the merest of effort. We saw your fight with the warlock. I didn't know there were any people alive to contest them."

Selane relaxed the glow of her power.

Dave sheathed Gloin and the others relaxed. The woman nodded to her people and they dismounted.

"Perhaps we could share a meal."

"That works for me," said Dave.

The woman eyed him curiously.

"He's from a different place," said Jenna. "He sometimes speaks strangely."

The woman nodded.

The strangers were shocked when Selane cooked meat using her power to avoid starting a campfire.

"I've never seen such wonders as this," said the woman, "or such strange looking people."

"We're not from your land either," Jenna explained.

"That I understand."

"My name is Dave. This is my wife, Jenna, Selane who is a white witch of the sisterhood, that's Graile the preeminent blade master of the world, here we have Angus, dwarf master warrior, Lissette, supreme elf huntress, and Kra'ac, mountain troll road grater."

They all looked at him and shook their heads.

"Perhaps I should talk, husband," said Jenna.

"You said you saw my battle with the... what was the word?" asked Selane.

"Warlock," she replied. "They're minions of the Emperor and his dark master. With the power they wield, none can stand against them, at least not until now. My name is Red Sylvia. These are my friends. We've banded together for mutual protection so we might survive the scourge sweeping this land, and in our little way to strike back at them from time to time for their grievous crimes. We've all suffered loss, but were fortunate to escape to freedom, for whatever that's worth."

"I'd like to find out about this emperor and whatever else we need to know," said Dave. "The patrols are everywhere and they're getting thicker each mile we go. You guys must be really good to evade them."

"We've been forced to develop survival skills," Sylvia replied, "but mostly they ignore us because we're so inconsequential. We pose no real threat and what we manage to do is little more than mischief. We have no real power to affect them. You, however, have killed a warlock. I've never heard of that being done. You've gained their full attention. You've been lucky to remain undiscovered, because they assume you would be going the other direction to flee the land at the border. You're going straight toward the imperial city. This I don't understand. Why would anybody choose to go there?"

"We're on a quest," said Dave. "That's why we need to know what to expect when we get there."

"I can tell you what to expect. You'll find the end of your lives. Although you're clearly an unusual group, skilled I'm sure, dangerous undoubtedly, but the Emperor employs power, his wife the empress employs power, their priests are warlocks in their own right, and that doesn't take into consideration the imperial army, which is vast. It's very easy to go into the imperial city, but none leave it alive. Of course, beyond the pure evil of that place stands to fortress of Mortus. There resides the dark lord that rules over all. I cannot tell you about him, because no one sees him and lives. If you marched upon the Emperor's city at the head of an army of millions, you couldn't feel secure in victory, and to go to Mortus, once in their control you would pray for a quick death."

"That sounds pretty grim."

"That's what has brought me to your camp. I was curious if you're some rare avatars filled with unstoppable powers, or if you're simply misguided heroes destined to your dooms. You're seven against the mightiest empire on this planet."

"The way you put it does sound pretty bad. I'm going to be honest with you. I'm not from this planet. I was born on another world in another universe. My father is from here, my mother was not. My father was lost a long time ago when I was a baby. My mother died at home and then my uncle came to my world and brought me here. He said this world is in big trouble and I can help. Somehow we got split up on the way here, so I'm looking for my uncle, and I guess to find out what happened to my father. Since I've arrived, I've been changing. I've got some power of my own. These friends I've met here are special people. I like to think we're following destiny. Maybe that's naive, but pretty much explains it. Do you always wear that wrap?"

Sylvia stared at him for a time, and then slowly removed the headgear and facial cover. She was a nice looking woman with long dark blond hair. Dave smiled and she returned his smile.

"I don't normally go about with my face uncovered to those I don't know. You can take this as a sign I've decided to trust you."

"Thank you," said Dave. "We're good people."

The group chuckled.

The rest of her people unwrapped themselves. There were twenty men and five women. They varied in ages from several who looked to be barely teens all the way up to a grizzled old man with white hair and wrinkles.

They ate their meal as they continued to talk.

"In spite of what I've said to you, I suspect you intend to go to the imperial city," said Sylvia.

"I believe the answers we seek are there," Dave answered. "In spite of the hazards, my uncle led me to believe I had to do this, and this world's survival hinged on it. I don't think I've got any choice."

"The others of you…

"We've chosen to share his fate, whether for good or ill," said Selane.

"He's my husband," Jenna added. "My place is at his side."

"You're truly brave souls. Perhaps that's rooted in your confidence in your strengths, or conviction for your cause. I'm sorry to tell you, it will not be enough. I would invite you to stay here and join us. You would be a great boon to our little bands, but I know you would go on anyway."

"Like I said, I don't think we have any choice," Dave repeated.

Sylvia got a thoughtful look and turned to whisper amongst her people for a time. She turned back and looked at Dave.

"We all wish you well in this suicidal endeavor," she said, "for none of us see any chance of success for you, but we wish to help you as we can. We'll escort you as I've established a network of bands such as us. You couldn't continue to stumble blindly forward for much longer before the imperial forces found you. Your next fight might be against a column of soldiers, or an army of them. Perhaps you will face ten warlocks, or a hundred. We can take you to safe places along the way and we can probably deliver you to the door of the foul city. From there, we're helpless to aid you. As I said, none that enter the Emperor's domain ever return."

"We would appreciate that," said Dave. "What can we do for you in return?"

"If you succeed in this impossible quest and bring down the Emperor its payment enough. You'll have a nation that will shout your name with joy until time comes to an end."

"That's a long time," said Dave.

Everybody laughed at that.

Sylvia moved over and sat beside Selane.

"Tell me about this power you wield. Is this something learned?"

"There was power born within me," said Selane. "It's not something within all people. Most people don't ever find it, if they have any power within them."

"Do you know if others have power?" she asked, excitedly.

"Do I know if you have power?"

"Yes," said Sylvia. "I would wish to have the means to properly punish these imperial dogs for what they've done."

Selane turned directly to her. "Relax and clear your mind and I'll examine you."

Selane put her hands to Sylvia's head. Her hands and Sylvia's head began to glow softly. They closed their eyes and sat in silence for a long time. Dave felt the usual prickly sensation when he sensed power in use.

After a time Selane took down her hands and looked into Sylvia's eyes.

"There is a seed of power within you. It's something that would require time and patience to draw out, nurture and develop. I cannot say at what level you would function. What you saw from me may not be within your abilities."

"It would be enough to have magic," said Sylvia. "I would no longer be completely helpless against them."

141

"Nor would you be immune to them," said Selane. "If you confronted a being of greater power, your end would be quick."

"I understand."

"If it's your wish, during the time we travel together, I would be willing to guide you in seeking your power."

"I would be so grateful," said Sylvia effusively. "I would pay you any price, do whatever you ask, anything at all."

"I require nothing from you."

"Don't so easily discount my desire to repay you for your services. I'm much more an asset than you know."

"I'll remember that."

Red Sylvia

It didn't take long for the quest to realize the benefit of Sylvia's help. They traveled farther each day, faster, and went through the best routes they would never have known about. Each night there were confederates of Sylvia along the way ready to safe guard them in sheltered places.

Sylvia was intense and driven in her lessons with Selane. Each night they sat in silent communion as Selane skillfully examined Sylvia's mind and then touched her power, as she had with the others. The changes in Sylvia were marked as her eyes were opened to a new world. Sharing intimate secrets hadn't been an issue for Sylvia. Pursuing her inner flame far outweighed the shame at exposing past indignities.

Dave realized that whatever had been Sylvia's life was very traumatic. He could tell by how strongly Selane reacted and how deeply it continued to affect her long afterwards.

During their travels, they had a near miss when a patrol rode out of a village unexpectedly. Fortunately, they were nearby some trees and Selane threw up a concealment to cover them all. It was a harrowing deception because the patrol was led by a warlock. Sylvia smiled at her troops because they could be so close to a warlock with impunity.

"Don't become overconfident about this," said Selane. "Within a matter of moments, they would have discovered us, and that would have been a dire matter. A magical fight is a thing to avoid at all costs."

"Of course," said Sylvia, but it was clear she was very taken with the budding power within her.

Selane glanced at Dave. He nodded to her so she knew he was concerned too.

Later that night, after dinner, Dave decided to broach the matter with Sylvia who was sitting with Selane, Jenna, and Lissette talking in low tones. As always, Kra'ac was just behind Selane. Angus had come over to sit beside Lissette, and even Graile was there, sitting beside Jenna. Sylvia's people and the local gang hosting them were not far away, listening intently.

Dave walked up and sat down in front of Sylvia.

"Got room for one more?"

Sylvia eyed him thoughtfully.

"I have some amount of notoriety," Sylvia explained. "That's not something of my choosing or my desire. Amongst my peers, they point to me as the beginning of the resistance against the Emperor, an inspiration. As I've previously told you, our efforts are minor in scale. We annoy them, but we pose no real threat and don't do substantial damage. That's why they've not gone to the effort to hunt us down. I'm sure that would change someday. Currently, they have ample fodder amongst the general populace to supply their needs in the imperial city. When their culling ever gets to the point where victims are harder to find and to round up, we would be high on their list for capture. The question posed to me now by your wife was my beginning and what it is that drives me. There are many concocted stories that make me sound noble and brave. That was never true. Bravery is your group marching toward an uncertain end against an invincible foe, but at any rate, I was born not far from the terrible city.

My parents worked for the empire in low level jobs before things turned as bad as they are now. The old emperor was well into his dotage, his wife long dead. He was really a figurehead, with the high priest exercising actual power. In a way, that's still true. The emperor had no surviving issue to follow him to the throne in spite of numerous wives, so the high priest decided he would pick a successor. It wasn't a matter of great interest to the people. One tyrant was not much different from another, but instead of selecting a man with some semblance of command presence, intelligence and experience, the high priest came up with young man meant to dazzle with superficial appearance. His name was Valderane. Soon afterwards, they found a stunning young woman, Madra, who became the new empress. They were perfect for the high priest, pretty puppets to manipulate. The old emperor met with a sudden unexplained death soon afterwards. Immediately, things changed for the worst throughout the land. My parents suddenly found themselves without jobs, replaced by dark minions of the priesthood. Terrible blood rites were introduced into the temples and human sacrifice and misery began. The priests formed a corps of warriors separate from the army called the blood guards who were sent out by the priesthood to enslave the people, which was really a cover to establish an endless supply of victims for the savage rites and heinous practices of the priests and their dark religion. What specifically they do in there no one knows. I was in my teens when they came for my family in the night.

My father knew we were doomed, so he fought back, telling my mother to take us away to safety. Mother wouldn't part from him, she sent my sisters and me out of the house to flee for our lives, but we became separated in the pandemonium and mayhem. I hid until sunrise and then tried to find my family, but was nearly captured and fled the city out of fear. What happened to my little sisters remains a mystery, but is a sin tormenting me still that I didn't save them. I wandered without any goal other than surviving each day. It was pure chance I met a strong young man who was also fleeing the capture of his family. He took me with him and we left the area.

With him, I had a protector and eventually we married. It wasn't an actual marriage, because there were only us and we spoke words pledging ourselves to each other and made our own union. We lived on the run hiding and scavenging as best we could, and for a time I knew happiness in his arms. We lived together for a year, wild, but free. We traveled far from the imperial city and began to think we'd escaped our fate. We took up residence in an abandoned farm and set about trying to create a life.

One night we heard the hunting horn of the priesthood. A patrol discovered us as they searched all area farms for victims. That particular patrol separated their men to cover more farms and they left five behind to hold us. They came into the farmhouse with trouble in their eyes. Two of them took me down to have their sport while the other three faced off against my husband. Driven mad with rage and unarmed, he attacked the assailants. It was a terrible fight and he was wounded grievously, but had no thought for his own pain. A big man, he managed to wrest away a sword from one of the soldiers, killing one. The man holding me down sprang up to help his mates while the man on me was lost in his pleasure - his scabbard beside me. I pulled out his dagger and stabbed him in the neck and killed him. Crawling out from under him, I grabbed his sword and stabbed one more of the enemy. My husband had killed the remaining two, but his wounds were mortal and he died in my arms. He cried at the very end because our life together was over and he couldn't bear to part, leaving me defenseless. Desolate with grief, I had no time to waste because the patrol returned too quickly. Fleeing naked out the back door, I ran to a place I knew in the woods where I could hide from their pursuit. I was fortunate that it wasn't winter or I would have frozen with the long wait. Much later, I crept back to wash away their blood and stench. I got dressed and buried my husband. I put his body in the ground, and along with it, buried the person who I was. For revenge I planned to take against the empire, I took the name Red Sylvia and met Jobert over there, as I wandered aimlessly. He was my first recruit, saved my life, taught me to hunt and how to survive on my own. He taught me to use the sword and the dagger I had stolen. We fashioned a bow and he taught he to shoot. As we moved about, other stragglers joined with us and our band began to grow. We realized before long we couldn't sustain a large stationary force, so the idea of numerous small bands took root and now I don't even know how many of us there are across the land. We don't openly engage the army, but when situations favor us, we exercise punishment on them. So as you can see, I'm no hero, just an angry woman who was lucky to find skilled friends. I buried my husband ten years ago and with him any thought of a normal life and a family. I'm a name turned into a legend, but the reality is just an illusion."

"That was terrible," said Dave sympathetically. "I'm sorry for what happened to you. I think you're a lot more than a lucky woman. To do what you have without benefit of power like we have is remarkable."

"Now I have power too," she remarked, her eyes gleaming. It gave Dave an uncomfortable feeling.

"It's pretty new, Sylvia," he said to temper her enthusiasm. "Don't bank on too much too soon. You don't want to put yourself in a bad situation thinking you can do more than you really can. Selane has been training and practicing since she was a little girl. I'm still amazed when she does her thing."

"Does her thing?" asked Sylvia. She looked at the companions and chuckled.

"You become accustomed to his speech with time," said Lissette, "a long time."

Suddenly Sylvia's eyes went wide with fear as she looked behind Dave. Bear had crept into the camp, right past the sentries without being seen.

"Hey big guy," said Dave, petting the deathcat.

"This is your beast?" asked Sylvia, incredulous.

"He's our friend," said Dave.

"That's a death cat," said Sylvia in awe. "I've never seen one before. I've only heard stories."

"Bear is a wily *hombre*," said Dave, affectionately, hugging Bear, "Aren't you?"

The friends came over and petted Bear also.

"You're truly a gift from above," said Sylvia. "To tame the greatest predator in the world, it's beyond incredible. Now I'm sure we're on a blessed mission. I pledge to follow you to the gates of hell."

"I think that the gates of the imperial city are challenge enough for the time being," said Dave.

* * * *

As the group trekked on, the journey to the city of the Emperor became increasingly difficult with open places being covered by occupied farms, larger villages and towns of gradually increasing size. That meant there was considerably more traffic moving about for them to avoid. At last they changed their clothes to try to look like locals. That was nearly impossible with Kra'ac's size.

Sylvia's people caused distractions whenever they came near a patrol so the quest could slip past unseen.

The once distant mountains now loomed large as they reached the outskirts of the vast city and entered urban areas for the first time. The outskirts of the city were rough areas, heavily infested with criminal elements preying on the unwary. One gang of thugs tried to jump them, but had no idea who they were dealing with. Graile was in the lead along with one of Sylvia's local guides. Swords flashed, subduing seven attackers, before Angus could join the fight. Kra'ac's appearance ended the courage of the thugs, those few who remained ran off in fear.

"Not much of a battle," said Graile.

"Indeed," said Angus. "It was good exercise though. I was getting a little soft without any fighting."

Graile chuckled.

"Well said, master dwarf."

Continuing their winding path through back alleys and side roads, they stopped at a small house for the night. It was the home of one of Sylvia's people.

"We keep an eye out for the blood guard," he said. "You'll have a safe night here."

He had no more than finished his statement when a deafening blast of the hunting horn blared.

"That's the call from the imperial palace," said the man. "Somehow they have means to amplify the sound so it's heard all across the land. Some say its evil magic they wield. It's not a direct threat to you. We hear it often."

Dave went to Selane.

"If there's magic being wielded, I usually feel it," he said. "I don't sense anything with that horn. It does give me the creeps though."

"It may not be magic, or it may be of some strange type I don't know. Perhaps we need to be closer to the source to get a sense of it. I don't have all of the answers, Dave. This is all new to me also."

* * * *

As they traveled farther into the city, the buildings improved along with the prosperity of the residents.

"We're entering sections where favored of the regime reside," Red Sylvia explained. "They retain employment, although I understand it doesn't come without a price. They must swear allegiance not only to the emperor, but also to the teachings and the ways of the priests. It's a terrible concession, because it means they must attend and revel in the foul rites those priests have devised. To be associated with that vileness is appalling. When they return to their homes from witnessing the horrors of the palace they're visibly ill. Suicide is common among them. That will give you some idea of what I say about the evil ruling this land. Whatever you intend to do, it must be well thought out my friends."

"Do you have any safe houses farther ahead?" asked Dave.

"Only one… There's a courageous family who chose not to take their lives. Instead they decided to seek us out and join our resistance, but aren't in a position to regularly meet with us. They only appear at infrequent times when one of them can slip away. They're closely watched so it's life threatening for them every time they aid us. I cannot take a force of my people in there. I'll guide you myself. We're close to the point where you must continue on your own if it's still your will to enter the palace. I strongly urge you to go no closer. Perhaps if we watch from here for a time, an opportunity will present itself to strike a blow for our cause."

"I appreciate what you're saying, Sylvia," Dave replied. "Now that we're here, I'm as frightened as everyone else."

He looked at his brave friends.

"We've been through so much already. I want to give you a chance to heed what Sylvia is saying. She's right. We're foolhardy to risk going in there and I don't want to put you at risk. Maybe that's why my father came alone, because he couldn't bear to have his friends get hurt. If anybody wants to back out right now, no one will think any less of you."

They looked at him grimly. No one said a word.

"So be it," said Sylvia. "I expected no less of you."

Her people eyed her with regret and concern.

"I cannot take any of you with us," she said. "You know that large groups draw notice in a place they're watching. If this venture doesn't go well my friends, know that I love you all and I've been proud to be your friend. Now leave quickly."

Dave saw tears in Sylvia's eyes as her dear friends slipped away. She wiped her eyes and turned.

"Come, let us get about this."

Waiting until dark, they worked their way cautiously through the affluent sections of the city. For the first time, Dave got a glimpse of the imperial palace in the distance and it wasn't what he expected. Instead of a foreboding black fortress like in a science fiction movie, it was actually very beautiful. The architecture was first rate with multiple floors, skilled stone craft and decorative friezes. Heavily rune carved wood workings, wrought iron fixtures, and colorful pennants flapping in the light breeze, said a benevolent king resided there. The main building was huge with large wings going in multiple directions. Although there was a main gate, it was clear the gates were never closed. The battalion of sentries didn't guard the outer face for what came in, they guarded against whatever might try to escape from within.

"Quickly," whispered Sylvia when Dave paused to look.

By the time they got to their destination, it was fully dark. Sylvia left the group hidden in an alley while she went to the back door of a house.

She was pulled inside quickly and was nearly an hour before she came back.

"We had a frank discussion," she explained. "They very reluctantly agreed you could come in."

They crept out of the alley and into the door of the house.

A man and woman sat on a sofa quaking in terror.

"This is Mavin and Shara," said Sylvia.

"Thank you for your kindness," said Dave.

"You can rest easily," said Selane. "I'll put a magical protection over your house. None will trouble you while we're here."

"Truly?" asked Shara. "You're a witch?"

"I am," said Selane, "but we come from across the mountains. We're not like those who torment you."

"If that's true, it's a blessing," said Shara, looking at her husband.

"I'll return shortly," said Selane and went out back and created her construct.

She came back into the house and smiled.

"The priests cannot see through your magic?" asked Mavin. "There's a rumor a warlock was slain in the field. It's aroused the palace into a frenzy. It was you who conquered the warlock."

"I had no choice," said Selane. "It wasn't my wish to take a life."

"You've come to a place where life has no value," said Mavin. "Spilling blood is the purpose of the priests."

"Have you been inside the palace?" asked Dave. "Sylvia said that they force you to watch what they do."

"Yes," said Mavin. Both of them lowered their eyes. "It's an abomination. We've been fortunate to be low ranking workers so we're forced to see fewer of those atrocities than most. It's not something that you can get out of your memory, what we see. If they see you look away, you're in danger of being dragged down there to be sacrificed too. They require that you scream for more from them. It drives many people to madness and suicide."

"What do they think they're accomplishing slaughtering their own people?" asked Dave.

"It's said that the master requires it," said Shara. "He revels in the torment."

"Have you seen the master?" asked Selane.

"No one sees the master," Mavin ansxwered. "His home is in Mortus, though he sees all everywhere."

"So they torture all of these people to death?" asked Dave.

150

"That's the fate of some," said Shara. "They degrade others for amusement. The priests pick some to be their slaves until they tire of them and find new slaves. The same is true with the emperor and the empress, who have large numbers of slaves at their mercy. The life of the slaves is worse than if they were killed in the sacrifices. If it were possible to flee and to escape the empire, the masses would do so, but none ever succeed. They're always captured and brought back to be made an example of."

Dave looked at his Jenna. She sat listening closely. She saw him looking and smiled at him.

Again, Dave worried. All of these people depended on him to have the answers for every problem. He was tempted to gather them up and head straight back to the mountains.

"What's the layout of the palace?" asked Graile.

"We've not been through most of it," said Mavin. "Our duties are very simple. I serve in the kitchen and dining area. My wife works in the laundry and serves as a maid going into the suites of the empress. We don't go in the main entrance we go in side entrances. She's seen more of the palace than I and she has seen little of it. It doesn't pay to be curious. One avoids attention as best they can. Even with that, we suffer our share of indignities. It's not good to be a woman in the palace, I would leave Shara home each day if I could, but they wouldn't allow it. They would come for her."

"I understand," said Dave sadly.

"It's a part of life here we must deal with," said Mavin. "They have the power to do whatever they wish."

"I'm surprised this country hasn't collapsed on its own from inner rot," Dave observed.

"There's power here that sustains them," Shara explained. "It's said it comes from the master. Although I've never seen him, I know his might. When the master comes to Mortus, we feel his touch here too, all of us."

"The master isn't always at Mortus?" asked Dave in curiosity.

"They say he also dwells in another world and comes down from time to time to visit his wrath upon us. I'm not a scholar to know the truth of this, but that's what they say. I can verify his touch though. It overcomes you and wrests away your control. It's terrifying to be helpless like a manipulated puppet."

"Is there any forewarning?" asked Graile. "Do you know when he approaches?"

"Not really," said Shara. "It's suddenly there within you."

"Is it common, does it happen a lot?" asked Dave.

"No," she replied.

Dave scratched his head. "That doesn't help in trying to plan. I think we all agree to get in and out as quickly as we can."

Graile stepped up. "Is the palace heavily guarded?"

"There are many soldiers, but there are also many warlocks," said Mavin. "I don't know how many."

"I don't know of the palace ever being attacked before," Shara added. "No one has ever mentioned such a thing."

"I think tomorrow we should scope things out for ourselves," said Dave. "Watch the traffic to get an idea of their routines to figure out any openings."

"How can you do that?" Mavin asked skeptically. "They watch constantly. They see all."

"Selane can work up a concealment spell," Dave explained.

Selane looked uncomfortable with the idea, but didn't dispute him.

"If that's your wish," said an apprehensive Mavin.

"If I thought we were putting you in jeopardy, we wouldn't do it," Dave further explained.

"I can only trust in your words," Mavin replied. "If Sylvia has faith in you, we will also."

"Thank you, Mavin. We should get some sleep and get ready for tomorrow."

For the first time, they slept separate from each other: Dave and Jenna in a bedroom, Kra'ac lying on the floor in Selane's bedroom with Lissette, Graile and Angus in the living room on the sofa and in a chair.

In the morning, they left with Mavin and Shara when they went to their jobs; except Kra'ac, who they forced to stay at the house. He was not happy when Selane left him behind.

"If she is harmed," he growled at Dave, "I will hold you personally responsible."

Selane turned and came back. She pulled Kra'ac aside and talked with him for a time before he went meekly back into the house.

"What did you say?" asked Dave when she came to his side.

"It was a private conversation," said Selane. "Don't concern yourself with it."

As they followed streams of people walking toward the palace, they kept their faces obscured by hoods. Selane picked a place where they could have a view of the street going into the main gate while resting in a protected area. She quickly worked a construct and the group reclined in relative safety to watch the foot traffic flow."

"Can we talk?" Dave whispered.

"Yes," said Selane, "but speak softly."

"Were you worried about doing this, Selane?"

"I don't know what forces are awaiting us inside the palace. My subterfuge might work on lesser magical entities, but beings of great power may pierce the veil and perceive us. This is all new ground for me. We may be in great peril."

"We need to know how to get in safely. This is a risk we needed to take."

"I'm wary nonetheless. Jenna, Lissette, and you Dave, all of us should extend our perceptions for any sign of enemy magic. If thcy'rc searching, we need to sense them before they take action against us."

They waited and watched for the bulk of the day warding the group. Graile and Angus were left to pay attention to the guards at the palace and the traffic. When Mavin and Shara came out of the gates they filtered over to the agreed meeting spot and returned to the house.

"Did you gain the insight you desired?" asked Shara.

"Getting in is no problem at all," said Dave. "The guards didn't check anybody. If we just followed you guys in, I don't think they would even notice. If we dressed the part, we'd be just more workers."

"What about him?" asked Mavin, nodding toward Kra'ac.

"We couldn't really disguise him," said Graile. "There are no others of his stature here in this land."

"I will not allow Selane to enter the palace without me at her side," said Kra'ac firmly.

"If we try to get you in, it may blow it for all of us," said Dave.

"You will need me with you," Kra'ac replied firmly. "We're too few already."

"We're too few, that's true. Did anybody pick up on magical wards and protections? I didn't sense anything at all. I didn't get that tingle of magic in use."

All agreed they had not.

"This seems too easy. It's possible, since they believe there's nothing to fear, the big guns are kept stashed away in the closet."

The group didn't comprehend what Dave was saying and looked confused.

"Moving right along," he said, "I say we walk in tomorrow. If anybody challenges us, we just start working like we have jobs there. Although, I agree it would be great to have Kra'ac with us, there's no way to get him in."

"I don't agree to this," said Kra'ac.

"I'd like to go in there with an army," said Dave, "but it just isn't possible. We're just going to check things out a bit. We'll be back at night and we can work out a plan. We don't know what to look for or where to go in the palace Kra'ac. We've got to find that out first."

"I have honored your wishes, but this time where there's serious danger. I cannot agree to stay behind while you're all imperiled. I have a life bond with Selane and will not put that aside."

"I don't have an answer, Kra'ac."

"I will go with you tomorrow. On that I will not compromise."

The group sat stone faced at his resolve.

* * * *

The following morning they all put on cloaks to disguise their looks and trooped after Mavin and Shara. Kra'ac bent down as much as he could, but he was also much wider than the others. The guards looked at him, but made no move to stop him.

Getting them inside the palace proved to be no problem. Once in, they tried to casually look around. They were in a side hallway off the main area. Shara looked at them sadly as she went down stairs to her work area.

Grabbing various rags, mops and implements, they began to mimic a cleaning crew and worked their way closer to the center of the palace. When guards or dignitaries came past, they diligently cleaned whatever was near. The ruse seemed to be working very well.

They came to the end of the hall and looked into the alcove, which was like the hub of a wheel, with hallways in all directions being the spokes.

"Let's split up to draw less attention," Dave whispered. "Try to check out the other halls and see where they go."

Angus and Lissette went as a pair, Dave and Jenna another and Kra'ac followed Selane and Graile. They all cleaned their way down hallways and back - mundane places where the palace staff went about their support services. Once, Dave even saw Mavin pass by. They glanced at each other, but said nothing.

They all had come back to the alcove and were about to move into the next hallway when a loud tone sounded throughout the building followed by the sound of marching feet. Everybody around them dropped to the floor prostrate with their heads down in obeisance. The quest did the same.

A large troop of soldiers marched past them and went down a hallway straight ahead. When the people started to get up Dave quickly looked to see who had passed them. He could only see the soldiers at the back of the column and could not see who, if anyone, they were escorting.

The soldiers wore gold uniforms trimmed in red.

After a few moments another tone rang out from one of the hallways.

Following the tone, they cleaned their way along until reaching ornate massive heavy rune carved doors. Huge guards manned the levers used to open and close the massive doors and other soldiers lined along the walls in a file.

Behind them a young woman cried in fear as guards dragged her along toward the throne room. As the guards opened the substantial doors, the group looked inward as best they could without appearing too conspicuous.

The room was huge with glittering crystal chandeliers and fixtures, opulent furnishings, great tapestries, sculpted pieces, and paintings. Golden hued light filled the space as the emperor and empress sat on two large thrones across the way. A noticeable display of wealth pervaded the room and clothing of the occupants; a large number of people in were attendance

"Jackpot," whispered Dave.

The friends started to clean their way back out of the hallway toward the alcove when another deep tone echoed loudly.

Dropping to the ground with faces to the floor, they heard the march of more boots approaching. A large column of soldiers marched past, but suddenly halted. Dave felt cold chills, but wasn't sure he should look up.

"Please rise faithful servants," said a deep voice.

The seven of them stood up. Kra'ac was unmistakable.

"Amazing," said the deep voiced speaker. A tall solid man dressed in a purple robe, he had a beard, long black straight hair, a fearsome looking staff and great power. Dave reacted to the magic like his skin was covered in wasps. The man's eyes were deep wells of potency frightening to behold. On the front the robe was an emblem of a fierce looking golden colored creature poised to strike.

"Please take off those ridiculous costumes," said the man. "You're not servants here. You've come to meet the emperor. By all means let us see to that."

The others looked at Dave and he shrugged. They discarded the disguises and eyed the man warily.

"Welcome to the palace," said the man. "Please follow me."

* * * *

The tall man led their procession through the open doors into the vast chamber. Dave didn't see any sign of the girl dragged in earlier.

The entire room fell silent and stared at them. The man led them to the center of the room and stopped. Dave looked up at the thrones. The emperor and the empress were fairly young and incredibly attractive, but their eyes were filled with disdain.

"I apologize," said the tall man. "Where are my manners? My name is Ciaphus, I'm high priest of the order, and before you sit Valderane, the emperor, and Madra, the empress of the domain. May we know your names please?"

"Do not," whispered Selane.

Ciaphus closed his eyes and the friends felt his power reaching out to them, but they all blocked his probe.

"What?" he questioned, opening his eyes quickly. He eyed them thoughtfully.

Suddenly, Dave felt something touch his neck and shoulders and a sting as sharp talons sunk into his neck, shoulders and the back of his head. He tried to reach back, but his body was numbed and wouldn't respond, and he couldn't access his power. Somehow, he managed to turn his head and saw small gargoyle creatures had also mounted onto the three women. They were equally captive.

"They're called Ashoks," Ciaphus explained. "I'm told they're not native to this world though they've been here for a long time. We find them very useful. They're symbiotic parasites that join to their hosts and feed from your bodies, but more importantly, feed from your power. They wrest control of that power away from you. It's irreversible and they're one with you until you die. The lives you lived before are over."

Dave turned to look at the men. Their faces were red with strain as they fought against magical restraints imposed on them by a phalanx of warlocks who stepped out from the crowd.

"They cannot aid you," said Ciaphus. Soldiers surrounded the men and removed their weapons, and placed their heads and arms in heavy wood yokes. With no yoke available big enough to fit Kra'ac, the warlocks kept him shackled magically.

"Now, let us try this again," said Ciaphus as he walked down to Selane. Dave could feel the power the high priest used as he searched her mind. It wasn't the gentle probes of the women. This was a harsh and intrusive act, forcing his will on her.

"Interesting," Ciaphus said, stepping over to Lissette.

Ciaphus went next to Jenna, and finally to Dave. He spent more time with Dave and seemed puzzled.

Finally he turned to the imperial couple.

"This is a momentous day indeed, unlike any other in the history of the realm," said Ciaphus. "Let me introduce our distinguished visitors who have journeyed far from across the mountains to come here to us. This is Selane, a white witch of the sisterhood. That's a significant title for it means she's pure and potential candidate destined to become their next leader. It's she that bested the warlock in open battle, a feat never before accomplished by any living being. Beside her stands Lissette, an elf warrior maiden and also pure. She too wields power of a type and strength I've never encountered before. This is Jenna, former prima virga of the Warlen nation, recently wedded to this man, Dave, who fought in ritual combat against their champion to gain the right to marry her. By winning that fight Dave became the ruler of the Warlen. Jenna shares in this power and it seems they have a magical link of some sort between them all. It's a wonder for me to discover. These others don't possess power, but are interesting nonetheless. The short squat one is a dwarf, that man is a master swordsman, perhaps the finest on the planet, and the large one a mountain troll. As you can see, they're not myths, but real living beings. I fear we need to rethink our precepts and plans. What resides beyond those mountains is definitely a matter of interest to the empire and I'm sure for the master."

The emperor and empress got up from their thrones and came down to closely examine the group. The empress in particular was fascinated with the women, coming close to touch and inspect them while they were helpless, probing and prodding them thoroughly.

"See the challenge in their eyes," said Madra. "I don't see that in these fragile weak women the blood guards bring before us. It will be a refreshing change to crush their spirits until they come to heel. I will have them as slaves in my household, Ciaphus."

Ciaphus bristled.

"Take care, your highness," he hissed. "Don't forget it's the master who rules, you're but his representatives, as am I. You may have them for your amusement, but hear me when I say they must not be damaged or maimed. They're the property of the master. It's he who will decide their fates when he returns. These men you may put to work laboring to serve the master's plan, but they cannot be damaged either. I'm sending word to Gristelle, the queen of the black witches. She will owe me a great debt if I turn the white witch over to her. This man, Dave, he's my charge for there is much I need to understand about him. I have important matters to tend to now, but upon my return, I'll seek him out. In the meantime, he may labor with the other men. Don't cross the line, Madra, for you'll face the wrath of the master."

Dave could see Madra shudder with fear.

"You have black witches?" asked Selane fearfully.

Ciaphus smiled, "We do, young witch, and they will have much to teach you."

"Take them to my chambers," said Madra. A severe looking woman stepped forward with a number of husky women and they led the three women away. Jenna looked back with sorrowful eyes. Dave swallowed hard, he felt impotent with his power neutralized.

Ciaphus eyed Gloin and reached for it. Dave felt his power respond, but it wasn't through his doing. Gloin could access Dave even though he couldn't return the favor. The sword hummed menacingly as Ciaphus tried to draw it forth and just when he touched the hilt a powerful concussion knocked Ciaphus to the floor. Dave was unaffected by the blast.

Ciaphus slowly got to his feet.

"I don't understand this," he said, edging close to Dave, "but I will, my friend. There's no secret you can hide from me. I'll return soon enough and then we shall see about these mysteries. Take them away."

As they led him along, Dave was appalled over what transpired. Although the Ashok had taken away access to his power, it didn't affect his mind. He could feel everything still, and his helplessness was painful as the women were taken away from him. Feelings of guilt for stumbling blindly into the nightmare and dragging his friends along racked his psyche. Ciaphus statement that he would never be free from the Ashok troubled him deeply and the thought his life was over was an irreconcilable grief. His own mind was the worst punishment, castigating him for foolishness and lack of good planning. Kra'ac plodded along ahead; he'd always been a comforting sight with his strength and resolve. Now he looked like a broken man, yoked by powers he couldn't overcome and torn away from the young woman he'd come to cherish; his life pledge to protect her at all costs made empty and hollow.

They were taken down to a foul place far below the palace. The stench was overpowering with numerous slave workers toiling in misery and hopelessness. They were draining and cleaning pools of noisome liquids and the chutes that fed them from above in the palace. It was more than sewer runoff. Some to the chutes were reddened like blood was flowing in the lines.

"I think this is the residue of the priests and their unholy rites," said Graile softly.

"Quiet," said a guard as they were handed implements and ordered to work with the others. It was a meaningless task trying to clean what was continuously fouled with an unending stream of detritus. Over the next week, things which Dave saw in the pools made him ill and gave him some idea of what they did upstairs in their temples.

"Damn them," he muttered.

The friends were barracked in an adjoining room, but being there didn't free them from the overpowering odor, and they were given no opportunity to cleanse themselves. It was a miserable existence.

The only time they could talk was at night.

"Does that leech pain you?" asked Graile.

"No," said Dave. "It's just numb in the area where it sits. I think it injects some kind of venom to control me. I know it sucks my blood, or fluids, but I don't feel it. I can feel the draw on my power sometimes. It's barely a trickle, but I know when it's sapping me."

"Perhaps we can pull it off," said Angus. "If I had my club I could smash it apart."

"Somehow I doubt it's that easy," said Dave. "Ciaphus said it's there for life. I don't know what happens if you try to take it off."

"Let me try," said Graile. "What have we got to lose?"

Graile crept out of his bunk and reached for the Ashok on Dave's neck. It started to hiss, and when Graile touched it, he was zapped with a burst of power and fell to the floor.

"Graile!" they cried. He lay unconscious and didn't awaken until the following morning. He awoke with a painful headache.

"I feel like I was hit by a boulder," he rasped. "That thing has a nasty kick."

The guards rousted them up and back to work.

Another week passed of backbreaking toil bent over, working in the filth of the palace with no end in sight. The absence of hope was their greatest enemy and after two weeks started to take a toll. Days blended together in sameness with a combination of continuous work, beatings from the guards, verbal scorn and too little food and water. Being unable to wash was another galling indignity.

Dave thought often about the women and Jenna in particular. He didn't want to think about what they were facing, but it plagued him constantly. It ate at him and fueled an underlying rage, a rage he could not excise with the presence of the Ashok throttling him, depression was not far behind as weeks turned into months in captivity.

The return of Ciaphus brought their exile in the cesspool to an end, but by no means was the end of their torment. He appeared suddenly one morning, as they slogged about in the tunnels tending the pools, accompanied by a number of warlocks and a troop of the emperor's palace guard. He looked at the friends in disgust and they ignored him.

"Climb up out of there," said Ciaphus curtly. "Guards, have them cleaned up and made presentable. Take them to the slaves to be bathed and bring them to me when it's done."

Wordlessly, the friends followed the guards away. Dave saw their fellow victims look on with pitiful eyes, also anxious for release from their misery.

Taken upward to a separate area, there were numerous women waiting who doused them with water and removed the caked on filth. Once the worst of the grime was gone, they were taken into bathing pools to be thoroughly cleansed. Once dried, they were dressed in simple tunics emblazoned with the emblem Ciaphus wore.

Mustered from the bath area, they were led back into the palace proper and taken to a room where they sat down to wait while a large number of soldiers and numerous warlocks watched over them.

Ciaphus took his time to visit the group. He walked into the room slowly and stood in front of each friend, putting his hands to their heads and examining them. He searched Dave the last.

"It's as I thought," said Ciaphus as he sat down and opened an ancient tome. He read for a time before setting the book aside.

"Your time under the palace has given you a new perspective. We can go about our business now that you realize your lives are mine completely. There's no hope, no escape, and no miracles. The charmed life you lived, Dave, was a brief divergence from what's real and what's inexorable. There are powers beyond any man. I, of all people, know that all to well. The master defies description. I can only tell you that to him, we're nothing, less than nothing. He holds this world in his hand and it's only with his forbearance that we're allowed to survive. It's good for you that you met me before you followed your foolish plan to face the master. I've read your mind and I know everything. You know this, Dave. You've done much the same with your women in your mutual sharing."

At the mention of the women, Dave felt a serious pang.

"She, who you call wife, it was in a different life, Dave. Oh yes, I know your thoughts and feelings now too. You all have new lives. It's best if you put the past away because what's ahead of you will be challenge enough. It's the same for them. Gristelle has moved here from her hidden stronghold she is so taken with the little white witch. I've never seen her so animated and anxious about any task. Your arrival is such a boon for the empire in so many ways. If you dwell on what was your past, it will not serve a good purpose for you. There's nothing that you can do to change your fate. You were meant to be here in my control. Together, you and me, I'll show you a new path, a better way. Someday, you may look back on this time and see the folly of your old path, and you'll thank me for pulling you forward into reality."

161

"With this thing stuck on my back, what are you saying?" asked Dave.

"I'm sorry I cannot promise you the adventure and the acclaim a young man craves," said Ciaphus. "That was never in your future, only in your dreams. Your reality has a much greater purpose and will mean a lifetime of service to the empire unmatched by any other living being."

Dave focused internally seeking his center and power. He'd done this everyday since the Ashok had taken him. The result was always the same.

"It's a waste of both our time, David. There's no release from the Ashok. I've already told you that."

"Troll," said Ciaphus. "You're intriguing to me. Your selflessness and your dedication to the little white witch are compelling, noble actually. Of course, you know the truth the fancies of your mind could never be a reality. A witch would never be the mate of a troll, and she was their highest maiden. Still you're relentless even against hopelessness. I would wish for my own followers to have half of your resolve. She's with Gristelle now. There could only be one outcome from that. Gristelle is a force even I must be wary of."

He nodded and the door opened. Slaves came in and served tankards of water to drink. The slaves left and Ciaphus resumed.

"Master dwarf, I see some of the same elements in you that I see in your troll friend. You bluster at the elf mistress, but secretly she's melted your heart. Elves and dwarves don't intermarry, yet you have a thought in your mind along that line. I think she doesn't realize your hopes, but it no longer matters. She too has a new life, one which will not include a dwarf."

Angus had a sullen look on his face.

"Sword master, you're not one to seek a wife, or rather, you're one who would seek women who are the wives of others. You've joined a band of companions who shame you with their purity and their nobility. Should we tell your friends about your secret longings for their women? I think with time we can find work for you in the imperial army. I think you'll comprehend the futility of resistance sooner than the others. Your great skills would be welcome in our army and I think you could quickly rise to a position of some importance. It's something to think upon."

Graile eyed Ciaphus coolly.

"I have a matter that requires my presence, but tomorrow we'll begin a new dialogue. We'll reason with each other as men. I'll answer your questions honestly. I have no reason to hide anything. You're no threat to me in any way."

The warlocks led them away to modest quarters, but at least they were together.

"We're in for a real test," Dave mentioned, looking at the others. "Since he can read us like a book, we can't hide anything from him. He wants to wear us down, like we'll eventually decide to join their side. I wish I could tell you how to protect your minds from him, but I don't think there is a way. All that we can do is go through the motions and make him think he's winning. Does anybody have any ideas?"

Graile spoke. "What he said in there, you know, about me having feelings about the women..."

Dave bristled. "Graile, he's a snake, don't worry about it. The women are beautiful. I'm not surprised you found them appealing, we all did. Don't let Ciaphus drive wedges between us. Every one of us has weaknesses and I suspect he'll try to take advantage of that. We'll have to do our best not to react to him, even when he says outrageous things meant to incite us. That's his goal."

Graile seemed relieved. "Thank you, my friend. He's right that I've not been the best person in some areas. It's a weakness I need to remedy."

"We can save that for another day, Graile."

"What he said about me was true also," said Angus. "I've thought about asking for Lissette's hand. It's impossible, but its how I feel. I know she had no thought of me other than as a nuisance. Now it's too late. I think that Kra'ac desires Selane."

They all looked at Kra'ac.

"Trolls aren't ones to talk about such things," he said, "but I will not deny I care for her."

"Love is a strong feeling," said Dave, "and is probably why he jumped on that first. It's very evocative and he wants to evoke us. Guard everything and show as little reaction as possible no matter what he says or does."

"I think he will not keep us together for these talks," said Kra'ac.

"I suspect you're right," Dave replied.

"What if the three of us try to rip that thing off your neck?" asked Graile.

"It used power against you," said Dave. "It can probably draw as much as needed to meet any threat. I don't know what would happen to me if it could be torn out. Maybe I would die now?"

"If that's true, perhaps we truly are doomed," said Graile. "We're companions to you Dave, but you're the real force. Without your power, we could only make brave and futile endings."

They paused and reflected on the sad possibility, which looked like it was becoming more probability.

"Dave, do you wonder what's happening to the women?" asked Graile.

"I'm sure it's a nightmare, my friend. If I start to think about what they could be facing, it stirs me up and I feel sick. I try not to think about it. That makes me acknowledge to myself what an idiot I am for causing this to happen to them and to us."

"The fault is not yours," said Angus.

"Actually it is, but I've learned not to go down that road. I can't even get suicidal, this thing wouldn't allow it."

"I wonder where they've taken my blades?" asked Graile.

"Here's one of them," said Dave.

"Gloin is a part of you, Dave. You saw what happened when Ciaphus tried to take it from you. It gave me hope, because he would have us believe he's invincible, yet Gloin floored him when he tested its power. I wish he'd tried again. Gloin can kill the unworthy and would have solved one of our problems."

They all chuckled.

"Is it not true?" asked Graile.

"I suppose it is," said Dave. "Thank you all for being here for me. I can never repay you, but I want you to know it means a lot to me, even if we rot in this place. You're all good friends."

"If it's true that he can be felled, perhaps these other things he says are not to be trusted either," said Graile, "such as that abomination."

"Now that would be really good news," said Dave.

Ciaphus came for them early the following morning. Kra'ac's prediction came true - they were led away to different rooms.

Ciaphus took Dave to the throne room, where the emperor and his wife sat in plush chairs on the floor of the chamber with smug looks on their faces. Few other people were present.

"Greetings, Ciaphus," said Madra.

"Highnesses," he replied.

"You're Dave," she said. "How have you enjoyed the wonders of the palace? I understand that you've played a vital role in maintaining our operations. For that we're very grateful."

She smirked insolently.

"How have your mighty friends fared?" asked the emperor.

Dave stood silent, trying to ignore the affronts.

"Oh, you might like to know that your women folk have adjusted well to service in my retinue. Though they were lacking in certain skills being raised in a barbaric land, our patience and diligent instruction brought them to heel nicely," the empress explained with relish.

"I was very diligent with them," said Valderane. "It was a great pleasure for me to serve as their teacher and their mentor. It's been a true pleasure to see them progress with our gentle care. We've made them greater than they were before."

They both laughed hilariously.

Dave seethed with rage, knowing Ciaphus was in his mind monitoring every reaction, emotion, and response while exerting great effort of will to calm his storming feelings. He thought back of his mental journey into the abyss in Raja Kai's cave to call back Jenna from the brink of death, and his experience of venturing into the midst of the divine beings. He wasn't wielding his power, yet impossibly he felt the raging internal emotional storm pass away nonetheless.

"Would you like for me to tell you about your wife who has forgotten you," said Valderane maliciously. "Should I tell you what she...?"

"Silence!" snapped Ciaphus. "It's enough. We're leaving now."

He grabbed Dave by the arm and hustled him out of the room.

He stopped in the hallway.

"What you did, I don't understand," said Ciaphus pointedly. "It was not the use of your power, and yet in a way it was. It didn't evoke the Ashok. Explain this to me."

"I don't have any answers," said Dave honestly. "The things I've done, it's like they're instinct or something. Believe me, if I could have wielded any power, you would be looking for new rulers."

Ciaphus smiled. "Well said."

"Were they trying to yank my chain?"

"They're particular types of people. It's their nature to do such things. Are you surprised by what they revealed? The women are intact, though their challenges have been great, greater than your own."

"Ciaphus, you can read my mind. I won't pretend that I don't want revenge. What do you expect from a husband?"

"I would expect nothing less from you. I can understand that reaction in you very clearly."

"Maybe you're all are so warped you don't comprehend the feelings and the motivations of normal people. Valderane knew my hands are tied so I've got to think there was some design to this whole thing. You intended for them to incite me. It worked. If I do nothing else with the rest of my life, I will find a way to get back at Valderane."

"I do understand you. You think that we're so different, we're not."

"I don't think so. If that dude had your wife, you don't think you would, eh, well you probably don't have a wife. You don't seem like the husband type."

"We have mates in the empire. I do not, you're correct. I've devoted all of my energies in the service of the master."

"If you had a girl, you would be vulnerable. That's what the real truth is, and why you're single. You wouldn't give that edge to your rivals. I know at some point in your life, there had to be a girl that you cherished. Think of her at the mercy of Valderane. That guy is a dog, and you know it."

Ciaphus eyed him thoughtfully. Dave saw a hard glint pass across his face before he dismissed the idea.

"Why don't you come right out and say whatever you have on your mind. You knew he was going to say that with me being helpless to do anything about it. Was this some form of subtle torture so I'll worry about Jenna now until it drives me crazy?"

They went into Ciaphus private chambers and sat down at his table.

"There was a moment in your response that was puzzling. You drew back on a memory, an experience, but it was confounding to me. I didn't know if it was a dream, because such a reality could not be. It gave you

166

strength and comfort though no power was wielded in the process. Explain this to me."

"What's to explain? Jenna was captured by the Konocks. She was in the process of passing over to the other side basically she was dying. Somehow I broke through the barrier and pulled her back. Under the current circumstances, it appears I didn't do her any favors by saving her."

"That's a preposterous story. It's impossible, yet strangely there's the ring of truth in your telling. I believe you when you say you have no means to explain your actions. I need to explore this deeply. It's a significant matter."

Placing his hands to Dave's head, Ciaphus probed his mind roughly, searching for clues and for signs of Dave's experiences. Dave felt like he was thrown back in time to his first encounter with the other side. He relived the struggle to unravel the mystery of the barrier of the vision, how he solved it, felt the rapture as he grasped the orb and was transformed. Again, he saw living beings of absolute purity. His soul cried out for their help, but abruptly he was ripped back to reality. Ciaphus was panting heavily.

"It cannot be," he said, over and over again. "This is some charade that you've crafted to snare the unwary."

He stared intently at Dave, but he was not intimidating at all. Ciaphus was obviously badly shaken, daunted by the vision.

"We'll continue our work tomorrow, Dave."

"Sure, I've got nothing else to do."

Guards took Dave back to the quarters. The other three men were already there waiting and they all looked haggard.

"Are you injured, Dave?" asked Angus.

"Not physically. Ciaphus took me to see the emperor and empress and they dropped a bomb on me about our women to gauge my reaction. It was funny though. Ciaphus was grilling me and sifting through my memories afterwards. He ran unto that experience when I crossed over and it knocked him for a loop. I've never seen him out of it like that. He sent me to my room right away. You guys don't look too good. It was pretty rough, eh?"

"It was indeed," said Graile. "In all of our cases, they have a plan and a goal in mind. For us, we must find the resolve to withstand their onslaught, and avoid their snares. It heartens me to see your strength against the dire designs they use to entrap us."

"They made a mistake keeping us together," said Dave. "We can still band together for mutual support."

"When they assail me," said Kra'ac, "I don't listen to their lies. I focus on the day I will have my club in hand again and the wrath I will exercise."

"I'm glad you are on our side," said Dave.

"What did they say of the women?" asked Angus.

"It was pretty bad," said Dave. "It's best not to think about it."

All of the other men grimaced with a mixture of understanding and rage.

"There will be an accounting," said Kra'ac.

"I still remember that day before the throne of the emperor how fearful Selane got when they mentioned something about a black witch coming for her," said Dave. "I don't know what all that meant, but I'm sure it was terrible. I do what you do, Kra'ac, I dream about being free to settle scores, and have a long list of dirt bags I would visit."

The men nodded.

"What angle are they using on you?" asked Dave. "Ciaphus is going through every experience I've had, but I think it's confusing him. I have no way to clarify it for him. He keeps trying to act like he's on my side and says we're not different at all."

"In my case, you saw a sample of their approach," said Graile. "They try to work at my many flaws to show me how unworthy a person I am, that I don't belong in your esteemed company, that I should abandon the quest and declare for them. They promise me loot, prestige in their society, women, whatever I want. If I don't, they say you'll all fail and I'll be left alone to face their master."

"They make sport of me," said Angus, "that I'm the least of the company, a poor choice with nothing to offer. They dangle Lissette before me, but say she has revealed great scorn for me, and I'm less than a crawling animal on the ground in her eyes. She's sought great champions of the empire and forsaken any thought of the quest and me. It was a galling affront to my dignity and pride, but with passing of time, the sting is lost. Now it's a monotonous drone I don't pay attention to. If I'm unworthy of Lissette, they aren't the judge of that."

"They assail me constantly on how I have failed so often in my life," said Kra'ac. "I made a sacred pledge to ward Selane, and they easily wrested her away from my protection. They say I'm merely an oversized oaf not worth their time and attention. It would be better if I end my life. A noble person like Selane could never think about me as anything other than a servant. She too has sought higher persons here in the empire. I'm not even a memory to her now."

"You guys all know they're talking garbage," said Dave. "Stay strong, but it sounds like you already figured out how. Let them natter away. It doesn't matter to us."

Dave locked hands with each of them.

"I want to say something else," he said. "If the worst comes about where there really is no hope, I don't want to live with this thing feeding off me. It may not allow you to tear it off, but you may be able to kill me and release me from this life. That thing would be left without a food source. Maybe it would die too. That would be good to get rid of such a nasty varmint."

"We hear you Dave," said Graile, "but that's not an option that we would exercise until the very end for us all."

"I just wanted to put that out there so you know how I feel," said Dave.

* * * *

The following day Dave went to Ciaphus chambers. Ciaphus eyed Dave confidently.

"I want to apologize for my discomfiture yesterday," said Ciaphus. "I took ill with an overnight misery, but it has passed. I'm well again so we may continue our conversations."

"So talk," said Dave.

Ciaphus smiled.

"You're very strange," he said. "Please make yourself comfortable. Do you care for some wine?"

"I'm good," said Dave dismissively.

"I would like to hear your explanation about the scene we visited," said Ciaphus.

"It's pretty simple," said Dave. "Apparently the great beyond is universal in every universe. My mother died back on Earth from a disease, but when I somehow broke through the barrier here to your heaven, she was there. I guess that means our final destination after we die, no matter where, is one single divine place."

Ciaphus looked unsettled with Dave's explanation.

"I can believe what you say to an extent," said Ciaphus. "When I have communion with the master, I sometimes get glimpses of his world. It's a higher plane of existence. I don't think it's a repository for the dead brought back to life."

"Maybe you aren't looking at the same place as I am," said Dave. "In our world, there is good and there is evil, heaven and hell. You might be looking at the other end where the bad people go."

"Bad people," said Ciaphus skeptically. "Do you propose that you're good and I'm bad?" He started to chuckle. "I've seen darkness in every single being I touch. It never fails. I have seen darkness in you, Dave."

"I never pretended to be perfect. I just don't choose to make my weaknesses an excuse to do all of these vile things done here. You think that you have no accountability, Ciaphus. You're wrong."

"Of course I have accountability," Ciaphus responded. "The master has no patience for failure. If you work in his name, you will be held responsible for your works."

"I think you picked the wrong side, Ciaphus."

"You think there's strength across the mountains to contest with the master? You're deluding yourself. What was the end result of your mindless quest into the unknown? You and your companions are helpless for all of your life now, because you were unprepared for the test. For such an august group, you proved a poor leader. You had great might within, but squandered your opportunity. Now it's too late."

"You're right, I messed up. I can't change that though. What's the purpose of wallowing in self pity?"

Ciaphus smiled ruefully. He eyed Dave carefully, like he was learning secrets of the universe from Dave's reactions.

Reunion

Three months passed since Dave had last seen Jenna and the other women. Each day he was interrogated by Ciaphus, followed by menial labor tasks heaped with plenty of scorn and abuse from the guards. It was the same for Graile, Angus, and Kra'ac. In every case, each friend hunkered down against the monotonous tactics and waited until evening to talk together.

"I will say that Ciaphus is relentless," said Dave. "If he thinks he's making progress, I don't understand it. I haven't changed one bit, but he keeps hammering away trying different angles and approaches. He told the guards to taunt me about the women, which they started recently. You know the kinds of things they say…"

"We hear the same," said Graile. "I'm not quick jumping to a conclusion that they've crumbled and fallen. I believe our women have strength equal to or greater than our own. Look how we've come together to draw strength from each other. I feel the women have done the same thing. During our journey, we all looked at Selane as our great comfort and our pride. She couldn't be so easily subdued."

Kra'ac's eyes burned with fierce pride.

"That's part of what doesn't make sense to me," said Dave. "Ciaphus isn't stupid and has got to know all of this. Maybe we're looking at this wrong. We're making assumptions about what he's up to. If we have it wrong, that might explain why we're allowed to have this time together."

"What are you thinking?" asked Graile.

"I feel like we're in a holding pattern, like Ciaphus is going through the motions. Think about it, we get interviewed about the same tired things that haven't worked for them for months, we get these nasty jobs to do, but isn't anything we can't handle. They keep us clean, healthy and well fed. Their main point of abuse is to taunt us about the women we love. Maybe we aren't the key piece in play here. Maybe what's happening to them is what's really important. We have no way of knowing for sure, but that's my suspicion."

"I can believe that," said Angus. "Of the four of us, you're the only one of us with any power, Dave. All of the women have power. I think they would be greater prizes to our enemy. Only you would have a place in their plans, Dave. We're merely fodder, no different than any other of their slaves."

"That's not true, Angus," Dave objected. "They've kept us together. If they wanted to kill you off, that would have happened long before now. Ciaphus is up to something we aren't seeing."

"We'll continue to be vigilant," said Graile soberly.

They went to their noisome daily tasks but minus visits with their interrogators that day, however when returning to their room that evening they all had a feeling of some dark omen close at hand.

Ciaphus came to their room late.

"Tomorrow, your life here in the palace comes to an end. It's time to move on to the next phase of your journey."

"What does that mean?" asked Dave.

"Tomorrow is soon enough to receive your answer. Rest well this last night." He turned abruptly and left.

"Uh-oh, I think things are about to go south in a hurry," Dave muttered.

"I cannot say I'm unhappy about it if it's true," Angus reflected. "I've had enough of this meaningless life under their boot. If I'm meant to meet my end in this god forsaken place, the sooner the better I say."

Graile nodded. Kra'ac looked grim and flexed his muscles in irritation.

"We need to be prepared for anything tomorrow," Dave cautioned. "I don't think its execution day. Like I said before, they could have killed us at any time. Maybe we're helpless, but just in case of some slipup on their part leaves us an opening, we've got to go for it. *Carpe Diem...*"

"I would like to make a good ending," Graile agreed. "If only I had my blades, but Dave I must say this magical yoke they have on us leaves me with no hope. If I cannot fight, I'm useless."

With no answers, Dave shrugged.

* * * *

All had a restless night and trouble sleeping. Guards came early in the morning, took them to the breakfast meal and hurried them back to their room. Ciaphus appeared shortly thereafter.

"Come," he said.

"Where are we going?" asked Dave.

Ciaphus didn't reply, just turned and left the room

The four prisoners followed him to the throne room.

"Here we go," Dave muttered to the others. "This should be a trip."

"Quiet," said Ciaphus, turning to face them. "Control yourselves in there."

They were escorted by a large number of his warlocks and a troop of soldiers. When the doors opened the emperor and empress hurried into the room, pulling on their clothes.

Ciaphus marched directly to the thrones.

"Ciaphus, this is too much," said Valderane irritably. "We're not subject to your whims. We require proper notice and an appointment for an audience. You're not our superior. We're the appointed of the master."

"Interesting you should mention that," said Ciaphus. "Have you fulfilled my charge to you? Have you summoned them?"

Another door opened and Dave's heart leapt. Selane, Lissette, and Jenna were led into the room accompanied by a considerable troop of rugged warrior women. His joy quickly evaporated as they were brought over to stand opposite Dave and his men. Dave hardly recognized them they were so changed in appearance, and those changes went deep to a fundamental level. Changed posture, slave woman garb and an air of indifference were appalling. Dave glanced at the other men who were equally shocked. Disdain and contempt covered their pretty faces, looks totally out of character for the women they'd known previously. Barely glancing at the men, they showed no interest at all in them. Selane had always carried herself with great dignity - very regal in her bearing and command presence. Lissette had projected confidence, competence and great allure while seemingly untouchable. Jenna was stunningly beautiful with delicate angelic facial features and petite form. All of those wonderful qualities were missing as Dave looked on with concern and regret. These women were strangers.

The female prisoner guards tensed as Ciaphus stepped over to examine the women, but said nothing as he examined their minds only.

Humph," he muttered and turned toward the thrones.

"Now perhaps you'll explain why you called us out of our beds so early," said Valderane with irritation. "They're unharmed as you can see, though they're made more worthy."

The empress chuckled.

Dave was watching the women. They all winced and looked down at the floor at the emperor's reference to their indignities. Dave's anger smoldered. He knew the futility of searching out his power, but exercised the empty gesture anyway. The result - the same as always - his power was shackled

"Speak, high priest," said Valderane. "I'm in no mood for your games today."

"We're not yet all in attendance," said Ciaphus.

Valderane and Madra got an uncomfortable look on their faces. They waited a short time before the doors were opened again. In walked a potent woman, easily as intimidating a presence as Ciaphus. She walked up to Ciaphus with challenge in her eyes. Dave could feel their great powers stirring to life. His skin itched greatly.

"You had better have a very good reason for this, Ciaphus," she said as they glared at each other before she suddenly turned and walked straight to Dave. She looked into his eyes and then he felt her scan him deeply.

She got the same curious and confused look he'd seen from Ciaphus. She studied him thoughtfully. She was beautiful and terrifying all at the same time. Even with the use of his power available, Dave suspected she would have been frightening.

"I'm Gristelle," she said. "You're Dave, the great enigma. As I see you, I understand why you've aroused such excitement in Ciaphus and his priests. I also know everything of your former life. Your women are no longer yours. I think you can see that."

Dave shrugged. "It's tough to give you an appropriate response with this thing on my neck. I would have liked to have a nice stirring conversation with you."

She eyed him in surprise at the grim look and the challenge she saw in his eyes.

"I would have liked to have that conversation also. You're the first man I've found to be intriguing in any way. I understand now what I saw in your women as I looked at their lives. It doesn't matter now, because that life ended and they've since begun new lives."

"Right," said Dave.

Gristelle chuckled and looked at Ciaphus. Ciaphus had a wry smile.

"I wish I could pursue this, but I have serious matters to deal with, Ciaphus. Tell me why we're here."

Collecting himself, Ciaphus paused.

"I've received contact from the master."

The tone in the room changed abruptly.

"These seven will be prepared and taken to Mortus to face his judgment. We'll leave tomorrow morning."

The imperial couple sat stone faced and frightened. Gristelle was livid.

"Did you have a question for the master, Gristelle?" asked Ciaphus pointedly. "Does he need your permission to do his will? Do your plans for these women exceed his?"

Dave thought a fight might ensue. He could feel their power cascading dangerously, but suddenly Gristelle backed down.

"I'll return to my home," she said grimly. Dave was bewildered at the reaction of the women who all were on the verge of tears when Gristelle turned and approached them. She whispered to each and kissed their cheeks before leaving the room.

Ciaphus triumphantly turned to the emperor.

"It seems you've won this contest," said Valderane.

"They'll be sequestered and warded by my warlocks from this moment," said Ciaphus. "Don't attempt to intercede, Valderane. Your custody over these women is over. Tomorrow I'll come for them and we'll depart promptly for Mortus."

"You may leave our presence now," said Valderane sullenly. "They will miss me, Dave, for I've become dear to them," he said as a parting shot. "They lost all thought and caring for you in a single night."

Glassy eyed and distracted, the women didn't pay any attention to the men as they were led away by the warlocks, nor did they respond to the emperor and empress.

Dave went back to the room in a black mood and was astounded to see what was laid out on their bunks.

175

"My swords," said a surprised Graile. "Everything is here."

"Tomorrow you will dress in your own clothes," said Ciaphus. "You'll don all of your weapons, although they're useless to you. When you're presented to the master, you'll be as you were arrayed when you arrived."

"One exception," said Dave gesturing to the Ashok still attached to his neck. "I didn't arrive with a passenger."

"There's nothing that can be done about that," said Ciaphus sadly. "We'll leave early, so don't dally. I give you this day for your own as a gift, free of any duties. You should use the time to ponder your lives. I suspect this will be the last gift you'll ever receive. The touch of the master isn't a pleasant experience. I know we've our differences and you see me as anathema, but I speak truly when I tell you that I wouldn't choose this fate for you."

"It sounds like we've got a death sentence," said Dave.

"I cannot anticipate an outcome in Mortus that will leave you in a better position," said Ciaphus. "Each time I've served in the presence of the master, it's been terrifying beyond imagining."

"Well, thanks Ciaphus," said Dave. "I think you're being sincere for once in your life. I can't say it's been a whole lot of fun here, but I hope you'll see I get some measure of dignity at my funeral."

Ciaphus eyed him regretfully.

"I've told you there are forces far beyond the scope of mortal men, you already know this. There's nothing I can do but try to survive the audience myself, for any in that room are in mortal peril."

"Ciaphus, if it's my time to go, I'm ready, all of us are. You know I'm going to a good place, you've seen it in my mind. Think about where you're going when your number is up while you can still do something about it. On my world, there's nothing that can't be forgiven. Think about it."

With a look of great distress, Ciaphus silently got up and left.

The following morning Dave donned clothes purchased so long ago at the trading post. He looked at his mates dressed in their own clothing and they smiled at each other.

"At least I'll look good," said Angus.

"That's a matter of opinion," said Graile.

They chuckled.

Graile pulled out a sword from the scabbard and took a few test strokes just as the guards came and escorted them out of the back of the palace to the stables. Dave saw Mavin glance at him as he walked past. Dave smiled bravely. Mavin looked away so as not to be noticed.

The friends stepped into sunlight for the first time in many months. Spring had passed into summer, although it wasn't a place that had sweltering days. Their mounts were waiting, including Kra'ac huge stallion.

The women were brought out separately dressed in their own clothing. Although they physically looked like the women Dave knew from before, they ignored him disdainfully.

Ciaphus looked over the assemblage - a full battalion of imperial soldiers and a large troop of warlocks - before he rode away at a gallop. Departing, they rode in the opposite direction from where Dave had entered the city. Before clearing the outskirts of the city, they stayed at inns several nights, eventually heading for a nearby mountain peak through towns and villages. Few people would even look up at them as they passed by. Their women were roomed separately and they were never allowed near them. The settlements ended abruptly - nobody chose to make their home anywhere near Mortus.

Dave began to think about what was ahead. The idea of his demise was something he hadn't really thought a great deal about. Now that the possibility appeared to be at hand, he felt sad. His life ending on this uncertain footing with his wife bothered him a great deal. With the Ashok holding him in check, he felt less than a man - a pitiful caricature. Certainly he was no conquering hero come to free this world.

Day after day they rode, camping in sparse wilderness each night. Ciaphus posted heavy sentries both with soldiers and warlocks.

"I wonder what he's concerned about?" asked Dave. "There must be some dangerous stuff out there if he's this worried."

"Indeed," said Graile. "Mortus must have magical defenses. Whatever creatures that could live in such a dire place must be deadly indeed."

"It's his problem," said Dave with a shrug of his shoulders.

Kra'ac stared at Selane every chance he got, but she never looked back or acknowledged him. Jenna only glanced at Dave once when he was near enough on his horse. He smiled at her. She gave him a contemptuous glance and looked away.

Dave shook his head sadly and rode away.

At night, he'd lie down and stare at the night sky. Just before he fell asleep, something familiar flitted through his mind, but he couldn't place it nor maintain the sensation. At first he was curious, but soon abandoned the thought.

The following night he experienced the same sensation. He tried to concentrate on the feeling, but it was very elusive like a butterfly. If he did nothing, the sensation returned and seemed to find him.

He didn't mention the mysterious phenomenon to anybody in case Ciaphus was monitoring them. Only one night passed when he didn't have the contact. The following night it was back. Ciaphus seemed consumed with the journey, casting about constantly for hazards and snares.

The mountain that seemed to be their destination was farther away than it seemed. They traveled for another week before the peak appeared closer.

Ciaphus nervousness increased the nearer they got and the warlocks became agitated also. Dave felt the presence of something magical, which blotted out his strange nightly sensations.

Soon, they traveled into a wasteland that looked to have been the site of a terrible cataclysm, whether a great battle, or a natural disaster, Dave couldn't tell. What few plants growing there were stunted and barbed. Three days passed crossing the barren place before they came upon a paved roadway that led to a huge granite cliff face of the mountain. Where the road ended at the cliff, Ciaphus began a chant and evoked his power. The cliff began to shimmer and then melted exposing an opening into the mountain. Ciaphus led them into a long tunnel leading to a cavern. Torches lit automatically as they passed by. When they entered the cavern, Dave saw the huge fortress of Mortus. Just like the imperial palace, it was a beautiful structure skillfully made of stone anchored in the bedrock, with elaborate woodcraft and wrought iron metal. It was located in the center of the vast cavern. The walls all around began to glow, illuminating the fortress and the road leading to it. The fortress didn't have great spires; instead it was curved and low built with few multiple floors. There was a great gate, which was closed. As they approached, the gates opened automatically.

Riding inside Mortus, Dave suddenly got a strong sensation of something familiar, but it was there and gone in an instant. Looking around, he saw nothing, but sensed something new and powerful. He didn't know if it was something good or bad - just something strong. It didn't feel threatening to him.

Ciaphus led them to a courtyard where they dismounted. Timid servants slunk out of the building to tend to the animals, taking them away to the stables. They all entered the building slowly. The escort was very edgy and looked around at everything. Dave didn't feel anything threatening and that surprised him in light of Mortus' reputation as the center of abject and all consuming evil.

Entering a large room, Ciaphus directed them to all sit in a section of tiered seats against one of the walls. This was the closest Dave had been to their women and he put an arm cautiously to Jenna's back. She looked at him crossly, pulled away in disgust and went to sit on the other side of Selane. All three women whispered to each other and eyed Dave with hostility, which upset him a great deal. Wounded in spirit, he climbed up several rows to take a seat separate from the women. The other's joined him, having witnessed being torched by his wife and her scornful reaction.

"I don't know when the master will arrive," said Ciaphus. "In the meantime, there will be things for us to do. I must see to several critical matters. You'll stay here for a short time until we come to take you for your tasks."

The women closed their eyes and appeared to go into a melding. Dave felt them on a small scale. Some type of union, but without benefit of their power. They paid no attention to anybody or anything else in the room.

"This isn't good," said Dave. "I don't know what was done to them, but it seems to have worked."

"You're right about them being the target," said Graile.

"Apparently, but I didn't want to be right about that. I'm really worried about them. Of course it's very possible it makes no difference at all with the master coming, but until he gets here, I'll keep trying to find a way."

The women didn't vary in their meditation or end their communion.

Suddenly, a ripple of pure evil passed through the room and the occupants. Everybody, including the guards and the warlocks, gasped in terror. Dave felt ill and vulnerable. The feeling passed quickly, but the side effects lasted for hours and none of them could talk about it for a long time. Finally it was Kra'ac who spoke.

"The master has surveyed his domain."

"If that was a sample of what it's going to be like," said Dave. "I hope it ends quickly for us."

"It seems the master didn't physically come, but only sent us his greetings," said Graile. "That's fortunate because our time would be short in his presence."

The traumatic experience had ended the women's melding and they looked around fearfully.

Ciaphus didn't return promptly, as he'd promised, and didn't return at all that day. That night, the women were led away to a separate room from where the men were housed.

Dave thought about their days in the inn when they'd used the two adjacent rooms - a lifetime ago. He couldn't shake the feeling of hopelessness that gripped him. Continuing to think about escape seemed futile.

The following morning, they were fed together. The women sat apart and ignored the men, continuing their private conversations.

Ciaphus entered the dining room and began to give directions to his minions who then took each of the seven away separately. A warlock led Dave to a small room where he was blindfolded and questioned by a stranger. They were generalized questions in nature and reminded Dave of Ciaphus old methods of interrogation. This cross-examination went on for several days until the fortress experienced another visitation from the consciousness of the master. This episode was equally traumatic for everyone, but particularly affected Ciaphus, requiring several days of his recovery and brought about a change in his tactics. The stalling was over.

Ciaphus came into the room with the men.

"Tomorrow you'll be taken to meet a man. This will be very important for you especially, Dave. I cannot explain this, but you'll understand what I'm saying when you get there. I was visited by the master and it's convinced me to take this action now, while I can."

The men looked at each other in confusion.

"What's up, Ciaphus?" asked Dave.

"Our talks have given me much to think about. What I've seen in your mind has caused me to rethink some things."

"If that's true, are you willing to talk to us about our women, Ciaphus? They seem to be really messed up."

"I was not a part of their ordeal, Dave."

"Maybe you didn't personally do anything, but you've got an idea what they went through."

"It's not something I have time or an inclination to do. The past is gone. I'm here about the future."

"You were stringing us along while our women were getting hammered. Don't tell me you had no part. You're the damn High Priest, Ciaphus. There's nothing that could happen without you signing off on it. Now what did you allow to be done to them?"

Ciaphus turned determinedly and glared at Dave.

"Hear my words carefully. I told you that I'm but one servant of the master. Gristelle is another major force. She's wrought what you see in them. She has her abiding goal and she was dogged to succeed in that endeavor. Do you hear what I'm saying? I chose not to destroy you and your friends. It was well within my power to do so. Don't castigate me for the work of Gristelle, and the imperial couple. Their influences are prominent in the current state of your women. What did you suffer other than indignity? You incurred no real harm at all. I allowed you to gather each night to maintain your spirits. Your women didn't have benefit of any kindnesses, but that's not important now. We've come to a place where all of our lives are suspended in the balance. Doom is just around the corner. If you don't become focused on surviving this crucible, this world will face disaster. The master could appear at any time and then it will be too late."

"Why wait until tomorrow?"

Ciaphus looked at Dave pensively.

"This may be a better time. You may be correct about that. I'll leave you now to see if the way can be cleared and will return as quickly as I can."

Ciaphus walked out of the room and glanced both ways in the hall before walking away.

"Do you think this is some ploy that he's perpetrating?" asked Graile. "I find it hard to believe anything he says, and trusting him would be impossible."

"I take what he says with a grain of salt," said Dave. "I figure we have nothing to lose hearing him out and seeing how this goes down."

"This isn't what I expected at Mortus," said Angus. "After all of the dire tales of doom, I find this place to be less threatening than the palace."

"Don't forget that taste of the master's touch," said Dave. "That was creepy."

Dave eased open the door and glanced down the hallways. There were guards in each direction.

"I wish I could slip into the room next door. I want to have a talk with the women and hear what they have to say."

"Don't take the risk," said Graile. "From what I saw, they might call the guards down on you. They show no inclination to resume our former relationships."

"I would have never believed it could come to this."

Just then Ciaphus came back to the room.

"It's not possible tonight. We'll follow the original plan to divert you tomorrow to meet him."

"All right," said Dave. The others nodded.

"Take your rest," said Ciaphus. "We don't know what tomorrow will hold."

"He's really spooked," said Dave after Ciaphus left. "I guess we should follow his advice."

They bedded down and eventually dozed off. Dave thought about Jenna being so near by as he fell asleep.

* * * *

Next morning they dressed in battle gear and armed themselves. Dave stepped calmly into the hallway while the guards eyed him closely. He went to the door to the women's room and knocked.

Lissette opened the door, her eyes hard with challenge.

"We're going armed," said Dave. "Take your weapons today."

He walked away before Lissette could reply to him.

Ciaphus called them together when he arrived.

"Come with me."

Dave stood unmoving, forcing the women to fall in line behind Ciaphus before the men would move. A file of warlocks flanked them on both sides as they walked briskly down a long staircase within the depths of the fortress carved into the bedrock of the mountain. When reaching the floor of the cavern, they followed Ciaphus to a stone wall completely covered with runes and glyphs. Ciaphus raised his power to open the

182

door carved in the stone. As Dave stood there he had a strong sensation of the familiar again and glanced around the cavern, but saw nothing.

The warlocks turned and left. Ciaphus nodded toward a dimly lit room. They all stepped inside. It took a moment before their eyes adjusted to the poor light. A withered skeletal old man sat, staring into a translucent pane. Behind the "pane," now more clearly resembling an urn, a continuously roiling cloud of glowing unknown material boiled. The substance within the container was multicolored and flowed with rapid currents.

"What is that?" asked Dave.

"A great secret of Mortus," said Ciaphus. "I cannot explain it to you."

"Why are we here?" asked Graile.

"Sitting before you is the man you were intended to meet," said Ciaphus. "I will leave you here with him as I have duties elsewhere and will return later. Hear what he can teach you. I don't know what that will be."

As Ciaphus opened the door, a sudden blur of movement crashed into him knocking him backwards hitting his head on a table knocking him unconscious.

Bear stood before the shocked group.

"Bear?" asked Dave.

Squatting on his haunches, he stared then growled at the terrified women. Suddenly he stood up and walked up to Dave and sniffed him. Bear eased around behind Dave and stared at the Ashok. Rising up on two legs, he rested his front paws on Dave's shoulders and in a blink of an eye closed his jaws on the Ashok. The leech screeched as Bear popped it into his mouth and consumed it in a single crunching gulp.

Dave staggered for a moment. His power returned to him instantly and reacted instinctively to meet his immediate needs. Acting like anti-venom to the Ashok poison, the power eliminated the bane and healed the wounds to the neck and head, leaving no scars.

"I'm healed," he said unbelieving. "It's gone and I'm back to normal."

Bear stalked to Jenna like she was prey. She cowered from the deathcat. He ripped off her Ashok and ate it whole, then didn't pause in freeing Lissette and finally Selane. They were too stunned to say anything. Selane seemed in a fog for a moment before she regained her composure, then went to the other women and healed their wounds with her restored power. Dave came over to her and did the same thing to Selane's wounds though she acted unhappy at his nearness. None had any remaining residual sign of the Ashok wounds.

Dave went to check on Ciaphus who was breathing steadily, but appeared to have a serious head wound.

Then Dave went over to the strange man who was staring vacantly at the pane. An Ashok was attached to the man. Dave called Bear mentally and the cat came over and ripped the venomous creature off the old man.

The Secrets of Mortus

The haggard spindly man blinked after Bear removed the Ashok.

He tried to speak, but it came out as a rasp. Dave poured a cup of water from a pitcher on a nearby table and held the cup up to the man's mouth. The old man drank some water and choked. After composing himself, he drank more and that seemed to help him focus.

"How?" he whispered.

"The Ashok?" asked Dave. "Bear ate the thing."

"Impossible," the man whispered.

"Obviously not, it's off your back and down his throat."

The man turned his head and looked at the death cat sitting benignly aside licking his paws.

"Am I dead?" asked the man, his voice getting a little stronger.

"No. Who are you?"

"I'm a prisoner," he replied, squinting and looking closely at Dave. "There's something about you. What's your name?"

"I'm Dave."

"Dave?" he asked in wonder. "This cannot be."

"Yeah, I'm Dave," he repeated. "What's strange about that?"

"My mind is foggy after so long a time, you must excuse me." He drank more water. Dave poured another cup. The man drained it and color started to show in his cheeks.

"Who's your mother?"

"Her name was Mary Cray."

The man's eyes watered.

"Was?"

"She died."

"She died?" asked the old man, suddenly stricken with grief.

"She got cancer," said Dave remorsefully. "There was nothing we could do to save her. The doctors tried everything."

The man started to sob wretchedly. It brought back Dave's pain.

"David," said the old man finally. "My name is Doran, I'm your father."

"What?" asked Dave, unable to cope with the magnitude of the shocking revelation.

"I'm your father," Doran repeated. "I've been confined here since you were a baby."

"What is all of this?" asked Dave shaking his head in disbelief as if the man was lying. "What happened here? What is that thing?" He nodded toward the pane.

"When I married your mother I was young and strong, the most powerful wizard of my time. I tested every theory, tried new and dangerous things and I read ancient tomes to glean the knowledge of the ancients. I far exceeded my peers and in the process I grew to see myself as more than I was. I expanded my abilities greatly because we were faced with a terrible danger. You know of the master. He came into the world and began to savage all within his reach. I chose to confront him with the thought I could rid the world of his malice. I journeyed here to Mortus in my pride and arrogance and came within his presence. He easily yoked me as if I was nothing more than a newborn babe. He shackled me here and used powers far beyond me to create this abomination you see. I have a vast well of power within me. This thing taps that power and funnels it out to the empire. The warlocks are enhanced and those select chosen few like the emperor and empress who have no innate magical abilities are artificially empowered. They cannot wield it like you or I. It flows through them and responds to their commands. They channel it to exercise their whims. I have no ability to staunch the flow, or control its use in any way. I'm simply a deep well for them to tap."

"We'll just pull you out of there and put an end to that," said Dave.

"You cannot," said Doran. "They took away my legs so I could never walk away from here, and the magical binding holding me cannot be broken. It's blended into my living fabric like a deep stain."

Dave sat down beside his father.

"There must be something I can do."

"Tell me about your life with your mother, son," said Doran, ignoring his comment.

"She was an inspiration to me and everyone else who knew her. She never let anything get her down was kind to everybody, selfless to a fault. All she cared about was that I was okay. She was lonely, though, not having you, but she never took up with another man. She suffered in silence."

"Oh my precious Mary," he wailed. "I couldn't get free to come back to you, and I couldn't let you know what happened to me."

"My uncle came to her funeral, he brought me here."

"Bralan..." said Doran sadly, "my faithful brother. He begged me not to come here, but I didn't think I could avoid it. The master was utter havoc and mayhem personified. Something had to be done."

"He was pretty broken up, Dad. I had no idea who he was. I didn't know I had any family. Now this is going to sound weird, but I saw her again."

"What?"

"When I came here I started to develop these powers. My girl, Jenna, she was in trouble and actually was on her way to dying. Somehow, I went over to the other side and pulled her back. Mom was there, but was different... advanced to a higher state... she was really something," Dave explained.

Dave looked over at the women who were sitting quietly, but intent on what was happening between Dave and Doran. Jenna didn't appear to be moved by Dave's reference to her and they all still had closed looks on their faces.

"I've always thought we're on a journey, that death is merely a transition," said Doran. "This is wondrous news, my son. Now let me tell you some things you need to know. This fortress, Mortus, wasn't the repository of evil nor was the palace. These were great treasures of the ancients. The master took this place with his might and made it into the hell it is. There are wonders hidden here and in the palace the master covets. He has no need of beauty, power, or treasure, but instead revels in destruction, torment, and slaughter. Those priests do their work to please him, but heinous as they are, they're paltry compared to the master. Nothing can be enough to sate the bottomless pit of his hunger. At a whim he will slaughter his own servants as easily as innocent victims. Mortus is not evil the master is evil. When he's here, Mortus is deadly, otherwise it's simply an inert place."

"What can we do?"

"You cannot face the master directly. You would be helpless. He would shackle you as he did me. You would sit here in my place broken and helpless like I am, fueling their empire until the day your heart finally stopped beating."

"Dad," said Dave, glancing at Jenna. "She's my wife. We were really in love. I cherish her, but as you can see, they did something to her, to all of the women. Is there anything that you can do for her?"

"I cannot," he replied.

"You mean that they're warped this way forever?"

"I didn't say that. I said I cannot help them, for I've been here too long. Though my power is undiminished, my body is nothing but a shell, a rotting husk. The enemy has long thought the secret to this seemingly boundless power within me is a talisman, or an artifact I conceal. The truth is I'm the real power, just as you are. It's innate in us, a part of our essence. I can never escape from here except one way. I cannot end my existence. I don't have the power to do that, but you can save me, son."

"What? Are you actually asking me to kill you?"

"You wouldn't kill me. I would transfer my essence into you. You'd gain all of my knowledge and experience; your considerable power would be enhanced so there would be none from this planet who could stand against you. But I caution you son that doesn't include the master. You must never allow yourself to be drawn into a direct fight with him. You couldn't win. We're mere pawns to him."

"Dad, I can't do that."

"You see me in this sorry state. Would you wish to exist this way? Give me a chance to join my wife again, to become a being such as she is now. She's precious to me. I'm weary of suffering and wish to leave this plane of reality to join hers."

Dave looked at his friends. None of them said anything. Bear suddenly got up and came over to Doran and licked his face.

"Please, my son. It would be a mercy to me. End this travesty of robbing my might and sending my power to aid the evil in the empire. Take this difficult mantle and face your destiny, as you must. I'll be eternally grateful, because I can be with your mother and know happiness again."

"Can we at least talk a bit? I never had a Dad."

"We cannot. The master could come at any time. You must be well away from here when he does. Close your eyes. Put your hands to my head as I put my hands to yours. I'll do what must be done. Afterwards, you'll have all of my knowledge, abilities, and power."

"Goodbye, Dad," said Dave regretfully.

"Goodbye, Davey," he said. "I'm proud of the man you've become, my son. Your mother and I will love you always from the great beyond."

The magical process happened very quickly after they placed their hands. Dave felt like he had put a screwdriver in a light socket as he was zapped by a wrenching jolt. His mind was instantly flooded with thoughts, ideas, and memories and he felt the pool of his power suddenly percolate and erupt. He was radiating blinding light and his body was translucent, but almost as quickly as it started, it was over. Dave looked at his father's lifeless body. The connection to the device was broken. The pane went black and inert. Dave launched a blast to shatter the diabolical device.

"We need to move," said Dave. He snapped thc magical shackles on the men with a flick of his hand. Kra'ac smiled grimly and gripped his huge war club.

"At last," he said. "Now let us meet our enemies."

They got up and went to the door. Dave opened it with a thought. Warlocks tensed and tried to confront them. Dave brushed them aside like they were straw, blunting their magic easily. The friends marched boldly up the long staircase and back to the entrance. Each time they encountered opposition, Dave eliminated them without effort. Entering the stables, they found their mounts as the stable slaves cowered in terror. The quest mounted the horses and Dave led them out the gates of Mortus at a gallop. The alarm sounded behind them, but Dave felt no concern. There was only one opponent he worried about.

They rode out far onto the blasted plain before stopping for the night. Although not hidden from sight, from his father's gift, Dave now knew how to create magical protection far beyond what Selane had done. They wouldn't be threatened that night by anything of Faenum.

Dave tried to act normally, in spite of his newfound powers. The men looked at him like he was worthy of worship. The women eyed him darkly and moved apart from the men.

"I'm the same guy," said Dave. The men looked at each other and shrugged.

Dave walked over to where the women were seated. Their facial expressions were not friendly.

"Can we talk?"

They didn't reply.

"I know you had it bad, but that's over now. Whenever you're ready to talk, whatever you need, I'm here for you."

"You know we had it bad," said Selane in a hiss. "What do you know of our plight? How could you know how it was for us with what we endured?"

"I'm not looking to pick a fight. I was trying to patch things up."

Selane shook her head in disbelief.

"Do you see?" she said to Lissette and Jenna. "It's as Gristelle told us."

Dave was mystified by the contemptuous looks on their faces.

"What does that mean?" he asked. "I don't understand?"

"Do you think we're fools?" asked Selane.

"No," said Dave.

"You say you're here for us? That's not true."

Dave was frustrated. He tried to reestablished their magical link and meld with them.

"Stop!" shouted Selane. All three of the women had put up there hands as if to guard against him.

"You've come here now because you're a man and it's your nature. It's not based in any concern for us. It's your male vanity that motivates you. You were easily bested by Ciaphus because you were a fool, and we were fools to blindly follow your path trusting you would find a way to do the impossible. You had no plan, no miracle protection to safeguard any of us. What was going to happen to us stumbling into the palace was inevitable."

"I know that," he said sadly. "I made a terrible error in judgment and I'm so sorry for that."

"Save your worthless words of regret," said Selane spitefully. "It's too late and doesn't remedy what was done to us and doesn't relieve you of the guilt of your wrongs. These feeble words don't suffice as recompense. Can you even speak the truth of what you really want? You wish to hear us tell you what was done to us? You cannot cope with your own feelings so you try to put it upon us to assuage your guilt. What did you think would happen when our power was taken away and we were put in the control of evil? What do you think evil does to the innocent? You already know the answer. Lissette and I were pure. It was the emperor's first task to take that away from us, but was the least of our suffering."

Dave looked at Jenna who was staring at the ground.

"Did you think the emperor would spare her because she was your wife?" asked Selane contemptuously. "He regularly had his sport with all of us, but it was the empress who set about to torment us in innumerable ways and to make our lives intolerable with odious labor, endless work, demeaning us with her cruel words and insults and delighting in the shame and pain visited upon us without rest. She was insidious, imaginative, focused on that which she knew was most hurtful and twisted us without remorse. She was well practiced in how to deeply torment a woman from considerable experience. I'll admit in the beginning it was more than we could bear. For Lissette and me, he had taken away what could never be replaced and wounded us to our core. I burned with shame and I thought to end my life. It was then that Gristelle came to us. She was harsh in her examinations and saw my life with the sisters and my journey with you. She examined us all, but not with the malice of the empress. Not intent on doing us further harm, which she easily could have done, she chose mercy. Instead of grinding us into the dust, she began to heal and nurture. She gave us strength when we had none. Most importantly, she gave us knowledge and understanding we sorely lacked. She helped us to cope with our ordeals and put them into proper perspective."

"What do you mean? What perspective?"

"Being raped was a terrible thing, but she helped us understand that we gave it greater importance than it warranted due to our flawed lives beyond the mountains. It was a tragic act, but we thought too much of our purity. Because of that, we gave power to the emperor. He felt pride for what he could do to us and how we would feel because of it. He gave us an abiding hatred for men. They're all weak, driven by lust. We're no longer vulnerable in that way. She taught us to look inward and focus on what is truly important in our lives. We dismissed the actions of the emperor and the empress from our minds as things we couldn't control and took away their power to demean us. He doesn't matter, he never did. All that remains is your rage at the affront to your manhood, that another man has soiled your wife due to your incompetence. We don't concern ourselves with those petty things any longer. It's a flaw we've excised from our lives."

Dave got a sick feeling listening to Selane's tirade and bizarre pronouncements. Dave's own guilt was trouble enough to cope with. Now he felt humbled on top of it.

"Gristelle helped us to cope with our vile life in the control of the empress, but more important, she opened a door for us to see what they've achieved at her coven. The black witches have so far exceeded the sisterhood. They've been willing to explore every avenue, to look at new opportunities. They've managed to achieve perfection and together they've become one entity. There's nothing they require outside of their keep. This is why you don't see black witches traveling about. They have no needs they cannot fulfill from within their own. Their lives are the ultimate achievement and it's an honor to us she would take of her valuable time to teach us."

"I don't get it, Selane. This doesn't sound like you. There has to be more to this story."

She looked at him thoughtfully.

"You'll remember when I told you about my fight with the warlock, at his end I saw the grain of goodness buried within him. It's the opposite we're talking about here. Gristelle sought out the grain of darkness in each of us. She nurtured and developed it to show us another way that there isn't a difference between what we call good and what we call bad. They've had the courage to embrace both of their sides and it has brought them into balance. In her efforts to nurture the dark within us, she did not fail."

"You switched sides?"

"That's not the way to look at it. We've merely expanded and purified our lives. We've been given a choice with our futures. Gristelle extended to us the chance to join with the coven, even shackled by the Ashoks. She didn't have to do that with our shameful conditions. It was a great gift from her. She shared with us in their manner so we could experience the thrill and the sweetness of their way. It was rapture, the greatest experiences of our lives. They're truly one in fulfilling every need. We finally understand what's outside of the coven doesn't matter."

Dave could think of nothing to say.

"We'll be keeping our own company while we travel with you. We have it in our minds to go on our own path and join with the black witches."

"I'm going to make one request of you," said Dave soberly. "With our history and all we've shared in our lives, I think I should at least have a chance to reason with you and make my points. Before you so easily toss us aside, let me talk to you. Gristelle had you in her control and you were helpless against her. She could make you think anything she wanted. I don't think you guys have a true view of things. You're all smart women. At least take the time to think about this."

"We've come to agreement," said Selane, "but it costs us nothing to give you your moment. We've been through a great deal, and you did release us from the Ashoks. Remember we'll not allow you to meld with us. You wish to know our experiences in captivity, but we'll not share that with you."

Dave got up and stepped away from them. The other men had heard everything. They appeared defeated when he looked at their faces.

Dave lay down and closed his eyes and Bear crawled up beside him to sleep. Bear, who had always favored the women before, now eyed them grimly. They didn't show any interest in the big cat and actually showed fear. The few times they would come near him, he growled.

Dave tried to doze off, but heard the women who were chanting softly, wielding their power. He sat up and looked over. Sitting facing each other in a triangle, their arms were draped on each other's shoulders, swaying side to side with their heads touching together.

Dave probed carefully with his power and was shocked he couldn't differentiate between them. Magically, they were one entity. This worried him, but he was at a loss for what he could or should do, if anything.

Waking in the morning, he looked over at the women. Still in the triangle formation, they had each lain over to rest their heads on each other while they slept, like a defensive posture against attack.

Opening their eyes simultaneously, they sat up in a concerted motion.

"This is not good," muttered Graile. "I get an ill feeling from the women. I've been amongst enemies and felt less of a threat."

"I've got my magical eyes trained on them," said Dave.

"They are three to your one," said Angus.

"After Mortus, that won't be a problem. I'm more powerful. But the big thing is I have my father's experiences and skills added to mine. I know why he felt a little cocky. He was a potent dude."

They broke camp quickly and rode away toward the imperial city.

Dave's new attributes included much keener perceptions. He sensed they were being stalked, although nothing was seen around them in the flat expanse of the blasted plain.

He increased their pace for a time. The feeling of pursuit didn't diminish. When they stopped that evening, Dave purposefully prepared his magical construct with flaws. He didn't fear whatever hunted them, wanted to discover what they were and set a trap to draw them in.

In the dark of the night they came creeping into the camp. Dave could feel the potency of their dark magic.

"Awaken my friends," said a male voice from the darkness. "You have guests come to claim your hospitality."

Dave and the others sat up. Cowled figures stepped into the firelight brandishing staffs crackling menacingly with red power. Dave felt the women build their power for an impending attack. He stood up to forestall the fight.

"Welcome, Raja Dul," he said.

"What?" replied a surprised tall figure. "How do you know that name?"

"We met your brother," said Dave. "He sends you his love."

Raja Dul chuckled. "Somehow, I don't think so. We have philosophical differences. This is an interesting twist. You pique my interest stranger. What's your name?"

"I'm Dave."

"How did you come to meet my brother and remain among the living?"

"It started as a misunderstanding and poor communication, but we worked it out."

"You worked it out?" asked Raja Dul, disbelieving. "Kai was living as a Konock who feed voraciously on living flesh, but I cannot dispute that you must have spoken with him or you wouldn't know of me."

"Why don't you call off your dogs so we can talk?"

"I don't think it prudent for us to relax our vigilance. We were informed you escaped Mortus and disabled the high priest, Ciaphus. If you could do that, we have reason for great caution."

"It was an accident. He bumped his head on a table and was knocked unconscious. Is he okay?"

"He will recover. I sense great power here amongst you. It's strange because these women have the taste of darkness and have been touched by Gristelle. You have a different flavor however."

"It is what it is," said Dave casually.

"You have no fear of us," said Raja Dul reflectively.

"There's probably a good reason for that," said Dave with a steely look.

They eyed each other frostily. Raja Dul turned away his glance first.

"I think I must reconsider this visit. I don't fear you, yet I suspect it's a time for caution. I've never been bested by any opponent, but no one has ever escaped the dark fortress before. I'll accept your invitation to talk."

"Sure," said Dave.

Raja Dul walked over to the women who stood in their triangle formation. Dave could feel them building up power. Again they felt to be a single magical entity blended together completely. Dave also sensed Raja Dul's considerable power.

"Interesting," He tried to probe them, but they rebuffed his tendril.

"Don't do that or we'll punish you," said Selane viciously.

Raja Dul chuckled. "You think you could punish me, little witch? I'm like my brother. I could consume all of you and gain your power and essence into my fabric. Think before you make a threat you cannot enforce."

The women glared.

"Another day perhaps," said Raja Dul with a wry smile. "You're very appealing, but this isn't the time. There's much in you worth my attention, but examination would be better done in a different situation."

He returned to face Dave.

"I will not ask you to explain how you've accomplished such feats, because I know you wouldn't tell me. In spite of that, I'll give you a gift because you've survived my brother. Don't think we're done, and don't think you can escape the power of the master. He'll be coming and then you'll rue the day you were born."

"Thanks for the warning."

"You'll see me again. Next time we'll see who has the upper hand. I'm sure my brother explained to you I have tastes and proclivities of which he does not approve."

"He gave us a heads up. Let me say this though. I've had experiences you wouldn't believe and I can tell you one thing I've learned. In every living person there's good and there's bad. That's true of you too, Raja Dul. You can't do enough evil to totally wipe out the sliver of good in you. I don't know what you think you're going to accomplish with all of this blood you shed, but there will be a day when something will wake you up. No one is beyond salvation."

Raja Dul looked like he'd been slapped across the face. He stood speechless staring at Dave.

"Spend the night camped with us if you like. If not, I guess we'll see you next time."

Raja Dul looked contemplatively before turning and led his warlocks away.

"I feared they could do us serious harm," said Graile.

"They're dangerous," said Dave, "but I wouldn't have allowed them to hurt any of you."

"You know this for certain?" asked Angus. "I don't doubt you, but without being tested in a real fight, can we trust just your opinion when it comes to our survival?"

Dave looked at the women.

"I screwed up before, so it's hard to trust me again. I get that. All I have to go on is this inner guide. I don't feel threatened. I hope I'm right."

The women shook their heads like he had proved their case and went back into their klatch and ignored the men.

They continued their ride the following day. Dave could sense surveillance around him, but nothing came forward to threaten them. Raja Dul seemed to be gone. Kra'ac rode at the end of the column trailing Selane in spite of her hostility. Angus and Graile flanked Dave.

"Have you noticed that we don't hear that foreboding horn any longer?" asked Graile.

"You're right," said Dave. "I hadn't thought about that. It may be that my father's power is what drove that phenomenon. Now that it's unplugged, they're back to normal, whatever normal is for them. I wonder what else has changed in the city."

"We will find out soon enough," said Angus.

They traveled doggedly until the outskirts of the imperial city were visible in the distance.

"Do we ride through the city?" asked Graile.

"Yes," said Dave. "We'll get supplies there."

"Is that safe?"

"Nothing is safe, but I think we can manage. I can detect danger a lot better now. If the master shows up, we're toast anyway."

Another day passed before they entered the suburbs of the imperial city. An imperial patrol saw the group and tried to arrest them. There were only soldiers in the group. The women lashed out felling most of them by unleashing powerful blasts. It resonated uncomfortably in Dave, like fingernails on a blackboard. The stream of their power was red and malevolent.

"My god, they really have gone over," said Graile. "Did you see how vicious and hate filled they were. We could have driven off this troop easily. We didn't even require magic to deal with the soldiers. They reveled in the killing."

"I saw," said Dave.

"Word of the slaughter spread as each subsequent patrol turned away rather than confront them. As they drew closer to the city proper, a patrol did ride toward them, this time headed by a team of warlocks. They chanted and aimed their staff's at the women. Once again the women reacted before Dave could do anything. As a triad they loosed a torrent of red might that struck at the astonished warlocks. The warlocks fought desperately, but were quickly put on the defensive. The women spurred their horses and rode straight at their enemy. The soldiers fled. The warlocks tried to rally, but the women's hatred surpassed their emotions. Their powers collided and detonated. The women were untouched, like they were secure inside a protective bubble. Under the onslaught, the warlocks staggered back. When the first one fell, it crumpled their defense and they were flamed by the torrent coming from the women.

Dave looked on in horror as the women trampled over the warlock bodies with their mounts. Dave had to spur his horse to keep pace as the trio rode off at a gallop.

"Where are they going?" asked Graile.

"My guess is they're looking for a little revenge at the palace," said Dave.

"Can we not stop them?"

"I don't know. If we try to interfere we might have a fight on our hands. They look pretty rabid."

Driven to find the emperor and empress, the women paid little attention to the innocents in the streets, several times nearly riding down children. The only thing stopping the women that day was the distance to get to the palace. Their horses couldn't continue without rest, so they were forced to stop. Storming into a house, they cowed the family. Dave and the men caught up as quickly as they could, went into the home and were confronted by three sparking red staffs.

Dave put up his hands.

"It's us." He eased his way in the door keeping himself between the women and his friends who then gathered the terrified family and pulled them behind Dave for protection. The women finally ended the confrontation, but went back into their triad and started chanting.

The friends fed the family, a father, mother, and two young daughters, from their supplies. Dave then set up a protection for the men and the family that didn't include the women - a defense against them.

"Is this how it's going to be?" asked Angus. "They're getting worse by the day. They're starting to look different, evil."

"I hope not," said Dave. "I have no idea what to expect next. I don't have any answers. I just try to get through the day intact."

"Are you giving up on them?" asked Kra'ac.

Dave thought for a long time then looked at these strangers, who'd been trusted and loved friends, Jenna being Dave's spouse. They couldn't have been any more different than how the girls had been before the ordeal began. It was a complete and negative turnabout.

"I'm discouraged…"

Crisis

In the morning the women left promptly.

"Thank you for your kindness, Dave," said the father. "Kindness no longer lives in this city."

"Stay hunkered down and out of sight. I'm afraid some big changes are coming. Stay safe."

The friends hustled out to pursue the women. By the time they got to the palace, the women had already set off a firestorm. The guards at the gates were left as smoking hulks. Dave could feel the power the trio was evoking as they fought with warlocks inside the building.

"We need to hurry," said Dave. "They're going up against an army of warlocks. We've got to have their backs."

When they rushed in the front door they were beset by imperial guards. Graile acted as the tip of their thrust with blades flying. At last Kra'ac and Angus had a chance to vent their rage flanking Graile and Dave. Fighting like madmen, they scythed down enemy like straw. Dave erected protection around them from magical attack, while his cohorts kept him from physical harm. It wasn't hard to follow the trail of bodies left behind by the women - straight to the throne room. The trio's hatred had no bounds. Dave was shocked at the power they were able to evoke.

Entering the hallway to the throne room, Dave could see a huge phalanx of warlocks arrayed to defend the doors into the room. The women were steadfast in the triad sending powerful blasts staggering their opponents. Being greatly outnumbered didn't appear to be a factor in the fight. The women were the aggressors and the warlocks seemed barely able to answer their challenge.

Dave stopped just behind the women. He felt them respond as if he was another enemy, deflecting their salvo with an impenetrable magical ward. Dave assessed the situation quickly. The warlocks were fighting a delaying action. Dave sensed the mass power of warlock reinforcements creeping into position on each side on the catwalks to flank the women from above. Before they could launch their deadly attack, Dave loosed a mighty wave of blue power that swept through their ranks disabling many and driving back the rest - his blue power a stark contrast to the sea of red flame sizzling all about.

The warlocks defending the door lost heart and ran away. Selane blasted open the throne room doors and they marched inside. The room was half full with courtesans quaking with fear, but there was no one of significance in attendance.

"Come out your majesties," Selane taunted. "We've returned seeking the pleasure of your embraces. You said we would miss you, so we've come back. Will you not honor us with your favor? You so often extolled to us your greatness as we choked under your pitiless attentions when you taught us the meaning of humiliation. We've learned your lessons very well. Come and let us return your diligent efforts ten fold. We offer you an embrace you'll never forget."

Dave searched the room magically and then the rest of the palace. The warlocks were scrambling outside and away, but there was no sign of the emperor or empress.

Selane blasted away a door behind the throne. Inside the small room Dave could see this was a place where the emperor did some of his mischief. Selane leveled a torrid blast so potent it flamed everything in the room to ash then she cried out in rage because she was thwarted in finding the imperial couple.

When there was nothing left in the room to destroy, she paused and then came out into the throne room. Most of the courtiers had fled.

"Now what, Selane?" asked Dave. "They're gone. Have you had enough of this useless posturing? You don't impress me and there's nobody else here to see your petulance."

Selane eyed him grimly and for a moment he prepared to be attacked.

Selane suddenly began to walk out of the room. Standing at the entrance looking on in fear were Mavin and Shara. They cowered in fear as the women came near. Dave hurried over to them.

"Are you guys okay?" he asked. "We're going to leave now. I think you should come with us. It's time to leave this life behind for you."

They nodded.

"What's happened to our friends?" asked Shara.

"It's a long story," said Dave.

"I know of their plight," said Shara, as they hurried away after the women. "We all did. Never did I see the empress exercise such cruelty as what she put upon them. They suffered terribly and were brought low in every way, but they endured. When the black witch came they began to change. I'd spoken with them in their misery to offer my sympathy, but they hardened with the presence of that witch and rejected me. They weren't like this though. They frighten me as badly as the black witch."

"We all had a bad time," said Dave. "Obviously, they had it a lot worse. I'm trying to figure out a solution. So far I'm shooting blanks."

"I fear to leave our home," said Shara, "but I know it would be worse to try to stay here."

"You'll be with us," said Dave. Shara looked at Graile, Angus, and Kra'ac who were changed men too. The fighting had restored their confidence.

They had a clear path out of the palace. The women had preceded them and no one chose to confront them. Dave rode away with Shara on his mount and Kra'ac took Mavin. Riding rapidly, they quickly caught up to the women.

"This way," Dave said, taking the lead.

They went to Mavin's house so they could gather some clothing and supplies. Dave was surprised the women had followed him and sensed a slight change in them. Their battle in the palace hadn't netted them their prey, but had alleviated some pent up rage. They were calmer and less menacing in their countenance.

"We might as well stay here for the night and leave in the morning," said Dave.

Selane got off her horse. The other women followed her lead. They were still disdainful of the men and maintained separation by going into a separate bedroom together slamming the door. When Dave went to his bed he could sense their dark magic as they resumed their meld. Disturbing, it felt like a nightmare of wrongness come to life. On this night their reverie escalated beyond any previous level Dave had sensed, eventually building up to a crushing climax before they de-escalated and fell asleep.

"They're getting worse," Dave muttered.

* * * *

They all left Mavin's house and traveled out of the affluent area into the poorer sections. The city was in pandemonium and with the usual patrols missing, thugs were preying on the weak. The quest happened on a gang that had broken into a home and they could hear the family screaming inside.

"Wait," Dave said as he jumped off his horse. Graile followed him inside the house to behold an ugly scene. Dave was enraged with what he saw. Reaching out with his power, he lifted a large man away from the helpless wife and threw him at the wall with such force he blew completely through it. Graile attacked the other gang members who tried to aid their mate. Dave wanted to immolate them, but Graile blocked his way. Instead, Dave levitated the terrified wife off the floor with his power and she floated into his grasp.

"You're safe now," said Dave. "Where's your family?"

"In there. They struck my husband and injured him severely."

Graile easily finished off the thugs.

Dave, clutching the wife in a protective embrace, went into the room where the husband lay. Three little boys were cowering around their unconscious father who was bleeding from a serious blow to the head. The wife cried out. Dave sat her down and she hurried to her husband.

Dave knelt down and placed his hands to the man's head. He instantly knew how to heal the man. The wife cried out in awe as Dave's hands glowed with the power. Within moments, the man blinked and sat up startled. There was no longer any sign of a wound.

His wife hugged him.

"What's happened?" asked the previously injured man.

"The stranger brought you back from the deathly wound. He's saved you."

"How can this be?"

"We're leaving the city," said Mavin. "Come with us. You'll never have another chance to escape. Dave is a great wizard for goodness."

Awe struck, all the man could muster was: "Truly?"

Dave shrugged. The wife needed no prodding to take action. She quickly gathered clothes, some food and then the family went out to the horses. The mother climbed up with Angus, and the father with Graile. Dave took the three little boys back to the women.

"You need to each carry a boy" He handed them up before they could reply.

They rode away heading towards the mountain pass.

Dave sensed something else as he rode along. With the little boys in tow, the women couldn't meld and Dave could magically perceive each of them separately for the first time.

"Good," he muttered to himself.

"Did you say something?" asked Shara, who had her arms around his chest.

"Nothing," said Dave.

Traveling away from the city proper for safety reasons, the first night they stopped to make camp, figures appeared out of the darkness.

"Red Sylvia," said Graile.

"I feared I'd seen the last of you," she replied, grabbing Graile in a warm embrace.

"It's good to see you again," said Dave. She embraced him next.

"Mavin and Shara, it warms my heart to see you free of that cursed city," she said.

"It's a blessed day," said Mavin. "These are new friends we've brought with us." He pointed to the young family.

"Where are…"asked Sylvia.

"They're apart from us," said Dave. "They went through some bad things. It's better if you give them some space for the time being."

"I don't understand, Dave. They're my friends."

"There have been some changes."

"Jenna is your wife."

"Well, she was. I don't know what she is now."

"This cannot be. She loved you more than her life. Nothing could sway her from that."

Dave got a sad look on his face.

"Apparently something could."

"I will speak to them."

"No, it might be dangerous, Sylvia. They've been corrupted and their magic is red now instead of blue."

Sylvia eyed him and then looked toward the three women.

"Stay in our camp with us, Sylvia. I don't think they'd attack you, but it's better not to take any chances."

"I wouldn't have thought this possible knowing who they were. It's disheartening. If noble and courageous women such as they couldn't withstand the encroachment of evil, what's the fate for the rest of us?"

Dave wanted to be supportive and encouraging, but at the moment was down also. He simply shrugged his shoulders.

During the night when they were asleep, Bear rejoined them. Padding silently into the camp and lying down beside Dave, the cat was still there in the morning when they awakened. Bear showed no animosity toward Sylvia, her people, or anyone else, but continued to snarl at the three women.

In the morning, Sylvia watched the women closely as they separately ate breakfast and paid no attention to the group. When they mounted up the women didn't even acknowledge Sylvia or the others of her group who'd been their friends.

"I see what you're talking about. These aren't the women I knew. If I came upon them on the highway, I would take cover until they passed by. It must have been a powerful magic worked on them."

Dave turned toward her. "Thank you, Sylvia. I think you've hit on it. I don't know why I didn't see this myself. That makes sense to me."

"What did I say?"

"I couldn't figure out this catastrophic change in them either. I wouldn't have thought Jenna could stop loving me with no remorse at all. The person she was, well this just didn't add up. They were in the control of the head of the black witches with no ability to defend themselves. If anybody could work such a potent spell, I would think it would be her. If they were bewitched, there must be some way to counter it. Sylvia, you've given me hope. They claim to love the black witches and they're acting like black witches. I would bet my life that Gristelle is behind all of this."

Dave suddenly grabbed Sylvia and kissed her.

Sylvia laughed. "Stop that you silly man. I haven't had the romantic attentions of a man since my late husband. I can't get those feelings back in my life again."

"Why?" asked Dave. "You're still young in your early thirties. You're a nice looking woman. Why shouldn't you think about another husband?"

"You're scrambling my mind. Stop this minute or I'll be force to, well, I can't think of what to do. See what I mean."

Dave chuckled. It was the best he'd felt since before his capture so he hugged her again.

Dave told the men about his hypothesis.

"How do you go about reversing this spell?" asked Kra'ac.

"That, I don't know. I don't want to stumble into this and do more harm than good. I'll think about this as we travel. I hope this intuition that guides me will kick in. In the meantime we'll just put up with the aggravation."

"You need to break that spell," said Kra'ac irritably. "This situation cannot be allowed to continue."

"Sure Kra'ac," said Dave facetiously. "I'll get that taken care of right away, in spite of the fact that I have no idea what to do."

"Do not mock me. About Selane, I have no patience for it."

"I know that, I'm sorry. I'm just frustrated."

"There's none other who can do this task, Dave. It falls upon you alone."

They traveled away from the city, but their numbers grew as Sylvia's network joined the migration.

"They see this as their chance to escape the empire, Dave," said Sylvia.

"I have no problem with that. But it slows us down, we're an unmistakable target and we have no way to feed large groups."

"They know to bring food when they come. I realize what you're saying, but I couldn't turn them aside. I didn't have the heart for it."

"Okay," said Dave shrugging his shoulders. "We'll just plug along and do the best that we can."

"A benefit of gathering my people is that imperial patrols will not attack us with so large a force arrayed against them."

"Since you've mentioned it, I haven't seen any patrols."

"We have a very long way to go. This will not be an easy crossing. Don't assume they'll never pursue us."

"I'm so overmatched for all of these roles thrust on me. If we amass a big crowd of people on the move and an imperial army confronts us, I'm no general to know strategies of war."

"We would choose no other," said Graile, who rode up beside them.

"That's because nobody else would take the job," Dave replied ruefully.

"That's probably true," said Graile. He winked at Sylvia. She smiled at him.

"Men…" she said, shaking her head.

Traveling each day the sight of the imperial city shrunk and then disappeared from the horizon behind them altogether. Almost daily, their exodus accumulated additional bodies as Sylvia's diverse small bands joined the movement. One unexpected development to this migration was the local people began to follow them abandoning their farms and villages. They carried food, but it would never be enough for the entire journey to the mountains. Additionally, most of them were on foot. If Dave waited for them, it would extend the travel time by triple or more - a difficult dilemma.

His accumulating responsibilities didn't allow Dave the time and the opportunity for what he was most interested in, which was to solve the problem of his women. The trio rode with the group, but was never an integral part. Dave got the feeling they were biding their time and waiting for something.

The progress of Dave's "army" was slow. He worried about the traumatic decision to leave walkers behind abandoned to their fate in order to ride ahead and make better time. Though he didn't fear for his safety, his intuition told him they needed to get moving.

They stopped for the night. The camp was like a small city it covered so much ground. Already food was short.

Angus came over to sit beside Dave.

"We're getting plea's to feed the hungry, Dave. If we do that, we'll all starve. It would be better if we tell the civilians they cannot come with us. If we wait much longer we'll start to have trouble with desperate starving people stealing food, or fighting with others for it."

"What am I supposed to say, Angus?"

"The truth… We should have stopped them in the beginning. Now it's become a large problem."

"Do you want to take over as the leader, Angus? I wouldn't mind being impeached."

"If that means the mantle of authority passes to another, I don't think you would be allowed to impeach."

Dave chuckled. "Angus, you can't use a noun as a verb or vice versa."

They started to laugh which soon developed into a belly laugh.

"What did that mean, Dave?"

They burst out laughing again. It was a much needed catharsis for Dave to relieve the stress momentarily.

"What's this all about?" asked Sylvia who walked over when she heard them.

"Nothing," said Dave. They started laughing heartily again and Sylvia laughed too.

Others around them started to chuckle.

Dave glanced up and saw his three women walking toward him, but they were not laughing.

"Have you divined solutions to your many problems?" asked Selane caustically.

"No," said Dave, composing himself. "I would explain it, but you wouldn't understand. To what do we owe the honor of this visit?"

"The time has come for us to part from you. We'll leave in the morning."

"What? I thought I got a shot at talking about this."

"From this point, we're closest to the road that leads to the black witch's enclave. We'll not travel farther away from them. I told you this is our destiny, our proper place. The empire and the world of men hold no interest for us."

Dave looked into Jenna's eyes. She had a steely expression, cold and impersonal. He saw none of the love, which had resided there.

Panic and great distress overcame Dave, but he was at a loss at what to do. The trio abruptly turned and walked away without a backwards glance. He seemingly had been excised from her thoughts and concern.

"No," he muttered.

Sylvia put her hand on his shoulder.

"I'm sorry, Dave. If there's anything that I can do, just tell me."

Dave was a basket case for the rest of the day. When they made camp, he sat alone pondering the ultimate split from the woman he loved - an unacceptable outcome.

"Damn it," he muttered angrily. "If I could go past death to save you, I can save you now."

He arose ominously, preparing his mind for the fight. Gathering power, he focused his mind on his purpose. It was just after dark when he walked purposefully to where the three women were isolated. He could feel them as he approached. Forming a triad in the midst of chant, they became a single entity, oblivious and impervious as their dark power roiled around Dave like a noxious vapor.

They sensed him and immediately took a defensive posture, starting a magic to seal them away from him. Dave responded, bringing up his might until he glowed like a sun.

With serious intent, they struck a vicious blast of their hatred towards Dave that would have leveled any other magical person. He drew upon the vast power that was his own and his father's. His new knowledge guided him in the test and he deflected their bile without returning an attack of his own. Relentless, the trio battered him with salvo after salvo of titanic power. Dave not only countered their strikes, he consumed them so they wouldn't harm any of the surrounding thousands of people. The foulness of their red power made him ill.

The women changed their attack, seeking a way to shatter and destroy him. He perceived clearly they were intent on his death, because he'd become a symbol of their hatred for the emperor, and for all men. He would be the object of their wrath and the beginning of their war against men everywhere. The insane intensity of their emotions appalled Dave that they reviled him utterly.

Steeling himself, he didn't lack for power, but their vehemence affected him and he couldn't afford to be distracted in the middle of a deadly fight. His own guilt feelings were a negative factor he had to combat. A childish part of him felt the need to be punished for causing this nightmare to occur in the first place.

The women varied their blows trying to catch him off guard. It was the same for him as when he first fought with a sword, or first wielded the power - he instinctively knew what to do. His father's skills and experience made him an impossible opponent. He could sense the frustration growing in the women as their attacks continued to fail.

Suddenly they shifted, blurred for a moment and became a vast host. They started a terrible black chant designed to grate on his nerves. With power expanded incredibly, they tried to encase him in a suffocating bubble of death. It was not a small challenge for he had to evoke a level of power that could damage worlds to counter the assault.

For a time the contesting forces teetered in stalemate. With an incredible force of will, Dave threw back the black might and poured a golden surge of his own force into the triad. He sensed the connection to the black coven and the might they were wielding as a single vast entity encompassing the entire coven. As a unit, he could sense their shock that a force as massive as theirs could not put him down.

Dave spoke a word of power from his father's memory and the connection to the coven was blasted apart in an eruption of golden brilliance. The triad of the women disintegrated without the power of the coven to shackle them.

The women fell to the ground unconscious.

"My god," cried Dave as he raced to their sides, linking to them with his power. With all three in serious distress, he drew upon his father's knowledge to seek out their psychic injuries and began to heal them. Selane, lead partner of the three, had the worst wounds. Dave had to maintain the other two while he concentrated on Selane. Working determinedly, he lost track of time putting the shattered pieces of Selane's mind back together, just like she had healed Kra'ac's broken leg. He could feel the damages in Lissette and in Jenna, but could only sustain them, because he didn't possess the power to heal them all at the same time. The noisome residue of the dark magic had bled into their essences like a stain. Dave poured floods of the golden power through her like a cleansing stream. Her vile hue began to fade until it was gone completely. Selane was reconstructed, but he didn't find her soul. It was buried somewhere deep within her core barricaded against the evil. Dave sifted through her entire body until he came upon her hidden place. She cowered like a frightened child. He showered her with his love and coaxed her into trusting him. Once she opened the door, Dave joined with her and in the process he restored her to her original state and much more. She saw what Dave had seen when he had received his father's gift.

"*Dave*," came her thought as she resumed her life.

"*I need your help with them, Selane.*"

Together, they painstakingly repeated the process on the other two, but with both of them working in concert; they were able to speed up the healing process.

Though Dave didn't seek it, he was exposed to the memories of the life the women had lived after their shackling and it was appalling to know what they'd been through. The women's nightmare was far beyond what he'd imagined, and dwarfed the ordeals of the men. Gristelle's efforts had never been a boon

In his distressed emotional state, Dave was moved to great compassion leaving them to rest and recover from their traumas while he wobbled in exhaustion. When he finally opened his eyes later it was light outside.

"Dave," said Graile with concern.

"How long have I been out?"

All of the night and most of this day, what's the news about our women?"

"They think I set them right. They'll rest for a time before they can awaken."

"This is wonderful news," said Angus.

"You've done well," said Kra'ac who was cradling Selane in his arms. The terrible dark countenance was gone from all three women at last.

Angus sat down beside Lissette gently stroking her hair.

"This is a miracle," said Sylvia. "You need to rest further, Dave. We'll celebrate when you're all restored to vitality."

He slept through the balance of that day and the night before they all awoke.

Selane did the best of the three. She opened her eyes, looked at Kra'ac and smiled. It was the most powerful thing she could do for Kra'ac. He hugged her to his chest. Dave could see him whispering in her ear.

Lissette awoke next, but was still very groggy. Angus smiled.

"Where am I, dwarf?" she whispered.

Angus laughed and embraced her tenderly.

Jenna was disoriented when she awoke. Dave took her in his arms.

"Dave?" she rasped.

He poured some water to wet her mouth and she took a couple of swallows from the gourd.

"I feel strange, Dave."

"Just relax honey. I've got you. Everything is fine now. You're safe."

She smiled. "I had a terrible dream."

"Don't think about it. Let's get some food in you. It will help you to feel better."

"Thank you, husband," she said weakly.

With those words, Dave was stricken with a pang of emotion and he kissed her tenderly.

"Welcome back."

Her eyes fluttered. "I'm sleepy," she whispered.

It was several more hours before the women were awake enough to have a full meal. Dave, Angus, and Kra'ac never left their sides.

With the food, the women regained strength quickly. Sylvia sat with them while they ate.

"I was so worried. I feared we'd lost you. I couldn't believe you could be such… You're such powerful women."

"No, we're not," said Selane.

"Your powers humble me," said Sylvia. "I practice my craft, but it's like a small candle compared to the sun. If you could fall, what of minor people like me?"

"You don't understand," said Selane. "You shouldn't feel inferior to us. You're not. We've been taught a great deal about ourselves by what happened. We're more than humbled. We were forced to learn things about ourselves we didn't want to admit. Gristelle took the darkness in us and crafted new creatures. It was horrible to live through and mortifying to face what we became."

"You're back now," said Sylvia. "That's what's important."

The three women got an uncomfortable look on their faces.

"There's much you don't know," said Lissette.

The men returned and the women put smiles onto their faces, but Sylvia realized they were forcing smiles for the benefit of the men.

"Did you get enough to eat?" asked Dave.

"Yes, thank you," Jenna answered.

"We're going to be heading for the border station," said Dave. "Are you guys up to traveling?"

"Yes," said Jenna. "We'll not delay you."

"I've been delaying some tough decisions," he said. "All of these people following us are a big problem. We were never prepared to move the whole country and soon they'll turn on each other from starvation. I feel so sorry for them, but I'm afraid we need to ride away and leave the walkers behind. There's no other way."

"You must make that decision, husband."

"I can't even look in their faces when I walk past them. They keep looking at me like I can work some miracle and solve all of their problems."

Jenna looked at him thoughtfully.

"You're so beautiful, honey," said Dave and kissed her.

She looked away.

"Sorry, I know I can be a little overwhelming, Jenna. I'm just so happy to have you back."

"I've caused you nothing but worry and strife. You've been forced to put your life at risk too many times to rescue me. You didn't get a bargain picking me to be your wife."

"You're all I want, Jenna. That first day I landed in your camp, I was taken with you. You told me to move along and stop following you, as I remember it."

Jenna chuckled.

"You frightened me. You exploded out of this cloud and landed on me. I thought you were going to kill me."

"No way, I don't kill pretty girls."

"That is fortunate for me."

Painful Matters

Dave hated himself for what he had to do. He called together the masses and stood on a high point to address them.

"I'm sorry that I must talk about some hard things with you. When we left the imperial city, we planned on a small force moving rapidly to the border. We made no provision for large numbers of people going with us and don't have the supplies to feed so many. Also, we're slowed to a pace we cannot allow to continue as we have matters that require our presence in our home country as soon as possible. I don't want you to think we're abandoning you, but we have no power to feed and protect you. Being in such a large slow moving configuration, we make all of us targets for the empire. Regretfully, I tell you we must separate from you and increase our speed."

There was utter silence for a moment before the masses started to shout and plead with him not to be left behind.

"I'm sorry," said Dave. "I don't have any answers," but by that time there was so much tumult he couldn't be heard.

Dave turned away sadly. He went with his friends and went to their horses and rode away at a gallop. Dave couldn't bring himself to look back at the throng. Even with the parting, there was still a very sizeable group, because Sylvia's network continued to add to their numbers. Mavin and Shara were fortunate Sylvia had provided them horses so they could ride as a part of her network.

Camp that night was subdued. Although it was a necessary decision, everybody felt guilty about leaving so many behind unprotected and unfed.

Dave sat down beside his wife and handed her a plate of food.

"Thank you, Dave."

They ate in silence for a while before she spoke.

"You shouldn't blame yourself for what you had to do, Dave."

"I do. I've been the cause of a lot of misery in my time on this world. I know that the black witches were controlling you guys when Selane said those hurtful things, but if I'm honest, there was a lot of truth in them. It really was me who was responsible for our capture and what you guys endured could have been avoided. When I add things like this today, leaving those poor people behind, it eats at me. My errors keep mounting higher and higher. I'm more dangerous to the people around me than our enemies."

"You've made the best choices you could, husband."

Selane and Lissette came over and sat down beside them. Angus and Kra'ac were not far behind, and then Graile walked over and sat with Sylvia.

"You must understand those words were put in our mouth," said Selane. "What we feel ourselves is deep regret for what happened. We don't hold you responsible. We knew there would be risk and we chose to share that risk with you."

"Aye," said the others.

"What's so hard for the three of us to deal with was when you broke through the spell of the black witches that restrained us, you learned what happened to us in captivity," said Jenna. "You know the full truth of it. You know there was much more to our misery than the depravity of the emperor and empress. Their shameful acts are on them. We couldn't stop that from happening. What shames us is the gradual toll it took on us, wearing down our resistance. Because we saw no possible escape, it was too easy to accede to what was to become our new lives. We were things, objects and no longer persons. It made us vulnerable to Gristelle when she came to us. She spun a web of deceit and offered us a life of her creation living as one with them. We'd not lost our intelligence to discern her temptations, but we'd lost heart so we succumbed to the lure. She sought out the darkness in us, but more than that she played on our weaknesses and we didn't resist. On some level, all of us knew we were being led into wrongness. That culpability we have, in spite of what was done to us that we couldn't control, that's what haunts us now. You know the things that were done in the dark. You know the things that we did and how we felt. I don't know how you can even bear to look at us. I pledged to you to be your faithful wife, but you know I shamed those vows with my actions. I was more than weak. I craved the touch of the coven. I was turned black as any of them and acted the part."

"It was true for all of us," said Lissette. "Never in our history has an elf become as foul as I. All of you think we're restored to who we were. I don't know that we could ever be those high women again. The memories of it burn in my mind. I cannot drive it away. Hungers and lusts are in me now that were never there before. I'm unworthy to be your companion."

"I agree," said Selane. "If I ever was the standard and the finest of the sisters, which I question, that's no longer the truth. I know humility and shame. Sylvia faced rape, but she didn't wallow in the darkness, instead she stood up, fought back and became a stronger person. We became weaker women."

"We appreciate all of your support and your kind words," said Jenna, "but this isn't a burden any can bear other than we three. The crisis has passed about our being the tools of the black witches, but any thought that we resume our former roles is a matter yet to be determined. There's much we must do only we can address. We don't wish to exclude you from our lives, but we cannot stay in this condition where we are now. I hope you'll understand what I'm saying and you'll exercise patience with us, yet again. For a time, we're going to continue to remain apart from you. Dave, you understand what compels us, because you saw the ugly truth. We must deal with this matter to its conclusion and the outcome we cannot know whether it be good, or bad. I'm so sorry. We don't wish to add further to your suffering, our dear men. You've been patient beyond all reasonable expectations, but how we are now must be resolved one way or another. There's great darkness within us, which either we control, or it will control us. Dave if you wish to end our marriage, I'll understand and will not fight it."

They got up and went away to bed down on their own for the night and continued to sleep apart each succeeding night thereafter.

Graile patted Dave on the shoulder sympathetically.

"I think I put out one fire and another pops up right away," said Dave.

"That's the nature of life," said Graile. "There was never any guarantee it would be easy, or fair."

"That's reassuring, Graile."

"What they were saying about this malaise within them of which you have knowledge, is it something you want to talk about?"

"No. They want to keep it private and I agree with them. It's a really difficult issue and I'm worried. Gristelle opened a can of worms, a Pandora's Box. Putting the genie back in the bottle may be an impossible task, I don't know."

"That sounds ominous, Dave."

"I want to help, but they don't want it."

"Perhaps there's some type of compromise which they can reach."

"I'll see how they do on their own for a while and maybe I'll make that suggestion later, Graile. It can't hurt."

Continuing the journey they traveled steadily, covering as many miles as possible without tiring the horses. Dave was happy that at least the women would rejoin them during the rides. Jenna rode beside Dave, Selane rode beside Kra'ac, Lissette rode beside Angus, and even Sylvia came up to ride beside Graile.

With steadily increasing numbers as more of Red Sylvia's network merged into their ranks, they sent out large hunting parties to search for food. It was the only way they could manage to keep everyone minimally fed.

It was a much different trip than when they'd come. They had no fear of the imperial forces this time. Dave didn't sense any significant magical entities anywhere nearby and soldiers didn't confront them during the entire journey.

After six months since they'd first come through the pass, they neared familiar ground.

"I think we're within a day or two of the border station," said Dave when they stopped to make camp. "Selane, aren't we near where Bashar lived?"

"Yes. We promised we would take them with us. We'll ride in search of them, Dave."

She rode off with Jenna and Lissette into the evening haze. Summer had passed and it was well into fall. Flocks of migratory birds filled the skies squawking loudly as they fled away from the coming winter storms.

"This will be a cold winter," said Angus, looking up at gathering clouds in the sky. "I can feel it in my bones."

"That's old age you feel," said Graile, chuckling.

"I'll show you old age," Angus retorted brandishing his battle axe.

Kra'ac chuckled. During his time with them, he'd developed something of a personality and a sense of humor, something mountain trolls weren't known for. Unfortunately, his laugh still sounded like a rumbling cough.

The women didn't return for several hours and when they came back it was dark. They'd found Bashar and his family. Bashar was riding sitting behind Jenna with a child riding in front of her and Kela was riding behind Lissette with a child in front. The other four children were riding with Selane, two in front and two behind.

"My friends!" shouted Bashar happily.

"Hey dude," said Dave.

"We had faith you would come for us one day," said Kela.

"We gave you our word," said Dave. "It was a rocky road we had to travel, but we made it back."

"Were you successful in your mission?" asked Bashar.

"Sort of," said Dave. "We left some things up in the air back there, but we needed to get out of town in a hurry."

"You've gathered many friends," said Bashar. "You're now an army."

"A hungry army," said Dave.

"Thank you for remembering us," said Kela. "Is there anything that we can do for you to repay your kindness?"

"No," said Dave.

"That will not suffice," said Kela. "I will find a way to do something important for you. It's not enough that we simply accept your benevolence without some return of goodness."

"Really Kela, we don't expect anything from you."

"I have spoken my word about this. The matter is closed. I will find a way. We'll speak no more about it."

"Okay," said Dave, shrugging helplessly.

The children found Bear right away and showered him with hugs. He settled down to enjoy the adoration and purred.

Dave relaxed under his bedroll cover that evening feeling good Bashar's family was safely in the camp, like he'd done something right for a change. He would have been contented if his wife was lying under the bedroll with him. He could still always sense them as they evoked magic in their private camp. They'd battled their inner demons the entire

217

trip apparently without turning the corner. Whatever measures they were trying were not working.

On this night the women's efforts exceeded what he normally felt, but, as always, there was a crescendo of flurry and then nothing after. He dozed off - nothing had changed.

At dawn the drive toward the mountain pass continued. The morning was uneventful, but when resuming travel after the noon meal, the station came into view ahead and also long line of troops arrayed to block their way.

"I guess we can see where the patrols went," said Dave. "It looks like they're ready for a fight."

"I don't see the warlocks," said Graile. "They're here somewhere."

Dave extended his magic. He could sense power, but couldn't pin down a specific location.

"Call the girls up front," said Dave. Angus peeled off and rode back to the rear where the girls were riding and they joined Dave about half an hour later.

"There are warlocks around here somewhere," said Dave. "We need you guys to help me keep them off Sylvia's fighters when the battle starts."

"We outnumber the soldiers," said Graile, "but they're experienced troops while we're a loose militia of guerillas who've never faced a pitched battle."

"This was going to happen sooner or later," said Dave. "This won't be the last battle we ever see, but it might be the most important. If we can't break through and get through the mountains, we're sitting ducks here in the open when the imperial army shows up behind us."

"They've spotted us," said Angus. "Let's get to this."

Dave looked at his women who didn't show any hesitation. Lissette strung her bow.

Dave rode over to them.

"Let's try to stay together. I know you don't like it, but we should consider linking again."

"It wouldn't be the same Dave," said Selane. "It isn't our modesty. You already know our secrets. The change Gristelle wrought in us is the problem, and is what we strive to eradicate, but so far have failed. If we try to bond with you, it may harm you and we cannot guarantee that we can mesh with you as before."

"Okay," said Dave uneasily.

The imperial's sounded their battle horns. Sylvia's warriors, nervous and unsteady, glanced at each other unsurely.

The imperial soldiers gave a loud shout and began to march toward the quest. The guerillas appeared like they were ready to bolt. Kra'ac roared loudly and rode out to bellow at them. He banged his war club on his shield to incite the troops as he rode along their front. The guerillas responded to his bravado and their shouts grew into a roar. Graile rode out with Angus to join Kra'ac. They shouted also, whipping their troops into frenzy, and then charged. For Dave, it was exciting. He'd never been in a war before and fought a battle. He spurred his horse to follow his troops, with the women close behind.

With a loud metallic clash, the two forces met - metal hitting metal. The imperial troops were arrayed in armor and organized, but Dave's side was a charging cavalry attack. They crashed into the imperial line and buckled the column in numerous places.

Dave still couldn't detect where the warlocks were hiding. He unsheathed Gloin and waded into the melee striking any imperial soldier he could reach. The soldiers reacted by buckling to allow an easy path forward and Dave was soon cut off from his army as the soldiers filled in behind in a deadly circle of steel. The enemy assailed him aggressively, but even surrounded he was in no danger. They were no match for his skill and Gloin. He realized they weren't trying to kill him, only were trapping and delaying him. Suddenly, he felt the emergence of the warlocks joining the battle. Dave raised his power, which protected him, but couldn't fight the soldiers and the warlocks at the same time. Ignoring the imperial sword strikes was impossible.

He followed the action magically. The three women sprang forward to meet the warlock threat, reverting to the triad formation and pooling their power. When they launched the first salvo to counter a warlock blast, Dave was glad to see the flash was no longer red with dark power.

Greatly outnumbered by warlocks, the women were quickly forced back on the defensive. Selane took the lead in directing their attack. Her skills emerged blunting the relentless warlock advance.

Dave desperately tried to break out of the circle to help, but the imperial soldiers sacrificed extravagantly to keep him in check, no matter how many he killed. Dave's army was fighting bravely, but combat was new ground and they had to grow into the challenge. Kra'ac was unstoppable, bashing away swathes of enemy as he drove to free Dave and Graile a blur of motion scything down enemy soldiers. Angus roared, his war axe red with blood, as he hacked and battered to keep up with Kra'ac and Graile.

Dave knew the reason for the encircle strategy the instant Raja Dul emerged. Dul ignored Dave totally and went straight for the women, easily brushing aside Sylvia's warriors who tried to block his path and protect the women. The women were unaware of Dul's approach as they concentrated fully on the fight with the warlocks.

Raja Dul came up behind them and loosed a magic covering them like bags. Dave felt the women's magic suddenly blunted as they lost consciousness. Raja Dul grabbed the reins of their horses and galloped away.

Dave loosed a shout that turned into pure golden power as he lit up like a sun, discharging a wild blast that mowed down friend and foe alike. He charged out of the trap and was immediately confronted by the warlocks. They loosed a mighty unified attack of red hatred slowing his charge.

"NO!" Dave screamed, roaring in rage. He reacted to the attack, but he couldn't escape the battle to chase Raja Dul.

Dave fought without thought of the damage he would do, unleashing a salvo that struck the warlock formation rocking them back like a windstorm, but they wouldn't relent. Dave hammered them again and again until they began to crumple. First it was just a few and then more fell until finally Dave sent a prodigious blue ball of roiling might knocking down their defense. Those still alive escaped quickly and the imperial soldiers suddenly broke off the battle and escaped.

His men cheered wildly, but Dave was frantic for none of his friend's saw what happened to the women.

Angus rode over with Graile.

"Are you injured, Dave?"

"It was Raja Dul, Graile. This was a trap, a diversion. He just kidnapped the women while we were distracted."

Kra'ac rode up and heard what he said.

"Where did they go?" he shouted angrily.

"I don't know. Dul had the warlocks distract me so he could get away. He said he was going to eat them, like Raja Kai, to gain their powers and attributes. We've got to find him in a hurry."

"What do we do?" asked Graile. "Where do we go?"

"I don't know," shouted Dave in frustration.

Sylvia rode up beside Graile and touched his hand.

"We'll hold the station for you, Dave."

Dave closed his eyes and searched for the women, but Raja Dul had invoked a construct to cover his escape. Dave screamed in rage.

He spurred his horse, riding off blindly. The other men quickly followed, not realizing Dave didn't have a trail to follow.

Dave loosed a blast of blue power up into the sky. It detonated, sweeping across the landscape in all directions. He fired another even larger blast that nearly leveled them all off their horses.

"Take care with your power, Dave!" shouted Graile, but Dave was riding wildly lost in his panic for the lost women now in Dul's control.

Suddenly, from the mountains, there was an answering concussion. A shape streaked across the land toward them at great speed. The figure drew close in a short amount of time. It was Raja Kai.

"Follow me," he shouted, angling away from their path and heading toward the mountains.

Riding at full speed, they reached a huge rock formation in the middle of the open land. Raja Kai rode straight at the rock like he was going to crash into it. As they drew near, Kai spoke a word and a tunnel appeared. They rode into the tunnel opening and raced the entire length of it until they entered a large cavern.

Raja Dul was there and had laid out the three women, unconscious on a stone table, just like Dave had seen in the Konock cave. Their clothes neatly folded and stacked nearby.

"Not again," said Dave.

They all came to a halt and jumped off their horses.

"Welcome to my dinner table, my friends," said Raja Dul. "Welcome Kai. It's too long since I've seen you, brother."

"Dul, you must not do this."

"Why Kai, it's permissible for you to consume human flesh and gain their essence, but it's not for me?"

"I live in harmony with the Konocks, Dul. I endeavor to raise them up and don't actively work to take the lives of the sentient like these humans. It's just something that occurs from time to time."

"Ha. Kai, there's no difference. You crave this meal. I can feel it in you. These sweet beautiful delectable little females are the utmost

221

temptation, because they're the utmost delight. I will not allow you to interfere with what I have fairly captured. This avatar who could escape Mortus was so easily duped he lost his treasures to me and doesn't deserve them. I'll give them a much better existence as a part of me."

"No!" shouted Dave. "Jenna is my wife!"

Dul smiled wickedly.

"Though I wouldn't part with such a prize, I hear the pain in your plea. I'm not greedy. I'll give you your woman back and keep the other two, I'll eat the little witch as she calls to my deepest hunger, and Kai can eat the little elf."

For a moment Dave was afraid the Raja Kai would accept the offer.

"I cannot permit this, brother."

"You cannot conquer me, Kai."

"Nor can you conquer me, Dul."

"If you want to fight somebody, fight me," said Dave.

"No Dave," said Kai, "you don't know what you're getting into. It's not a matter of raw power. Dul and I have knowledge and skills to best you."

"I'm not going to stand by and let him do this to any of them," said Dave fitfully. "If I have to die so they can live, so be it. I will not go easily you son of a bitch!"

Dave began to glow ominously.

Raja Dul eyed him thoughtfully.

"I told you when we first met what I intended for these women, Dave, and that you were a unique person. I'm no less fascinated with you now as then. No one else could have reunited me with my brother. I'm grateful to you for that."

"I didn't forsake you, brother," said Kai. "You know I couldn't abide the path you chose. I live in hope you might yet turn away from the dark path and join me in the light. There's work enough where I could use your help."

"You call my path dark and yours enlightened, Kai? That's a travesty."

"I don't agree, brother."

"We've lived a very long time," said Dul, looking back to Dave. "Perhaps I can wait to have this succulent meal of these lovely women at a later time. They were born to serve this purpose, wouldn't you agree? I can recapture them at any time I wish."

"If you come for them, I'll be there to face you," Dave answered frostily.

"Well said. I can appreciate courage, even though it's misguided and impotent. You speak from honest belief and conviction straight from your heart. You're a courageous soul. I can still appreciate that."

Dul waived his hand and the women awoke and sat up confused and disoriented.

"Dave?" asked Jenna.

"Your clothes are right here," said Dave and he helped her to dress. Kra'ac helped Selane, eyeing Raja Dul with hostility the whole time, and Angus helped Lissette.

"I've not dined on troll before, that may be a dish that I would savor," said Dul.

"You can try," said Kra'ac.

Dul laughed heartily.

"Goodbye my new friends, this has been a rare pleasure being with you," said Dul. "I've given you back their lives and will look to even the ledger someday. You owe me a debt."

"Goodbye, Dul," said Kai.

"I think that perhaps we shall see each other again in the near future," said Dul, "circumstances being what they are in the empire."

"Think on my words and abandon that vile path. I would gladly welcome you home."

Dul got a thoughtful look. "I don't know if I can do that. Goodbye, brother."

"You showed mercy here, Dul."

"Did I? I was confronted by my equal and also an avatar of great power. I couldn't prevail, so I did the expedient thing. I have the taste of these pretty little things in my mind now and it will be an irresistible lure until I can finally sate that hunger. You know of what I speak, Kai."

"I do. You understand that we'll resist you."

"Yes. Though I'm anathema to you now, it was good I could see you again, brother."

Dave took Jenna up onto his horse and pulled her horse along. Selane rode with Kra'ac and Lissette with Angus. Raja Kai rode with them back to their camp where Sylvia was waiting anxiously.

"I feared for you," she said to the women as they dismounted.

"We knew nothing of it," said Jenna, "our last memory was the battle and then waking up on Raja Dul's table."

"That must have been terrifying," said Sylvia.

"I've been in that position before. My husband has saved me twice from that fate."

"There's so much I don't know in this world," said Sylvia.

Dave took Raja Kai aside.

"How did you know to be here at this moment when we needed you?"

"I could sense the approach of my brother, and your magic is like a beacon flaming as bright as the sun. I have intuition also and felt a serious event was before me, so I left my home to come here. When I saw the battle unfold, I realized Dul's plan and knew you needed me, or the women would be lost. I understood what my brother was telling us. He couldn't discard the hunger for your women if he wanted to. It will be a lifelong peril for you and for them. I'll ward them at your side, but his cunning is equal to me. I cannot guarantee he'll never find an opportunity to steal them away."

"This just keeps getting better and better, Kai. If it came down to a showdown between me and him, do I have any chance at all to beat him?"

"You have power beyond anything I've ever seen, but you saw what happened against him. You didn't know the nature of the fight and how to react, so you were easily thwarted. That's the problem for you. He would never give you a chance to level your full might against him if you ever learn to wield it. I sense you gained skills and abilities when you absorbed your father, but you have no experience with it. You'll gain that experience with time, but whether you can ever be equal to the menace of Raja Dul, I cannot say. He's not stronger than you, no one is other than the master, but he is wily, crafty, and skilled in killing from innumerable deaths he's caused."

"Is there any good news?"

"I'll think upon that. Perhaps I can glean some small glimmer of hope."

"Great," said Dave, shaking his head. "In the meantime, I'll try to gain experience."

"I'm sorry, Dave, but it's better if you know the truth."

Dave went back to Jenna.

"Are you feeling better?"

"It was different the second time. I was on a journey before this time was a blank. I had no awareness of my life or plight."

"It may have been that the Konock were praying for you, while Dul was just licking his chops. Somehow that must make a difference for your soul. I need to find a way to get you off the menu."

Jenna chuckled.

"I wasn't trying to be funny."

"It struck me that way."

"It's good to see you acting normal. I've really missed you."

"We've lost so much time together. It was worse for you, because you were aware of your circumstances. We were imprisoned within ourselves and to an extent not fully aware. Gristelle pulled the strings like we were puppets."

"She's another on my long list of people I need to settle a score with."

"I hope we can just return home and put this all behind us. I don't want to think about revenge. I don't want to deal with the empire ever again."

"I don't think that's possible, they're not going to just turn their heads to our escaping their clutches without some sort of serious response. Eventually this master dude is going to show up and we're going to need to get ready for some major trouble."

Selane and Lissette came over and sat down with them.

"It's hard to explain to you our feelings about Gristelle," said Jenna. "We don't hate her at all. Actually, we feel great affection. I know this doesn't make sense to you, but in her presence she wrought substantial and fundamental changes in us. She re-structured us into being one with them. It was a different lure than a married life with you. In its way it was very compelling. That's part of what we three are coping with. A residual effect is potent and remains in spite of what we do to remove it. That's why we seek to be apart. We're no longer worthy companions for our brave and noble men. Do you see?"

"I don't buy that, not one bit. I married you for better or worse, Jenna. I'm not going to let you, or Selane and Lissette for that matter, go down this alternative path. We're going to be there for you no matter what and find a way to get past it. If that means compromise, so be it. I want you no matter what."

"You know of our dilemma," said Selane, "but I don't think you grasp the gravity of the temptations for us."

"I know what specifically it is you're talking about," said Dave. "My opinion is when you were in the control of the black witches you did what they wanted you to do. First and foremost was you hated men and were on the verge of torching any and all of us on the spot. Once I broke their spell over you, what remains isn't a deadly threat any longer - more of a nuisance. It isn't any worse than what you got from your sisterhood, Selane. I can live with how you are now, even if you need to do your thing. Trying to achieve the impossible is frustrating you. You can't eradicate what's in you now, but maybe you need to take a different look at it and realize you're not hurting anybody else. I can work around it as long as I have you. I think if you ask Graile, Angus, and Kra'ac, you'll find they agree."

"I don't deserve you," she whispered, embracing him.

"Yes, you do. I'm no great shakes, but I'm all yours, so deal with it."

Jenna chuckled.

He kissed her tenderly and she returned his kiss.

"You should have let Raja Dul eat me. It would have solved a lot of problems for you."

"Will you shut up? I'll eat you myself if you think you're such a delicious meal. I have my doubts about that though. I think you might be stringy and a little chewy and full of gristle."

Jenna laughed heartily. The others joined her and soon the laughter spread.

"What's so funny?" asked Sylvia.

"Our esteemed leader," said Jenna. "He is a blockhead, to use his words."

"I've been saying that all along," said Angus. "Now you finally believe me. It's a about time."

"I've noticed how much time that Graile spends with Sylvia," said Jenna.

"He's a man," said Dave. "He gets lonely just like anybody else. I think that Sylvia is thinking about him too."

"Good, they would be a good match," said Jenna.

Going Home

Dave organized a sizeable crew to man the imperial border station to hold it while they started to send their people through the mountain pass. Raja Kai had disappeared without word to Dave.

"Did he say anything to anybody?" asked Dave.

"He spoke to us," said Selane. "He said he'll be watching us. We know the danger of his brother hasn't ended, and he helped us understand it never will. He gave us help with how to protect ourselves and how to sense Dul's presence when he comes looking for us. He bade us a safe journey. I must tell you, I've never felt fully secure in his presence, any more than his brother. Their hunger is palpable and they suppress it with great difficulty. I think it wouldn't be farfetched that he craves our bodies on his own dinner table as well."

"That may be true," said Dave. "While he's on our side, we need to learn what we can from him. I'll treat him as an ally until he acts otherwise. Are you ready to go home?"

All three of the women smiled and spurred their horses forward into the pass and started the climb upward.

"I thought we would be in for a difficult time when we came here," said Jenna, as they rode along, "but I never thought it would be as bad as it was. It's like my former life was a lifetime ago."

"I know what you mean," said Dave. "Earth seems like a dream rather than a part of my life. We'll be all right. I'm right here. Being together is what counts."

"Yes," she said, without much conviction, like she doubted herself.

Spending each day in the pass during their journey felt different. The empire was at their back and easy to think the threat of attack was over. Bear showed up, rejoined the camp, went straight to Jenna and lay down beside her with his head on her lap.

"See," said Dave. "Even Bear knows you're better. That black witch nightmare is over, honey."

"Hello Bear," she whispered as she petted his thick furry main.

"Selane, would you come over here please?" asked Dave.

She came over, accompanied by Kra'ac.

"Do you remember that day we found Kra'ac and you fixed his broken leg?"

"Of course I do."

"If I understand right, you repaired the damage by mending the pieces and shards and putting everything back in place and fusing it together."

"Yes."

"If there was a different kind of injury would it have been different? For example, what if a person was attacked by an animal that bit off a big chunk, did you need all the broken pieces to be there or could you have healed it anyway without them? Can you replace lost tissue, missing limbs, or other horrific injuries?"

"I've never considered that. No matter how badly damaged Kra'ac's leg was, I could mend it and put it back as it was. If that leg was missing, I don't know that I could create a replacement. I've never tried such a thing and never heard of it being done. I suspect there's a limit of what can be done with our power. What do you have in your mind to do, Dave?"

"I was just curious. I want to learn everything that I can. Kai said I lack experience. I'm hoping I can make up part of that gap with knowledge. If I can do things nobody else can, that's got to be a good thing."

Selane nodded. "I don't think creating a new limb is possible, but you've done so many impossible things, who knows what else you could do. We haven't seen any limits to your power, Dave."

"This probably won't be the last weird question you hear from me, Selane."

"I don't see it as weird. Seeking new knowledge will always seem unconventional. That's courageous, not foolhardy."

"We'll see."

Jenna crawled under the bedroll with Dave for the first time.

"Hey baby, what's your sign?"

"What? What does that mean, Dave?"

"Nothing," said Dave laughing heartily and hugging his wife. "It's just my poor attempt at humor. I'm glad you're back with me. That's what I mean."

The next day they rode on, steadily passing the high point of the pass where they could see their own land again.

"That's a sight for sore eyes," said Dave.

"It warms my heart to think I'll see my parents again," said Jenna. "I feared my old life was over forever."

"I told you things would work out."

When they completed the journey through the pass and came upon the confederation border station, the guards were concerned and wary.

"Who are you and why have you come?" asked their captain tersely.

"We're the travelers who passed this way half a year ago," said Graile. "We've returned from our visit to the empire."

"You bring an army of rabble at your back," said the captain.

"They're friends. Don't judge them merely on appearance. They've prevailed against impossible odds and are worthy of your respect."

"What are your intentions?" asked the captain abruptly.

"We'll travel through the confederation on our way to the Warlen."

Dave realized he hadn't thought about a plan once they arrived back in their own country.

"You're responsible for the actions of these immigrants," said the captain curtly. "We will not tolerate thievery or mischief on their part."

"We'll need to feed and to rest. We've faced great hardship."

"It's not our responsibility to take of our limited resources to give charity to strangers."

"We'll not cause any problems," said Dave.

The captain grudgingly stepped aside and the migration began. Dave looked back. He couldn't see an end to the trailing procession.

As they traveled to the nearest town, the citizenry closed their gates at the approach of so large a force.

"Ho, in the town," cried Graile. "You have guests to see to."

"We have no room for such a mob," cried a guard.

"At least let us arrange for some supplies," said Graile. "We've traveled a great distance and our supplies are in desperate shape."

"You shouldn't have made the journey," said the guard unsympathetically. "We've plenty of citizens in the confederation to fill our land. We have no room for squatters."

"We're travelers. We ask nothing of you other than common courtesy and some small assistance."

The guards debated before finally opening the gate.

"Only a few of you may enter to do your business," said the guard.

Kra'ac started forward.

"Not the big one," said the guard. He nodded toward Selane, Jenna, and Lissette. "How about those women, they'll be welcomed."

Dave rode up to the guard.

"We're not here for trouble, but we'll be coming in to get supplies. You may not choose for our women to ride into your midst, alone. I'll pick ten to come in, both men and women. After we finish our business we'll resume our journey. There are families among us with children, for god sake. Show some pity, man."

Dave began to glow as he brought up his power. The guard nodded fearfully and hurried back into the city.

"Graile, you pick the team. We'll meet you on the other side of the town."

The supplies they got were inadequate, but enough to stave off hunger temporarily and they camped by a river to replenish drinking water. Dave sent out hunting parties and over the course of a week, managed to bring in enough meat to get past the starvation threat. They didn't find any better receptions at the subsequent towns and cities - word of them had preceded their arrivals.

"This is real nice," said Dave. "What happens when the refugees start to come through the pass?"

"What happens when the imperial army comes through the pass?" asked Graile.

"I've been thinking about that. We need to organize everybody on this side of the mountains. First, I want to go and see Andron to see how he's doing with forming a central government for the Warlen. Hopefully, he's also made progress in forming an army. At least that would be a force we could use to confront the imperials if they come pouring through the breech. After that, I was thinking we should visit all of the other peoples."

"Are you serious?" asked Graile. "If you try to go to the trolls, the dwarves and the elves you're asking for trouble. Kra'ac, Lissette, and Angus are sure to be outcasts by this time. I can't imagine you also intend to visit with the Agia men and the other lower species who are little more than beasts. Beyond the land of the Warlen to the east is my homeland, which abuts the great ocean. It's a land of fiefdoms and small city states that war with each other continuously. I don't believe they could ever be brought to unite, even against a common foe set upon destroying them. They're shallow and corrupt people, little better than the imperials. You can see what manner of man I am, what I've done. The people I spring from see little wrong with indiscretions and my dalliances. My mistake with them is I got caught, not that I did it. Do you understand what I'm saying? They're low people not worth trying to save."

"Don't forget the sisters," said Dave. "We need everybody on our side. The sister's are the only ones that have power over here. I plan on setting up a wizard school or something to find and train the boys, but obviously won't help us in the short term."

"If Selane went back to the keep," said Graile, "she would be in the greatest peril of all of us. She's no longer pure. The sisters don't ask or care how it happened and would feel the need and seek to sacrifice her in the most gruesome way to make an example for any potential subsequent wayward prima virgas. This isn't a good plan, Dave."

"We've got to deal with it, Graile. We can't have enemies within our borders. I know it's a risk. I'll be there with her."

Graile shook his head.

"It's your decision, but I think it's a big mistake."

"We can talk about it. Everybody gets a vote."

"A vote would be worse than if you make the decision. It will put everyone at odds with each other. I'll guarantee you none of our companions will want to return to homelands and face the retribution of their peoples. In most cases it could be a deadly risk."

"This problem won't solve itself. It's like when we talked about going to the empire in the first place. None of us wanted to go, but it had to be done."

"I want to say this, but please understand I'm trying to give you perspective, Dave. Don't take this as an affront."

"I want to hear whatever you have to say, Graile. Don't worry about my feelings. This is serious stuff we're facing here."

"We all have faith in you. We chose to follow you into the empire. What happened to us there, I would say let it guide you now. Entering the palace was an ill conceived idea. I don't want to stifle your planning now, but just remember our past failures before we leap into any future entanglements."

"You mean my failures. I know, Graile. I wish I could come up with foolproof plans, but that just isn't me. I'm too much of a trial and error guy. With me, what you see is what you get. I've been telling everybody who will listen I'm a very poor choice as the leader of this tribe."

"So we're a tribe now?" asked Graile chuckling.

"Whatever. If you can think of a better description, be my guest."

"I have nothing, Dave. I laughed because as long as I've been around you, I've never gotten accustomed to your strange ways of speaking."

"I'm glad I'm such a hoot," said Dave sourly, "maybe I should sell admission tickets."

Graile laughed heartily.

"He's addled in the head," said Angus who had walked up and listened to their exchange. "I've got the answer right here." He brandished his war hammer.

"I can't disagree with you, Angus," said Dave.

* * * *

Dave's words had affected the women and they accepted his suggestion to look at themselves differently. The positive impact was they no longer sought constant separation from the others, allowed their men to be close and resumed old roles of leadership and responsibility. Although dark issues within them remained, they came to see their darkness was no different than the darkness in any other person. That was a quantum leap allowing them to regain their functionality and competence.

For Dave, he had his wife back and that was incredibly gratifying to feel her love again. To see her smile warmed his heart.

It also meant Angus and Kra'ac took the plunge and actually explained their romantic feelings to Lissette and Selane. It wasn't a surprise to either woman.

232

Kra'ac took Selane aside for his private talk. It was a strange contrast between his great size and her delicate form, but the tenderness he showed was very moving. Selane wasn't unaware of his desires, but he'd never actually spoken of it to her before. Her upbringing had never caused her to think in that direction, men were so reviled by the sisters.

For Kra'ac to put himself out there with the possibility of scorn, rejection and ridicule was courageous, much more difficult than facing enemies in battle. To pursue a woman coveted universally, of unmatched beauty, allure and stature was unthinkable, but he carried on.

Selane was imminently kind and gentle, knowing his vulnerability to her. Dave and the others couldn't help but watch and tried to pretend otherwise, but it wasn't a short interlude. Initially, Kra'ac appeared to be hurt by what she said, but as they continued to speak, his features calmed. What he was finally hearing was a much better answer to his pleas.

They were sitting on the ground and Selane got up and kissed him tenderly after a protracted conversation. Kra'ac seemed both pleased and distressed.

They both got up and came over to the group.

"Kra'ac has expressed his love for me. I'm greatly moved by his passion and devotion. I've explained to him the difficulty of my position in relation to the sisterhood. I cannot agree to be his betrothed at this time, but with much discussion I've agreed to consider the matter further. He worries I don't find him an acceptable mate. I explained that's not the problem. Any woman would be honored if he were their husband. He's a great man, honorable and decent. Because he's of a different race, I don't hold that against him. He's told me he wants no other woman but me. I'll allow him to spend private time with me to allow us to learn each other better, to share our thoughts, hopes and goals, and to discuss our flaws so we'll know each other completely. He's agreed to that. Dave, you already know our shame back in the empire, because you've been in our minds. I explained to Kra'ac what happened to us, what was done to us and what we did. I wanted to be totally honest with him. He's said there's nothing to repent and it's behind us now. It's unbelievable to me he can be so great a person as to accept me with this stain I bear. I'm awed by him."

Angus had gone off with Lissette for his private chat too. They came back soon after and heard much of what was said as Selane finished speaking.

"I've experienced many things in my life," said Lissette, "things far beyond the life of elves. I would never have thought to be wooed by a dwarf. It's a difficult matter. Our two peoples war against each other. Intermarriage has never been done. Master Angus proposed we change that fact by being the first to marry. I've told him I appreciate his diligence in pursuing me. In another world, I would gladly agree to make a life with him, as unlikely as that might seem. Here, however, it's a problem that may have no solution. He thought I don't care for him. That's wrong, for I do. What's the problem for both of us is neither of our peoples will accept such a union, of that I'm sure. Also, he's said that just because I'm no longer pure doesn't deter him from wishing to marry me, and I believe him, but it's an issue for me. Jenna, Selane and I have troubles remaining from our time as black witches. Until I can come to terms with that, I cannot be the mate of another and pledge my whole self to them. We're agreed to honor each other and to forsake all others, but a resolution to my problem is a first step I must accomplish before we could consider the other problems. I explained our sins and he assured me it was no factor for him. He accepts me as I am, flawed as that may be."

"If I understand you correctly Selane and Lissette, you didn't say no, am I right?" asked Dave.

They looked at each other sheepishly and shrugged.

"Well, there you go then," said Dave grinning broadly. "Let's be optimistic and look at the bright side."

Everybody chuckled.

"I have something to say," said Graile. "I've spoken with Sylvia, and she's agreed to become my wife."

The group stood in stunned silence a moment before they shouted and came over to hug and congratulate the couple.

"Are you going to be Red Graile now?" asked Dave.

Everybody laughed hilariously.

"I didn't think to ever have a man in my life again," said Sylvia. "Graile has melted my heart and soothed the loss of my former husband. Why he would want me I cannot understand, but I have agreed to be a wife again. I've had enough of empty beds and loneliness."

"He's the one that's lucky," said Dave. "You're a remarkable woman, Sylvia."

"Thank you. It isn't true, but I appreciate the kind words."

"Let's celebrate," said Graile.

An impromptu fest developed and their camp spent the evening dancing and singing, and there was considerable drinking - a wonderful respite after terrible times in the empire.

Sleep came late and all were slow to wake up in the morning.

Although they weren't technically engaged, Dave could see now both couples finally acted as couples. Kra'ac comically followed Selane around like a gigantic puppy, but, at the same time, her patience and fondness with him was heartwarming. Lissette and Angus verbal sparring was constant, but any animosity had disappeared and was just good natured banter.

Even Bear, the most feared predator in the world, picked up on the emotional changes by strangely acting like a tame pet and licking the women's faces affectionately.

"What a world you're creating," said Graile. "What's next?"

"I have no idea," said Dave.

The journey continued. About a week later they set about to have a wedding for Graile and Sylvia. Stopping at a town, they coerced a local holy man to perform the ceremony, which loosened up the town folk who nervously joined in the wedding aftermath. At the end of the day, the reception became another fest with plenty of loud music and singing, wild dancing and genuine good feelings for all.

Graile's honeymoon was little better than Dave's, with no place for privacy. Dave instructed they be allowed a tent set apart from the camp, but it didn't stop rabble rousers from annoying them constantly. Sylvia's people especially took diabolical pleasure in the abuse.

* * * *

With that piece of business wrapped up, Dave called a council of his leaders to discuss their plans.

"I've mentioned this to Graile, but haven't said it to anyone else. War is coming. We stirred up the empire and though it may take them time to get back on their feet. You know as well as I they will not let this whole thing slide and will be coming for us. We need to get ready. This country cannot stand up to the vast imperial army and their corps of warlocks. In the short term, we can station forces in the pass to keep the enemy from getting through, but that would only be a temporary holding action. Eventually, we'll be faced with full fledged war and when that time comes, we've got to have an army able to handle that fight. That means everybody on this side gets into the action. We've got a start with the Warlen, but it's just a start. We'll go to Andron first, but after we've got to make some difficult trips."

He looked somberly at his friends. They knew what was coming and didn't look happy.

"We're going to visit the dwarves, elves, and trolls. We must stop at the keep, to visit the sisters and there may be other peoples we'll need to see. I know this won't be easy, but we have faced hard things before. Mortus was no picnic."

"That's true," said Selane, "but you don't know what you're asking of us."

"I believe I do," said Dave. "We've weathered every storm. Granted we've taken some terrible knocks along the way, but I say that made us stronger. We're going to do this, because there's no other choice. Without the numbers of the dwarf, elf, and troll armies, the Warlen wouldn't be enough. Without the sisters, we have no other magical aid. They have to realize warlocks are real live magical enemies, and some of their people may die - not to mention the black witches. What do you think Gristelle is going to do after reading your mind about the sisters? She probably thinks they're easy pickings. If we don't win them all over to our cause we're doomed, folks. Another thing concerning the sisters, we've got to stop them from taking out the males who have power we can develop. I'm going to create a school to collect them together and start training them to be wizards. Maybe we can get the sisters to help train them."

"That's crazy," said Selane. "You don't know them like I do. It's doubtful they would allow me to come back to the keep, but an alliance is highly doubtful, and your idea to train boys is impossible."

"How do you think they'll like being black witches?" asked Dave. "Gristelle and her pals will roast the sisters."

"There are no words I could use to accomplish that which you propose," said Selane. "They wouldn't want to hear it and would fight us all of the way."

"Don't forget we'll be there with you," said Dave. "You'll have all of the power available you need."

"We cannot simply conquer them, if that's even possible," said Selane. "They wouldn't willingly be our tools. I'm sorry Dave. I don't see how this could be accomplished."

"I'm still working out the details."

Graile eyed him wryly.

"Going to my country would be equally impossible," said Lissette. "If we're not attacked and wiped out for just crossing the border, they can and will evade our search. We could travel forever and never find them if they didn't want to be found."

"I'm sure you'll think of something, Lissette," said Dave.

Appalled by the rebuff, Dave could see Lissette was going to lash out.

"What do you think, Angus?" asked Dave.

"My people wouldn't hide from us. They would show themselves, but would be no more welcoming than the elves. We'd face a battle for sure. The dwarves aren't tolerant of trespassers."

"Kra'ac?" asked Dave.

"Trolls are not social creatures. We have strife enough in living with each other. There's a reason people don't go to troll country. There's a very real probability you would be supper that night."

"What's with all of this cannibalism?" asked Dave. "Why can't everybody just get along? I don't get it."

They talked at length about Dave's proposal and failed to dissuade him from his path.

"Do you have a better idea?" he asked over and over again. They did not.

"Then it's settled," he said finally. "We'll travel to Warlen country first and go from there. I'm thinking we can make our initial border patrol from Sylvia's folk, the Warlen, and confederation soldiers. They will have to hold out against any imperial attack until we get these other pieces into play."

"The confederation didn't seem particularly open to our visit," said Graile.

"We'll change their minds," said Dave. "Either they cooperate with us, or else get their doors blown off by the imperial army. They don't really have a choice, just a matter of making them realize that."

They all shook their heads doubtfully.

"Am I wrong?" asked Dave.

Nobody replied.

"Do you have anything else to add, Red Graile?" he joked.

Shaking his fist at Dave, "if you call me that one more time, I will…"

Laughing, they broke up to go their separate ways.

Jenna settled down with Dave under the bedroll.

"I know you're doing what you feel you must, Dave, but I fear we're in for another terrible time. All of those tasks you've set out for us are daunting. Any one of them alone would be terribly hazardous. All of them together seem impossible."

"All that we can do is plug away, one step after another. I know it would be easy to stick our heads in the sand, but the problems won't go away, honey."

"I know, but I don't wish to go through the gauntlet again. I don't have your strength. I was too easily cowed and broken and was their thing to use in whatever manner they chose. I cannot explain what that's like and don't think you would ever be in such a state. You're indomitable of spirit and determined in purpose in all things you do."

"Is that what you think? The truth is, I'm just a loose cannon and out of control most of the time. I've been lucky, not skilled. Kai and Dul recognized that in an instant. As potent as I'm supposed to be, I didn't scare them one bit. The only thing I can say that I'm sure of is I've got to do something. I can't just sit back. I've got to get out in front of this thing, because there's a tidal wave coming. I have no desire to put anybody in harm's way, but unfortunately, we're going to have to live with the risk. If I had my way, I would have Andron hide you in a cave so you were safe from the war, but I can't be sure anywhere would be safe when they break through, and you know they will."

"Dave, the power of the black witch coven is incredible. I've never been amongst the sisters, but I fear they're a feeble counter to the black witches. Even if the best happens for us, can we prevail against the full might of the empire? What will we do if the master appears?"

"Tough questions, if I ever get any answers I'll let you know."

The End

The saga continues in The Gathering Storm, Book II of the Faenum Quest Series.